W9-CEE-128

THE GOLDEN HOUR

TODD MOSS

THORNDIKE PRESS

A part of Gale, Cengage Learning

GALE
CENGAGE Learning·

Farmington Hills, Mich • San Francisco • New York • Waterville, Maine
Meriden, Conn • Mason, Ohio • Chicago

LIBRARY OF CONGRESS CATALOGING-IN-PUBLICATION DATA

Moss, Todd.
   The golden hour / by Todd Moss. — Large print edition.
     pages ; cm. — (Thorndike Press large print thriller)
    ISBN 978-1-4104-7563-3 (hardcover) — ISBN 1-4104-7563-8 (hardcover)
   1. Political fiction. I. Title.
PS3613.O785G65 2015
813'.6—dc23   2014036951

Published in 2015 by arrangement with G. P. Putnam's Sons, a member of Penguin Group (USA) LLC, a Penguin Random House Company

Printed in Mexico
1 2 3 4 5 6 7 19 18 17 16 15

AUTHOR'S NOTE

The Golden Hour draws on my real-life experiences, but what follows is entirely a work of fiction. The golden hour principle of rapid intervention in trauma cases is a concept from emergency medicine that I learned when working as an EMT and ambulance driver in Boston. I am unaware of any published academic study so far that has discovered such a time pattern in politics, but there is a growing quantitative literature on drivers of conflict.

In the story that follows, any resemblances to actual people or events are coincidental. Timbuktu is real.

A Note on Time

Mali and Great Britain are both on Greenwich Mean Time (GMT), but Mali does not follow daylight savings time. Thus, in *The Golden Hour* Mali is four hours ahead of U.S. Eastern Standard Time while Britain is five hours ahead. Germany is six hours ahead.

"The advantages of backchannels are secrecy, speed, and the avoidance of internal bureaucratic battles."

— G. R. BERRIDGE,
Diplomacy: Theory and Practice, 1995

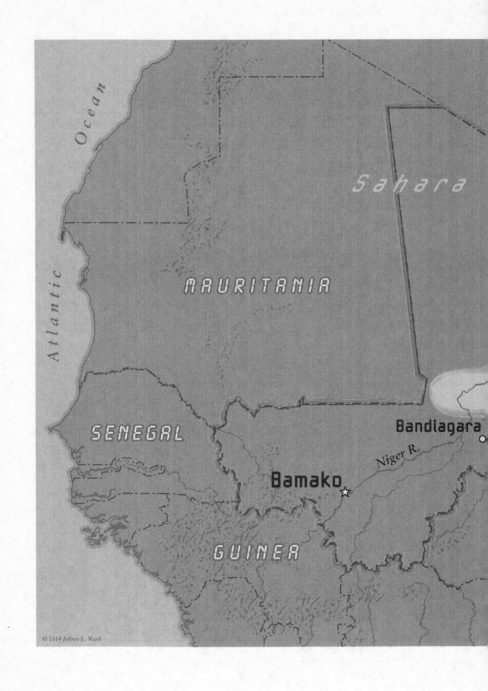

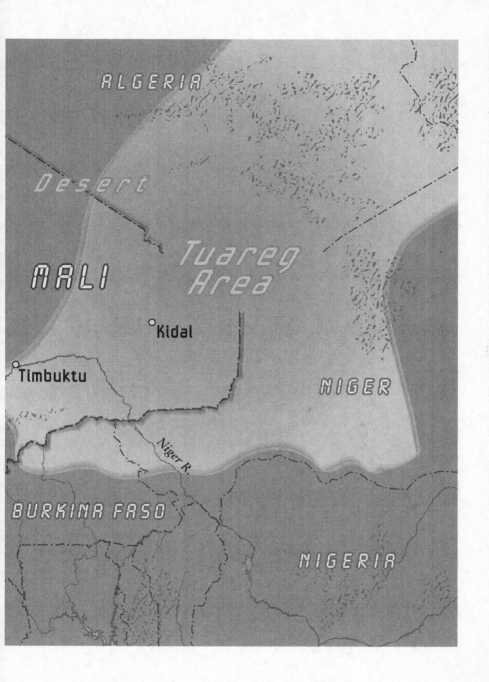

Prologue

BANGORO VILLAGE, MALI, WEST AFRICA
SIXTY-FIVE MILES NORTH OF TIMBUKTU
Camel meat.

At the thought, her mouth watered slightly. *A Philly cheesesteak with camel meat?*

Kate, dreaming of comfort food, couldn't be farther from home. For years, her father would joke, "I'm in Timbuktu," when he'd call from any of the remote towns of rural Pennsylvania he was constantly visiting. Now she was living a three-hour drive — or, for the locals, a three-day walk — outside of the real Timbuktu. *Beyond* the middle of nowhere.

The steel bolt clanged loudly as Kate locked up the classroom. She clamped on a bright yellow padlock. The key, also school-bus yellow, was on a leather lanyard around her neck. It was mostly for show, everyone knew, but the headmaster insisted that security must be maintained. Especially for the token library of a few dozen books, each preciously hand-delivered by Kate and the string of Peace Corps volunteers that came before her.

Why not camel? Tastes like beef. I could be the first. I'm a cheesesteak pioneer.

She licked her lips. It was futile, she knew, to fantasize about impossible snacks. But it was a ritual she justified as a normal reaction to homesickness. And the searing Saharan desert heat.

The sun was dropping toward the horizon and glowing in the rich burnt orange that exists only in the African sky.

Most of the students were long gone, the girls called home to haul water, the boys to tend the family goats. A few stragglers were still wandering around the school in tattered pale-blue uniforms, watching the foreigner lock up for the day.

Kate slung her backpack over her shoulder and turned down the sandy path toward her home. Other than the school, her house was the only concrete structure in the village. The rest — the huts, the granaries full of millet, and the tiny shops selling Coca-Cola, long bars of pink soap, jugs of cooking oil, and mobile phone scratch cards — were made of dried mud.

Even though dusk was nearing, it was still close to 100 degrees. Bubbles of sweat were sprouting on her nose and along her cheekbones, periodically sliding down salty paths onto her lips. Her long red hair, pulled back into a perky ponytail, bobbed up and down as she walked.

She was exhausted. But her long day was finally over.

"Miss Katie, Miss Katie! Hello! How are you? Miss Katie!" She waved back at a gaggle of small children, naked and dusty, hopping along the path.

"Hello. Good evening." Kate forced a friendly smile. *The price of being a local celebrity,* she reminded herself. And the first freckled redhead the village children had ever seen.

"Hello! Miss Katie! Bonjour! Hello!" They giggled and scampered off into the bush.

As she settled into her forty-minute walk, the very one she had made every day for the past five months, she returned to her thoughts.

She missed her family, especially her dad. Kate loved when they would go out for brunch, just the two of them, on weekends. For as long as she could remember, her father had spent the work-week away from Philadelphia, taking the train back home on

Fridays. His afternoons and evenings were usually also busy with work. But the mornings were for family. Kate had even chosen Penn over Yale to stay closer to home. So their weekends could stay the same.

Kate revered her father. To be like him, she knew she would have to see the world. After college, the Peace Corps seemed an obvious, almost unconscious choice. Kate had never even heard of Mali when she received her assignment. She had studied French in school so she could spend the summers in Paris. Or maybe the Riviera. Who knew they spoke French in the Sahara Desert? When she was told where she was going, she laughed, as surely Timbuktu was fictional. Like Atlantis. But her father sternly advised that she accept her duty.

So here she was, in Bangoro, teaching English.

Kate barely noticed the sunset that had helped her fall in love with Africa during those tough early weeks of adjustment. She spied a single white camel off in the distance, nibbling lazily at a dry bush. The sight no longer drew Kate's fascination, but rather pulled her mind back to cheesesteaks.

Lost in her daydreaming, she didn't notice that the village was unusually quiet that evening. Or that all the children had suddenly disappeared.

Kate followed a bend in the path and was startled by a Toyota pickup truck, spray-painted with the beige and green squiggles of homemade camouflage, parked in front of her house. Her instinct was to run away, but two men — their faces covered by black scarves, AK-47s slung on their chests — stepped into her path. She spun back toward her house only to find more men emerging from the cab of the Toyota.

Large hands grabbed both her arms firmly and, before she could scream, a burlap sack was slipped over her head.

■ ■ ■ ■

PART ONE: MONDAY

■ ■ ■ ■

1.

*KITTY HAWK, OUTER BANKS, NORTH
CAROLINA
MONDAY, 5:42 A.M. EST (EASTERN
STANDARD TIME)*

It started, unsurprisingly, with the low buzz
of a BlackBerry. Judd slowly opened one
eye. The phone was lying facedown on the
nightstand just six inches from his nose. Its
little blinking green light, barely perceptible
during the day, illuminated the pitch-dark
room in half-second intervals. *So much for
vacation.*

He grabbed the vibrating phone and
studied the caller ID. It was flashing "202"
but nothing more. A scrambled number
from Washington, D.C. He swung his legs
off the bed and sat up. Stealing a quick
glance to make sure Jessica was still sound
asleep, he pushed the answer button with
his thumb and whispered into the phone,
"This is Ryker."

"This is White House Operations. What is your confirmation code?" asked the robotic, clearly military voice on the line.

He paused. "Turquoise Mobutu Seven."

"Good morning, Dr. Ryker. Embassy Bamako is reporting a probable coup overnight in Mali. As of oh five hundred, we have no reports of violence, but there are military roadblocks around the city and the whereabouts of President Maiga are unknown."

"Okay," was all Judd could squeeze out, still shaking out the cobwebs.

"State is setting up a task force to run our policy response, and we should have a new Ops report in about an hour."

Finally waking up, he asked, "Is it Diallo or Idrissa?"

"Excuse me, sir?"

"Who is behind the coup? Is it General Oumar Diallo or General Mamadou Idrissa?"

"We don't know yet, sir. The ambassador and the station chief should have more information soon."

"Okay, thanks for letting me know. Please tell Larissa James she can reach me on my phone if she wants my input as news rolls in."

"Ambassador James is the one who asked us to bring you in. A car will be at your location at oh six hundred. They are twelve minutes out."

He exhaled a deep breath, and sat up straight.

"If that's your office, it better be goddamn important." Jessica was awake. "Don't they know it's your first day of vacation in a whole year?"

Judd tried to tap her reassuringly, but unable to see in the dark, he just patted the blankets while speaking back into the phone. "Okay, thanks. I'll look out for the car." And he hung up.

"Car?"

"A coup in Mali. I can't say any more. I, um, I don't *know* any more. I'm sorry." He got up and started to get dressed. "It shouldn't be more than a day or two. The kids won't even notice that I'm gone."

"I will," snapped Jessica.

Judd clipped his BlackBerry onto his belt and picked up his go bag, which was already sitting by the door. He planted a long kiss on Jessica's lips and then turned to leave.

"Don't let Rogerson push you around," she said. "Don't let him fuck you again," she added, stopping Judd in his tracks. He turned, gave her a slight, unconvincing nod, and then silently walked away.

As he stepped out of the rented beach

house onto the sand driveway, he cursed himself for not setting up the coffeemaker to be ready for just such a possibility. Just as he considered going back in to make a quick double espresso, he saw four beaming headlights approaching in the dark, barreling up the driveway. An all-black Chevy Suburban rolled up and abruptly stopped beside him. A tall, thick man with short hair and a wire looped behind his ear silently exited the front of the vehicle, quickly surveyed the area, then opened the back door while removing the go bag from Judd's grip.

Judd squinted at the bright lights from inside the cab. "Good morning, sir," said a young man inside whom he didn't recognize.

"Morning. We need to stop and get coffee." He ducked his head and climbed in.

The security officer closed the door, stealing one more glance around, then slid into the car, which was already accelerating. Judd turned around in his seat and waved good-bye to Jessica.

From the bedroom window, she watched the behemoth and its lifeless blacked-out windows speed away.

2.

Judd checked his watch. Nearly ten hours since the coup.

Judd had been on the phone and thumbing his BlackBerry since he left his family at the beach house. *Futility.*

The conflicting rumors had been flying on the Internet like a desert wind funnel: President Maiga had been poisoned by the Saudis, al-Qaeda had attacked the palace, the whole coup was a hoax, the Algerians had sent a brigade over the border, the CIA had bundled Maiga into a car and driven him to a secret prison in Timbuktu, and . . .

Judd shook his head. *None of it can be true, of course.*

The BlackBerry was hot in his hands. But it wasn't yielding what Judd craved. For the real information, Judd knew he must wait until he got back to Washington. For the

23

classified video-conference with the ambassador.

Things had been much easier, clearer, when he used to work with numbers. Hard data. Instead he now received a steady stream of assessments. Best guesses, usually. Or, all too often, deliberate misinformation. *Lies.* But he suppressed any thoughts of returning to his old life yet. No giving up.

Judd took off his glasses and dropped the BlackBerry in his lap as he tried to clear his head by staring out the window. He spied the road sign announcing their approach to the Beltway, the sixty-four-mile-long, eight-lane highway that encircled the nation's capital. Inside this moat was the globe's ultimate game of power and influence. To the outside world the key combatants were the public faces, the senators, the press secretaries, and the Sunday-morning TV talking heads. Inside the Beltway, the real action was a layer or two deeper among the Capitol Hill committee staffers, the K Street lobbyists, the wonks deep in the bowels of the Eisenhower Executive Office Building. Mostly unseen, they made the day-to-day decisions, wielding the power of the United States government.

How different from the genteel campus of

Amherst College. Life had been good. Teaching two classes a week, running a small team of graduate students collecting data for his research on political conflict in South Asia and Africa, and taking long walks with his wife and their two young boys in the Berkshires. He'd been within a two-hour drive of his hometown in Vermont, his grandmother at the family house in Burlington, the ballgames at Fenway Park.

The call almost exactly one year ago, so early on a Saturday morning, should have been the first warning sign. . . .

3.

"Judd Ryker, this is Landon Parker, Chief of Staff to the Secretary of State. I'm calling from Washington. I didn't wake you, I hope?"

"Uh, no, of course not, Mr. Parker," Judd lied. The alarm clock blinked a cherry-red 7:55.

"Let me get right to the point, Ryker. The Secretary's policy planning staff is setting up a new rapid reaction unit inside the department. They have been impressed with your work on crisis response times, especially your conclusions about the Golden Hour. We'd like to bring you in for a briefing."

Judd sat up. "Well, thank you. The new papers on Sri Lanka and Rwanda are only based on preliminary numbers, and haven't even been published yet. I wouldn't really

26

call them conclusions. I should have firmer results late next year when all the data is back from Colombo and Kigali. The Golden Hour is still just a theory."

"How about Monday, nine fifteen?"

"The day after tomorrow? In Washington?"

"Yes. Here at the State Department."

"Well, I am supposed to teach a class that afternoon, but I can try to find someone to cover."

"Good. See you Monday morning, Ryker. Someone will meet you in the lobby to clear you into the building and bring you up." Click.

Forty-eight hours later, Judd was standing in Foggy Bottom, a soulless zone of bleak office buildings on the western edge of Washington, D.C. He was wearing his best navy blue business suit, although the slight fray in the cuffs and the distressed-leather satchel slung over his shoulder hinted at his academic vocation. His tousled brown hair and retro G-man glasses also exposed him as a mere visitor to this particular neighborhood. Jessica had examined his outfit as he left for the airport and proclaimed, with approval, that he was appropriately shabby and "nerd cute."

Judd strolled up to the Harry S. Truman Federal Building, the headquarters of the U.S. Department of State, trying to suppress his unexpected nervousness. From the outside, the building appeared colossal, gray, and nondescript, hidden behind the gaudy American Pharmacists Association and the more elegant and subtle National Academy of Sciences.

As Judd stood on Constitution Avenue and looked up Twenty-second Street toward the security barriers, he realized that he had been standing in the same spot a few years earlier when he brought his kids to see the four-ton bronze Albert Einstein memorial. He hadn't even noticed the State Department headquarters just half a block away.

After passing through airport-like security and a tedious ID check, he was given a bright orange badge emblazoned with ES-CORT REQUIRED and was instructed to hang it on a chain around his neck. Once inside the lobby, he recognized the nearly two hundred flags from watching the nightly news.

An elderly heavyset woman with a long gray ponytail, who reminded Judd of the grumpy librarian at his elementary school in Vermont, approached him. "Dr. Ryker? I can take you up to the conference room."

In the elevator, Judd flipped through the charts he had printed out and ran through his presentation in his head. He had told this story a hundred times in seminars and over departmental dinners, but for some reason his palms were sweating. The elevator doors opened, and he was led down a long and drab hallway of flickering fluorescent lights to a door labeled 7-4504. The escort turned the handle and motioned for him to enter. "I'll wait for you here." Judd paused and took a deep breath. *I can do this.* Then he stepped inside.

It was like a portal to another world. The brightly lit conference room had dark cherrywood paneling with a bank of six large flat-panel monitors along one wall. *Just like in the movies.* About a dozen men and women, all in dark suits, were sitting in high-backed leather chairs around the table. Behind them, in a concentric ring, sat younger suits, reading papers or thumbing dials on their mobile phones. *They look like my students.*

No one said a word to Judd or even acknowledged his arrival. He took an empty seat at the table and waited.

A minute later, at exactly nine fifteen, a tall man walked in briskly from a side door. He was in his late thirties and had small round glasses and short-cropped hair. Immediately, the room went silent and the man nodded to no one in general, and then approached Judd.

"Ryker, I'm Landon Parker. Thanks for coming in. We've got no more than ten minutes, so I'll spare introductions. You've got the Secretary's planning staff here, plus the heads of each of the major regional and functional offices."

Parker turned to the others. "Folks, this is Professor Judd Ryker from Amherst College."

Back to Judd. "Okay, Ryker. The floor is yours. Take three or four minutes to leave time for questions."

"I'll try to make this quick. Thank you, Mr. Parker, for asking me to come here today." Judd stood up for emphasis. "In emergency medicine, a trauma patient's chances of survival are greatest if they receive professional care in the hospital within sixty minutes after a severe multi-system injury. This is known as the Golden Hour."

Judd scanned the room, hoping for hints of recognition. Nothing. He continued, "Although there is some debate about the precise length of time of the Golden Hour, the principle of rapid intervention in trauma cases is universally accepted. If you don't get help very quickly, you die. It's that simple." Judd nodded, but still no reaction from the audience.

"I believe we have found the same principle to apply to international political trauma. We can't run experiments in a lab, but we can pick up patterns in the data. The numbers can tell us." Pause. *My undergrads love that line.*

Judd waved his arms as he got more excited. "Using data over the past forty years, we studied two hundred thirty cases of political crisis in low- and middle-income countries. We found that the probability of resolution declines significantly over time. In fact, time is more dominant in the statistical analysis than ethnic cleavages, type of regime, or the other standard political variables." Judd waited a moment, to give the crowd time to let that settle in. *Am I losing them?*

"Most interesting, the time-resolution correlation is not linear. In plain English, this means we have found clear tipping points in time. For the outbreak of a civil war, the critical period is about thirteen or fourteen days. After two weeks, the chances of a speedy resolution decline by more than half. Similarly, if an illegal seizure of power by

31

the military is not reversed within about four days, the chances of reversal over the next year drop by eighty percent." Judd paused for effect. "In other words, ladies and gentlemen, the Golden Hour for a coup d'état is just one hundred hours."

Satisfyingly, this led to murmuring and scribbling among the crowd.

"I must stress that these results are still preliminary, and I have teams in Asia and Africa collecting additional data." *Caveats. I have a reputation to protect.*

"Are you finding differences across regions? Is Africa different from south Asia, or are they all pretty much the same?" asked one of those seated at the table, without identifying himself.

"No, we haven't found any of the regional variables to be statistically significant," responded Judd.

"Did anything change with the end of the Cold War or 9/11?"

"Good question. We haven't broken the data into periods. We could try that. I just don't know."

"What is driving the results on coups? How can you explain what's so special about timing? I understand the idea of a Golden Hour, but why does it exist?"

"We don't really know. We can theorize

that it probably has something to do with the dynamics of consolidating power after seizure. The coup makers must line up the rest of the security forces and maybe buy off parliament and other local political leaders before those loyal to the deposed president are able to react and countermove. It's a race for influence. But these are just hypotheses."

"What about international intervention? Does it matter if an external force gets involved diplomatically?" asked one staffer.

"Or militarily?" interjected another.

"We don't have classifications for intervention, so it's not in there," replied Judd. "The numbers can't tell us. So, we don't know. I guess we could —"

Parker interrupted abruptly. "But in your expert opinion, Ryker, does it matter? Would it make a difference? Does the United States need to find ways to intervene more rapidly in emerging crises in the developing world? Can we prevent more wars and coups by reacting more quickly?"

Judd looked around the room at all the eyes locked on him. *My numbers don't answer that question. Isn't that what you guys are here for?*

But instead he sat up straight, turned to look Landon Parker directly in the eyes, and said simply, "Yes."

And that was it. A few thank-yous and handshakes, and everyone left. Judd's escort took him down the same elevator and out to the lobby. He dropped his orange security badge into a clear plastic container with a slot at the top, not too dissimilar from the ballot boxes he'd seen used for voting in Nigeria. He walked back down Twenty-second Street for one more look at Einstein and to hail a cab.

The return trip to Ronald Reagan National Airport was only seven minutes. He might even catch an earlier shuttle back to Logan. As the taxi drove behind the Lincoln Memorial and over a bridge, he thought he might just make it back to Amherst in time for class.

Once in Virginia, the cab looped around and headed south, down the George Washington Parkway along the Potomac River. Judd looked over the water at the Washington Monument. For a brief flash, between the trees, he could even make out the Capitol building off in the distance.

The park along the riverbank was mostly empty, save a few joggers and an attractive young woman walking a yellow Labrador. Behind the dog walker, two dark green army helicopters in tight formation banked sharply over the river, then turned to the west and flew directly over Judd's taxi. Turning in his seat to follow their course, he noticed, sitting low and squat, a colossal stone-colored office building surrounded by an ocean of parked cars. The Pentagon.

The exit for Reagan was almost immediate. As he stood in the security line and waited to take off his shoes, he wondered whether any of this was worth it. *All this effort for ten minutes in a conference room?*

Settling into a chair in the departure lounge, he was reminded of his old professor and advisor, BJ van Hollen, who had urged him to take an interest in public service. His mentor had even offered to help Judd find a good job inside the U.S. government applying his analytical skills to solving real-world puzzles. Professor van Hollen had been openly disappointed when Judd opted for the academic life.

At least I have a good story for BJ. He'll be impressed the State Department called me. Why not?

Judd pulled out his phone and dialed a number. After several rings, a weak raspy voice answered, "Huuhh-looooo?"

"BJ? Is that you?"

"Yes," was the soft reply, followed by a

series of coughs so loud and violent that Judd was forced to hold the phone away from his ear. "Who's this?"

"It's Judd. Sorry to call you out of the blue. You sound terrible."

"I know. I've been a little sick."

"I didn't know. Is it serious?"

"No, no. It's nothing like that. And don't say anything to Jessica. It'll just worry her. We don't need that."

"Guess where I am."

"Here in California?"

"No. Sorry, I didn't mean that. I'm in Washington, D.C. I just finished briefing the State Department on my conflict metrics."

"Oh, really? That's excellent news."

"They called me."

"It's about time, too. I'm very proud. I'm sure Jessica is very proud."

"They were really interested in the Golden Hour. Asked lots of tough questions. I just thought you'd be pleased I was helping do something real."

"I am," said van Hollen before unleashing another barrage of coughs.

"BJ, you sound like you're dying. I hope you're seeing a doctor."

"At my age, I'm seeing too many doctors. I'm tired of it. Judd, congratulations on the

State Department. I'm sure they appreciated your help. And thank you for letting me know. Is Jessica with you?"

"No. She's home with the kids."

"Is she working again?"

"A bit. She took time off when Noah was born and all the travel became too much. But she's starting to work again. A coffee project in Ethiopia and rice somewhere in southeast Asia, I think. I'm never sure where's she's going. I can never keep track."

"Good for her," he said, sounding increasingly weakened. "I've got to get off the phone now. I'm sorry. Send my love to Jessica."

"I will. Thanks. And good-bye, BJ."

"Good-bye, Judd. Au revoir."

Judd slumped back into the airport chair. Satisfied the day wasn't a total loss, he relaxed, half reading through some papers he was supposed to be grading and half scanning the crowds for George Stephanopoulos or David Gergen.

Judd's flight was finally called, and he stood in line again, waiting to board. As he approached the front to hand over his ticket, his phone rang. The caller ID flashed "202" with no other numbers. *How odd,* he thought. Handing his ticket to the attendant, and trying not to drop all the

37

papers, he wedged the phone between his ear and shoulder.

"Uh, hello?"

"Ryker, this is Landon Parker. That was impressive. Especially the Golden Hour for a coup and the hundred-hour thing. Very illuminating. And timely, too. The Secretary is in Brussels today for the NATO summit and will be announcing a new State Department Crisis Reaction Unit. She is also going to announce the director who will launch and lead this effort. That person is you. Ryker, do not get on that plane."

4.

"This is three-one-four, we are two minutes out."

The security officer in the front seat was holding his right ear and talking into his left wrist. The aide sitting next to Judd was, as he'd been doing for most of the past four hours, tapping feverishly with his thumbs on his BlackBerry.

As the black Suburban crossed over the Arlington Memorial Bridge, returning Judd to the District of Columbia, his dreams of a lazy day of white sand and Carolina barbecue were long gone. Instead, he was reprising all the questions he should have asked Landon Parker that day twelve months ago. *If I only knew then . . .*

■ ■ ■ ■

He had been so surprised and thrilled at being asked, that he hadn't even considered asking about staff or a budget. It was just plain naïve not to consider how a new office, much less one led by an outside academic parachuting in, would be received by the existing system. All bureaucracies were turf obsessed, he knew. But he was shocked at the particularly virulent, dog-eat-dog subculture of the United States Foreign Service.

Maybe it was all the tours locked in the fishbowl of an embassy fortress in a faraway dangerous place. Perhaps it was the cocktail of hyperambition, natural human pettiness, and living just on the edge of Washington power. Being within reach of those with true influence can make it feel so far away. And even more desirable. Or possibly, Judd thought, it was just a spectacular irony that those tasked to build friends for America around the world would treat each other with such disdain.

The result for Judd Ryker was a beautiful oak-paneled office with a view of the Lincoln Memorial, a mandate to help the United States government respond more quickly to evolving crises around the world, and no means whatsoever to get this task done. Who would want some new guy with his charts and data sticking his nose into their business? No one.

In his first few weeks on the job, shooting had erupted in the Solomon Islands, an unstable archipelago in the South Pacific. Judd had been completely iced out. He'd even had solid new data on the causes of conflict in small island nations. Neither the Pacific team nor the Australia office director would even answer his calls.

A month later, riots broke out in Kenya after a disputed election, and this time the Assistant Secretary for Africa, William Rogerson, had wholly cut him out. He'd only heard about Task Force Kenya after it had already met and decided the course of action for U.S. policy. "Sorry, the meeting must have been moved. Didn't my assistant tell your assistant?" was the halfhearted reply.

But then it happened again, without even the pretense of a disingenuous excuse. Judd confronted Rogerson over being excluded from a Nigeria meeting. This time, the response was blunt: "Young man, when people get out of their lane, they usually get lost. Or run over."

Judd's frustration grew. He began to regret taking the job. *How can I speed up response times if I'm ignored?*

Judd turned to counsel outside the government. BJ van Hollen advised patience and perseverance. "These things take time," his mentor scolded him. "You know this."

His wife Jessica also encouraged him to build new allies and find ways to circumvent obstructers. "You are still learning your way around the building. Still figuring out how to play the game. Wait for your moment," she suggested.

But with each new failure, Judd's doubts grew. He even began to wonder, *Did Landon Parker set me up to fail?*

Impossible to know. At best, Judd began to understand that his office was a mere experiment, that *he* was an experiment. A lab rat.

As the driver pulled up to the security barriers in front of State headquarters, Judd fished his ID card out of his briefcase and held it up for the diplomatic security officer leaning into the vehicle window.

Judd ducked his head and slid the ID

chain over his neck. *Back in Washington.* A second officer stood at attention in the guardhouse, patiently waiting for a signal. A third officer slowly circled the car with a sniffing German shepherd on a leash.

"Thank you, sir." And then, "Lower the barrier!"

"Lowering the barrier!" Down came the metal barricade with a squeal and a hollow thunk.

After being waved through the front security gates, the car roared for fifty yards, then endured the same procedure again at the entrance to the underground garage. ID check. "Thank you, sir. Lower the barrier!" "Lowering the barrier!" Squeal, thunk, roar, and then down into the subterranea of the concrete government building.

At the bottom of the ramp, Judd's head bobbed to the right, then to the left, as the Suburban swung two sharp corners. His head came forward as the vehicle screeched to a halt in front of a set of Plexiglas revolving doors.

Before Judd could reach for the handle, the door opened and the officer was holding Judd's go bag. There was still one more security check before entry into the building was complete. Judd swiped his ID card against a keypad and fingered a six-digit

43

PIN. A little light shined green and a loud clack told him it was time to push through the door.

Vacation over.

When Judd arrived at his office, his assistant, Serena, was standing in the doorway holding a folder. Above her head read a small sign: CRISIS REACTION UNIT, OFFICE OF THE DIRECTOR.

"Task Force Mali is ready, over at the Operations Center. They are waiting for you." Serena was all business.

"Good to see you, too. Anything I need to read first?"

"No." Serena was now actively blocking the doorway. Her short, slight frame was more than matched by the serious look on her face and her no-nonsense jet-black business suit, just a shade or two darker than her skin.

"No other messages?"

"It's four minutes after ten already, Dr. Ryker. They are waiting for you at Ops." She handed over the file and gently pushed him down the hallway.

As he walked toward the Operations Center, he opened the file, and the corners of his mouth curled slowly into a faint smile. The folder contained a single piece of paper, almost entirely blank, except: "LJ call T+5."

Judd locked his BlackBerry in a small locker built into the wall next to the security booth. He flashed his ID badge to a uniformed guard at the door and pushed hard on the thick glass door, which gave way with a whoosh of rushing air.

"Thank you, sir. Task Force Mali and Bamako videoconference is Room G."

The State Operations Center was the twenty-four-hour beehive that kept headquarters in touch with America's 305 embassies and diplomatic outposts around the world. It looked like a cross between an air traffic control center and a small trading floor. Young foreign service officers and security specialists sat at terminals with headsets. The walls were lined with large screens, blinking maps, and clocks that flashed the hour of major cities in every global time zone.

Off to one side were several doors that led to highly secure conference rooms. Judd found Room G and pushed open the door.

The scene was much like the one during his fateful seminar for Landon Parker twelve months earlier. There were about a dozen suits sitting around the wood conference table, with younger suits in chairs ringing

45

the outside.

Up on the large screen was a familiar face, Ambassador Larissa James. She was flanked on either side by two men, one in military uniform and one in a rumpled tan suit: the defense attaché and the CIA station chief.

Judd slipped into one of two empty seats at the head of the table.

"Good morning, everybody. I assume we're waiting for Bill Rogerson. What's his ETA?"

"Assistant Secretary Rogerson is not here, sir," said a young staffer sitting along the back.

"Where is he? When is he expected?"

"Away. I have no location and no ETA for the Assistant Secretary. You are chairing the task force, Dr. Ryker," the staffer said, adding definitively, "Mr. Parker's orders."

"Okay, fine." *Lucky break.* "Let's get started. Bamako is plus four hours, everyone, which is fourteen hundred hours GMT." Judd nodded to the screen. "Good afternoon, Bamako. We've got the task force here. For Ambassador James's sake, and my own, let's make quick introductions. I'm Judd Ryker, S/CRU, State Crisis Reaction Unit."

Around the room it went, each in quick succession, announcing a name and an acronym, representing some corner of the State Department bureaucracy and the proliferation of issues and offices. There were reps for the offices of West Africa, North Africa, democracy, human rights, political-military, counterterrorism, economics, regional security, African Union, and consular affairs. Each two-person team, reflecting the strict hierarchy of government, had the more senior person at the table and one staffer, the "plus-one," sitting in the outside ring, at the ready to whisper a detail or pass a critical fact sheet.

The more experienced of those at the table sat with no paper in front of them, the blank table space a sign of supreme confidence of their grasp of the issues at hand. A single crib sheet was still allowable but, Judd had quickly learned, an unmistakable sign of weakness to the others. The thick binders of papers, stuffed with background, spreadsheets, and maps ready at a moment's notice to answer a question — or, better, to trump a rival — were strictly the purview of the outer ring.

They were all, of course, present on short notice in order to hear an update from the embassy and to provide input to U.S. policy during a time of crisis and decision making. Or, more to the point, to ensure their offices weren't cut out of any decisions that impinged on their respective boss's turf.

Just as the staccato of letters finished and the last person had laid their claim to be in the room, Judd impatiently turned back to the screen. "Ambassador James, what is the situation?"

"Thank you, and good morning, everybody. We've got conflicting reports, but we're fairly confident we have a coup unfolding here in Bamako, which probably took place in the early hours of this morning, local time. We think before dawn, roughly four a.m. The television and radio stations are all off the air, the army's on the streets setting up roadblocks around the palace at Koulouba and along the airport road."

Yep, classic signs, thought Judd. *It's a coup.*

"Thus far, the city is calm and we have no reports of violence in the capital or other major towns," continued the ambassador. "I can't get anyone on their cell phones in President Maiga's office. The foreign minister is in Beijing this week, so I haven't been able to reach him, either. Colonel Randy Houston, here, is our defense attaché. Colonel Houston?"

"Thank you, ma'am," responded the

48

military uniform sitting to her right. "At thirteen hundred hours Bamako time, about an hour ago, the regional security officer and I visually confirmed roadblocks around the city. The roadblocks on the highways leading to the palace and to main army barracks at Wangara are both manned by elite presidential guard, the Bérets Rouges or Red Berets. The road to the airport is also confirmed closed. The troops on the airport road are, however, black-hatted Gendarmerie, the equivalent of the U.S. National Guard. We aren't sure what this means, but it does suggest a highly coordinated military effort. This is not just the action of one rogue army unit."

"What about the rest of the military? Where are they?"

"We have private unconfirmed reports that Malian army regulars are on the streets in Kidal, Mopti, Gao, and Timbuktu. We have been unable to reach any of our contacts in the Ministry of Defense by phone. We do have Special Forces officers embedded with the Scorpions. At least one of those units is reported to be AWOL."

"Excuse me, Colonel, the Scorpions?"

"Mali's counterterrorism strike teams. The Scorpions are a new weapon in the global war on terror. We trained and

49

equipped them over the past eighteen months and now have advisors embedded inside each of the units. They are the tip of the spear of our fight against al-Qaeda in this part of the world."

"Thank you, Colonel," said the ambassador, turning back to face the camera. "Any other questions from Washington?"

"The airport. Is it open?"

"An Ethiopian Airlines flight reportedly landed about three hours ago without incident, but the military has now closed it until further notice. All other arrivals have been diverted to Dakar in neighboring Senegal. Air France has canceled its flight in from Paris tonight. British Airways has done the same from London."

"What about American citizens?"

"All official Americans in Bamako have been accounted for," replied Ambassador James. "There are eighty-five Peace Corps volunteers in-country and we will assess their status over the next twenty-four hours. An estimated five hundred private American citizens are also here, but we have no reports of attacks and no reason they are likely to be targeted. Consular Affairs has issued an alert to all AmCits to stay inside. We will also recommend deferring all but essential travel until the situation is clarified."

"Thank you, Ambassador," said Judd. "Do we know who is responsible?"

"At this point, we do not," replied the ambassador. "Mali has a long history of coups and countercoups. The last known attempt was early last year when the then–army Chief of Staff, General Oumar Diallo, tried to arrest President Maiga. Diallo was easily thwarted by Maiga's Red Beret presidential guard, but he escaped to Senegal and then made his way to Europe. Diallo lives in exile in Paris."

The rumpled tan suit, so far completely silent and motionless, mechanically turned his head and whispered into Ambassador James's ear.

"I'm sorry. I mean London," she corrected herself. "Diallo is, we believe, in exile in London."

"Is there any indication that General Diallo may be back in Mali today?" asked Judd.

"None yet, but we are checking," she replied.

The CIA station chief whispered again in her ear. The ambassador nodded slightly, then added, "The current army Chief of Staff is General Mamadou Idrissa. He is supposed to be on leave at his home village up in Dogon Country, near the border with Burkina Faso. But we have unconfirmed reports that he was sighted in Bamako last night. We are checking on this, too."

"What about a terrorist connection?" interrupted a staffer from the counter-terrorism office. He was so young that Judd assumed he was seated at the table only because his superior was too busy to deal with a small West African country. "Could Mali be under terrorist attack?"

"We don't think so," quickly responded the ambassador.

"But Mali does have active al-Qaeda affiliates in its territory. We have been tracking increased activity along the Algerian border and a recent change in smuggling patterns by Tuareg nomads along routes from Niger and Burkina Faso," the staffer continued.

"Yes. That's all true," said the ambassador slowly, failing to hide her annoyance. "But there is no indication whatsoever that there is any terrorism link to the unfolding events of today. Until we have a clear indicator, we are not jumping to conclusions."

Judd interrupted, "Okay, thank you, Madam Ambassador. Do you need anything from Washington?"

"Not right now. We are hunkered down. I hope to know more soon."

"Very good. In that case, we will reconvene in six hours. Thank you, Embassy Bamako."

Without giving anyone else the chance to object, Judd hit the disconnect button on the remote control and the large screen went blank.

"Thanks, everybody. See you all back here at four o'clock. Who's here from public affairs? We need to get a statement out. General boilerplate, expressing concern and that we are closely monitoring the situation, is good enough for now. All offices here on Task Force Mali are on the clearance list for the public statement. Let's try to push this out quickly, folks."

And with that, Judd stood, turned, and hustled out the door, anxious to get back to his office.

Mali, he thought. And the memories rushed back. . . .

5.

BAMAKO AIRPORT, MALI
EIGHT MONTHS AGO

Judd exited the Senegal Airlines Boeing 737 and paused at the top of the truck-mounted stairs. The Saharan heat seared his eyes, forcing him to squint through his slightly crooked sunglasses. *Africa hot.*

Two sandy beige single-story concrete buildings stood a few hundred yards away, with a simple black-and-white sign reading BAMAKO SENOU INTERNATIONAL AIRPORT. BIENVENUE À MALI.

Off to one side was a shiny, obviously new billboard with a handsome African man in a sharp blue pin-striped suit smiling broadly while talking on a tiny mobile phone. Beyond the Malitel sign, toward the far edge of the airport, was a low white prefab building with no markings or signs at all. Beside it Judd could make out the top of a black attack helicopter resting in the tall grass.

On the tarmac stood a small posse waiting for Judd. Several large men in suits and wraparound Oakley sunglasses surrounded a petite woman with short gray hair and tan weathered skin.

Behind them a train of three vehicles idled: a small Peugeot police car with flashing lights, a new white Toyota Hilux pickup truck with GENDARMERIE NATIONALE stenciled sloppily on the side, and a shiny black Chevrolet Suburban. The SUV had tiny American flags on small poles attached to each corner of the front bumper.

The other passengers snaked around the group to make their way to the arrival bay of the airport. When Judd got to the bottom of the steps, the woman stepped forward and extended a stiff hand. "Welcome to Mali, Dr. Ryker."

"Good to meet you, Ambassador James. You didn't have to come out to the airport. I could have met you at the embassy."

"No, no, I'm happy to. Plus, it's protocol. The Malians are very excited to have a special American envoy visiting. Let's go."

And with that she spun around and climbed into the Suburban. Judd ambled around the other side, where one of the men was holding the door. The police siren wailed and the rest of the security guards clambered into the back of the pickup. Judd ducked his head and hopped into the car. The door slammed shut with a slight creak and an unexpectedly heavy thud. *Armored car.* The caravan lurched forward, and the little American flags on the truck's bumper sprang to life.

Beats the death-trap minibus I rode in last time I was in Mali.

Ten seconds later, the cars abruptly halted in front of a concrete building. "VIP lounge." The ambassador shrugged. Judd followed her out of the vehicle and through a door flanked on both sides by stoic soldiers holding automatic rifles.

Inside was a column of men wearing bright blue and stark-white boubous, the full-length flowing robes common in this part of the world. The room had about a dozen shabby burgundy velvet sofas and two brand-new wide-screen televisions sitting side by side, one showing a soccer game, the other Al Jazeera cable news in Arabic with French subtitles. Both were on high volume. Above the TVs was a crooked portrait of a stern-looking President Boubacar Maiga, wearing a modest white cap and watching over the lounge with paternal benevolence.

But the thing Judd most noticed, amid the

sudden assault of noise and color, was the unexpected chill. In a far corner, a massive air-conditioning unit was blowing frigid air across the room. It fogged his sunglasses, and he took them off, sliding them into the inside pocket of his suit jacket.

The ambassador, apparently unfazed by the shocking change in climate, walked Judd up to the receiving line and introduced him to each man in succession. Judd shook hands, smiled politely, but the names and titles were a meaningless jumble. *I'm on the edge of the world's largest desert and I'm freezing.*

"You'll see many of them again later," said the ambassador after the introductions were complete. The men had retreated to the sofas and were busy fishing mobile phones out from inside their boubous.

"Ahmed will take your passport and bring your bag to the residence. Let's go."

Judd handed over his diplomatic passport and followed Ambassador James out of the lounge and back into the Suburban. The caravan, now joined by several more cars, sped out the airport gates, lights blazing, sirens wailing, and down the highway toward the city center.

"Sorry to hit you with all of this right off the plane, but I'm sure you're used to it by now, Dr. Ryker," she said, exposing a slight Texan drawl.

"It's Judd, please. And yes, it's been quite a trip so far."

"You're coming from Senegal, right?" Judd guessed she was in her late fifties, close to retirement, and probably beautiful back in the day. *The Foreign Service takes a toll.*

"Yes, and I hit Mauritania, Guinea, and Liberia before that," Judd said. "I'm leaving for Niger tomorrow evening."

"That does sound exhausting. I hope you'll be able to get what you need while you're here in Mali. It's a risk assessment, right?"

"Correct. We're meeting with all the country and security teams to be sure that our conflict and coup risk metrics are aligned with the data our people on the ground are getting. It's a ground-truth tour."

"Plus, you can get to know the people on the other side of the table," she added. "I've been in the Foreign Service twenty-six years. I've served in Honduras and Japan, in Congo and El Salvador. And one thing I've learned, no matter where you are, is that diplomacy is rarely about policy. It's all about personal relationships."

Judd nodded politely and turned away to

take in the city of Bamako. Along both sides of the road, people were walking, women with rainbow bundles atop their heads, crowds of young men waiting for bush taxis, little muddy boys riding donkeys. And goats, an endless throng of goats.

"Your first time in Mali?" she asked.

Judd faced Larissa James.

"I was here many years ago as part of a survey team with the Haverford Foundation. We were assessing community water management in Kidal. I actually met my wife, Jessica, here on that trip."

"How wonderful."

"She's an agronomist."

"So Mali has been lucky for you?" she smiled.

"Yes." Judd turned back to the window and the bustling cityscape. "So far, Mali has been very lucky for me."

6.

"Judd, they're here. Come out and meet the team!"

"Coming, Professor!" Judd replied from inside the tent. *Christ, it's hot,* was all he could think. *I should have gone on the Mongolia project. Or, better yet, stayed in my lab.*

Judd opened the tent flap and ducked his head to exit. Standing outside among several parked Land Rovers were Professor BJ van Hollen and a middle-aged African man with a short-cropped goatee.

"Judd, this is Dr. Papa Toure. He's come up from the University of Ibadan in Nigeria to help us with this project. No one knows water in this part of the world better than Papa."

"Pleased to meet you," said Judd, extending a firm handshake.

"Judd is the rising star I was telling you

60

about," van Hollen explained, rubbing his fingers through his thick graying beard, a habit from the classroom that he could never quite shake during fieldwork.

"I really don't think so," replied Judd, doing his best to deflect the uncomfortable praise from his mentor.

"Nonsense. Judd is one of my best students."

"How do you two know each other?" asked Judd, steering the conversation away.

"Oh, we've known each other for ages! Since Papa first went to the university. He was still a frightened little village boy back then. Papa, you were scared out of your mind!" exclaimed van Hollen, slapping Papa on the back and looking very pleased with himself. "It was your first time in Nigeria!"

"It was my first time outside of Mali," added Papa, returning the hearty smile. "It was my first time anywhere. What can you expect?"

"Ah, those were the days! We were all so naïve back then. Remember how we thought oil would make Nigeria the next Norway?"

"So long ago, BJ!" agreed Papa.

"And so foolish!"

"Yes, fools among fools! That was us!" said Papa. "But what does that make us now?"

"Papa is the most honest man in Nigeria,"

61

declared van Hollen, his face suddenly turning dead serious. Then he turned to Papa. "I'd say that makes you a prince among thieves."

"Ah, still a fool among fools," said Papa, shaking his head in mock disgust.

Their banter was interrupted by a loud rustling coming from inside one of the Land Rovers. The three men turned to face the noise. One of the truck doors swung open and out stepped a pair of tall slender black boots. Wearing the boots was a young woman in a tight white blouse and khaki trousers.

"And, *here* she is," announced van Hollen with a flourish.

The girl had long dark hair, mocha-colored skin, and bright blue eyes. Most of all, Judd noticed she was suspiciously immaculate for someone who'd just spent eleven hours on a dusty desert road. *So clean.*

"Lovely to see you, BJ," she said, slightly embarrassed. She gave him a warm hug and a kiss on both cheeks. Judd was transfixed. *A desert mirage?*

"Judd, this is our agronomist, Jessica White. She recently finished her doctorate at the University of Wisconsin. She's one of my new protégés."

She gave Judd a polite but distant smile.

"Madison has a strong Africa program," Judd offered.

She nodded.

"Judd used to be one of my students. Just finished. Brilliant work on conflict measurement. Cutting-edge data metrics. Luckily, I've convinced him to help me one last time before he flees the van Hollen nest. He's joining us on this Haverford Foundation project, but in the fall he'll be starting as junior faculty at Amherst College."

"Ah, yes, very good," said Papa. "Massachusetts. Impressive."

"Yes, I am extremely pleased," said van Hollen, rubbing his beard again. "I'm still hoping I can talk Judd into coming down from the ivory tower once in a while to work on real-world problems. But if he's going to teach, it might as well be at a place like Amherst. Isn't that right, Dr. Ryker?"

"Stop it," said Judd, trying to deflect his embarrassment.

"Judd here is better with numbers than social interaction," added van Hollen. "He's still working on his people skills. Right, Judd?"

"Amherst College houses the original Emily Dickinson Collection," offered Jessica.

"I didn't know that," said Judd.

"She's my favorite poet."

"Oh, *I am good.* I knew you two would hit it off," said van Hollen, pulling the four of them together into a huddle. "We are going to make a terrific team. I just know it. And Judd, my boy, you are going to love Mali. . . ."

7.

BAMAKO, MALI
EIGHT MONTHS AGO
And love it he did, for many reasons, Judd thought as he sat in the car from the airport. But thinking of that first trip now reminded him of something he'd been putting off for far too long.

Once the ambassador's SUV arrived back at her fortresslike residence, Judd excused himself and retreated to the guest room. He sat on the bed, cradling his phone and thinking about the call that he really didn't want to make.

It had only been a few weeks since BJ's death. He hadn't spoken with Papa yet. He had tried several times, once even picking up the phone and dialing the fifteen digits. But he'd hung up before anyone answered. Maybe he felt guilty. Maybe he wasn't ready to talk with Papa. Or maybe he just hadn't yet come to accept that his mentor was really gone.

Jessica, too, had been upset by BJ's passing. They'd both known he was very ill, but the end was still sudden. By sheer bad luck, Jessica had had to rush off to Indonesia to deal with a problem at one of her projects, and when the end had finally arrived, she'd been stuck in Jakarta and forced to miss the funeral. Judd had dropped their children at his grandmother's house and flown to California to be there. During the memorial service, he'd held up his cell phone so Jessica could listen from her hotel room on the other side of the world. She hid her emotions well, but Judd knew she was devastated. Judd was certain that she cried over BJ, but she never let him see it.

Judd looked down at his phone and then dialed a local number.

"Oui?" curtly answered a deep male voice.

"Yes, hello? This is Judd Ryker calling for Papa Toure. Is he there? Is this Papa?"

"Ah, Judd!" came the reply, a few octaves higher. "My American friend who loves the beer! I have been hoping to hear from you. I was just yesterday thinking about your wedding. I can't believe you've been married eight years already. I was remembering how the trees were changing color in Vermont in the autumn. That was really something for an African to see, you know. Ah, *mon dieu, très magnifique*! Speaking of beautiful, how is Jessica? How are the handsome boys?"

"Yes, everyone's all fine. They send their love."

"How old are they now?"

"Toby is five. Noah just turned three."

"Oh, so wonderful. I am sure they are strong. Just like their mother."

"Yes, Papa. I'm . . . I'm in Bamako."

"Now? You are here in Mali now?"

"Uh-huh."

"Why didn't you tell me? What are you doing here? I don't work much for Haverford lately. Just checking on some of their water projects now and again. Ever since Miriam passed and my son moved to Dakar. I still teach at the university, which doesn't pay but it keeps me busy. You didn't say you were coming. I'll come collect you from the hotel."

"No, I'm not here with Haverford, either. I'll have to explain another time. I am working tonight and have to leave tomorrow. I'm — I'm sorry. I don't think I'll have time to meet up on this trip."

"Who comes all the way from Massachusetts to Bamako for one day? It is absurd. *C'est ridicule!*"

67

"I'm working for the government now. The State Department. I just started a few months ago. It's a special project looking at conflict risk. I can't really tell you too much more."

"I see. Ahhh, the American government. You are a big man now. *Un grand homme.* Very good. The professor would have been proud."

Judd was regretting calling his old friend. Phoning Papa without making time for a face-to-face visit was a mistake. After so many years working with foreigners, Papa of course knew about Americans' different ideas toward social obligations. But now Judd worried that he was causing offense.

"Yes, the professor. BJ is very much missed."

"Judd, I am ashamed that I failed to make the funeral. The journey to California was just too far for my old bones. I hope you understand and forgive me."

"Of course, Papa! We all understand. Please don't apologize."

"It was not proper."

"I'm the one who is sorry. I've come all this way and won't be able to see you. I'll be sure to come back to Bamako soon. I promise. And when I get here we'll have many beers and catch up. I just wanted to call today to check in on you."

"I understand. But I have to ask you: What kind of special conflict is here in Mali that requires such a strange trip? To come all this way from America for one day?" Papa's inquisitive instincts, the same ones that made him such an excellent researcher and collaborator, were kicking in.

"Oh, nothing out of the ordinary, Papa. Just the usual government worries about coups and war in Africa. I guess they picked me because they like my work. I mean, they like *our* work."

"Are you going up to Timbuktu?"

"No."

"You must go."

"I would love to. I've never been to Timbuktu. But no time on this trip."

"Ah, Judd, no. You must go to Timbuktu, Judd. Things are going on up there."

"Yeah, I know," agreed Judd. "I guess the Tuareg traders have been resisting outside control for two thousand years, so we shouldn't expect an easy resolution anytime soon."

"No, no, this is different. Not just the usual troubles. New things are happening. Bad things. Ask your friends in the American government. Ask your people."

A loud knock at the door interrupted.

69

"Dr. Ryker, the palace called and the president is ready to see you." It was the ambassador. "I will wait for you in the car."

"Yes, thank you." Judd belatedly covered the phone with his hand. "I'll be right there."

Then back into the handset, "Papa, it's so good to hear your voice. I do want to know more. I promise I'll be back soon and I owe you a dinner."

"You are going to see President Maiga? Look at you! You really are a big man, eh, Judd?"

"I wish it were true. Let's try to speak soon, and not let it go so long this time, okay? Keep well, Papa."

"We have a proverb, Judd. 'Salt comes from the north, gold comes from the south, wisdom comes from Timbuktu.' "

As Judd climbed into the car, Ambassador James handed him a single piece of paper, "This just came in from your office." It was a clipping from the *Washington Post,* dated that morning, under the headline: "Senate Pushes New Sanctions for Global Drug War." Serena had highlighted several sections:

"Senator Bryce McCall (D-PA), chairman of the Senate Foreign Relations Committee, is poised to add a new penalty against countries deemed uncooperative with American global counter-narcotics efforts. . . . At a press conference, surrounded by his extended family including his two young daughters, McCall announced, 'We can no longer tolerate countries that accept American aid but turn a blind eye to drug kingpins operating with impunity. We must protect our country and our children. . . .' The McCall Kingpin Amendment will mandate that the State Department report back to Congress an annual assessment on every country's level of cooperation in curtailing the illegal drug trade. . . . Any country deemed to be insufficient will be subject to immediate financial sanctions, including the suspension of foreign assistance. McCall has been a longtime advocate of a harder U.S. line on drugs, and this is his latest effort to increase pressure on countries he believes are abetting the international narcotics trade. . . . Aides to the senator confirmed that the principal targets are politicians in Central America with purported links to drug cartels, but they dismissed concerns that the McCall Amendment, if passed, would overly complicate relations with other countries. . . . The McCall Kingpin Amendment is expected to pass both houses of Congress this week, while the White House has indicated the president will sign 'any bill that protects American children.' " Judd folded the paper in half lengthwise and tucked it into the inside pocket of his suit jacket.

He turned back to Ambassador James, who appeared, for the first time, visibly a little nervous.

"We are approaching Koulouba. That's the palace. I would have preferred that my embassy team brief you before you meet the president, but the palace was insistent that President Maiga wants to see you now. I don't think Maiga will spring anything on us, but you can expect him to ask about intelligence sharing and for more malaria money. He is making a big deal about malaria. One of his campaign promises was to eradicate malaria in the north, and they are already falling way behind schedule."

"What intel sharing?"

"We've got a Code Orange program with them. Looking for terrorist groups, infiltration of foreign jihadists, watching the borders. Nothing out of the ordinary. Mostly we track smugglers who just want to be left alone. But a few bad guys flying the jihadist flag are making trouble."

"And Maiga cooperates?"

"It's in his interest. He's mainly nervous about any plots against him. The intelligence is partly to keep an eye on his own commanders. Like most of Africa, the real threat is from within his own ranks more than from a foreign invader."

"And? Is he at risk?"

"There are rumors. There are always rumors," said the ambassador. Judd noticed she looked down when she answered. *Is that a tell?*

"I've heard the same thing in every country I've visited. What else do I need to know about the president?"

"Boubacar Maiga spent his thirties in America, mostly working his way up through SunCity Bank in New York. So his English is perfect and, unlike most of the other presidents in West Africa, he's not enthralled with the French. After New York, he came back to Mali and set up his own firm, including BamakoSun Bank, the country's first completely private local bank. He quickly used his connections on Wall Street and in London to swallow up his competition. That made him a tycoon and very wealthy, but also many enemies. When he turned fifty, he abruptly sold BamakoSun and ran for president. That was two years ago now and so far, so good. Maiga has allowed the press and opposition to operate freely and encouraged new investment. Economic growth is up and poverty, while still high, is on the decline. Maiga deserves his reputation as one of our closest and most reliable allies in Africa."

"That sounds too good to be true, Ambassador."

"If I'm going to call you Judd, you can call me Larissa."

"Okay, Larissa. What is the real story?"

"That is the real story. He's vetted. That's why we have President Maiga sitting next to the Secretary of State at the upcoming Democracy Summit in Jakarta. We had to fight East Asia to the mat for that seat."

"I know Mali, and it can't be all so rosy."

"Well, Mali is nothing like Nigeria. But we are pretty sure that some of the top military brass is involved in smuggling. The region is rife with traffickers in guns, cigarettes, and drugs. Mali is now part of the route from the coast across the desert and into Europe. General Mamadou Idrissa is the commander for the northern Timbuktu Zone Six and probably on the take. He's a nasty piece of work. You'll likely meet him at the palace."

"I'll want to ask about the north. But what's the northern commander doing down here in the capital, by the president's side?"

"Good question. We don't know. He seems to be around the president all the time."

"What about Maiga? Does he have his hand in the cookie jar?"

"He seems clean. Rich enough, I suppose, to avoid the temptation."

"Yet he can't rein in Idrissa?"

"I believe he's trying. But he has to be careful. Mali has had four coups since independence and many more failed attempts. Just last month, the head of the army, General Oumar Diallo, was forced to flee after trying to organize a putsch. He caught wind that Maiga was planning to fire him, so he tried to seize the palace. But Diallo's guys didn't even get through the front gate. Someone tipped off Maiga's personal security, probably French intelligence."

"Not us?" Judd raised his eyebrows.

"Not as far as I know," Larissa responded quickly, with a slight shrug. "Maiga's pro-American, so I'm sure the French have been trying to court him."

"And Diallo?"

"He fled to Europe. Doesn't seem to be making any new trouble. But Diallo always had grand ambitions and a healthy ego. He definitely wanted to be president. I expect he'll try again one day. He's the First Lady's cousin."

"General Diallo is related to the president?"

"By marriage, yes." Larissa had clearly told this story many times and was amused at Judd's naïve surprise. "Mrs. Maiga and General Diallo grew up in the same village. We think their mothers are half sisters. It's always the internal family squabbles that are the most bitter."

"Yes. Yes, they are."

The convoy with Judd Ryker and Larissa James reached the road leading up to the Presidential Palace. At the corners, young soldiers with hard helmets sat behind sandbags and leaned on heavy .50 caliber guns mounted on tripods. Along the main road other soldiers lay underneath the bulbous bellies of South African armed personnel carriers that Judd had seen in many other countries. Larissa poked Judd in the shoulder.

"Maiga just bought a new fleet of those hippos," she grimaced. "They are fine in the city, but no good up north in the sand. Not the best use of our counterterrorism dollars, but that's what he said he wanted."

As they rolled up to the main palace gate, Judd sat up straight. Passing military checkpoints, even with diplomatic security in an ambassador's armor-plated vehicle, made him nervous. But they were waved through without slowing down. *Must be those little American flags.*

Several guards with AK-47s slung over their shoulders and wearing red berets jumped to attention and saluted the Suburban as they passed.

The circular driveway at the front of the main building was lined with men in sparkling-white boubous. As they exited the car, Judd and Larissa shook hands with each of the men, who then fell in line behind them as they entered into the palace. Men with shoulder-mounted television cameras jostled each other for position as the entourage passed.

They were all led into a small waiting room, painted light green, with a large TV in the corner. The sofas were also green and brand-new, with dainty white crocheted covers on the arms that reminded Judd of his grandmother's old farmhouse in Vermont.

Just as Judd had exhausted his small talk with the entourage and was starting to fidget, they were mercifully led into the president's office.

President Boubacar Maiga, wearing a crisp royal blue boubou, was sitting at an enormous ebony desk signing some papers. Behind him hovered the Malian flag on a pole, and large photos of Mali's cultural sites adorned the walls. Judd recognized the Great Mosque of Djenné, the world's largest mud building. He also eyed photos of the smaller but no less significant Great Mosque of Timbuktu, painted boats along the Niger River, and the villages built into cliffs in Dogon Country. In front of the desk was a semicircle of a dozen heavy burgundy chairs.

"Madam Ambassador!" Maiga looked up, removed his reading glasses, and swooped out from behind the desk with surprising speed for such a large man. Maiga spread his wings like a giant blue bat, and hugged Larissa James, enveloping the diminutive ambassador.

"And Dr. Ryker. Welcome! Welcome to Koulouba! I understand you are already an expert on Mali and have helped my country with our water problems. Thank you for coming back to honor us with your visit."

"Yes, Mr. President, this is Dr. Judd Ryker." Larissa was recovering from the bear hug.

"Thank you, Mr. President. I am honored to be back. Thank you for making time to see me."

Maiga extended a beefy hand, and the two of them awkwardly held the handshake while cameras snapped away. Still holding Judd's grip, Maiga turned to a TV camera.

"We welcome our American friends here today. The visit of such a high-level official from the government of the United States of America shows our close partnership. We will today discuss cooperation on malaria, road construction, and bringing American businesses to Mali."

All eyes and cameras turned to Judd. Larissa gave him a little nod of encouragement.

"Yes, thank you. I am pleased to be in Mali today and to meet with President Maiga. America is a good friend to Mali. We will, um, we will discuss many things today." After a long pause, Judd simply nodded. Maiga then released Judd's hand, and waved away the press.

The three of them took their seats in the center, with each entourage taking their place down the line. Behind Maiga stood a tall soldier at attention. His uniform was several sizes too large for his skinny frame, but a chest full of ribbons and a flat-topped cap with stars announced he was a general.

"Mr. President," Judd began. "I'm here on a regional tour to evaluate the potential for conflict in West Africa. My office deals with crisis reaction, so I'm here to discuss the situation in the north."

"Yes, yes. The north. We are working closely with our American friends to fight malaria in the north. It is going well, but we need to accelerate if we are going to reach our targets. We need more bed nets and the next-generation insecticides from American companies. I was promised these."

Judd turned to Larissa, who accepted his cue. "Yes, Mr. President. I have passed your request to Washington and I appreciate your patience. Dr. Ryker will, I am sure, reinforce that message when he gets back to headquarters."

"Yes, Mr. President," added Judd. "I know the U.S. government is slow, but I will speak with the malaria teams in Washington and see what can be done. What about security in the north?"

"I have been waiting for eight months on the insecticides. Do I have your word you will make inquiries on Mali's behalf?"

"You do, Mr. President."

"Very well. Our military is working hard to control the north and to control the borders. We are talking to the Tuareg leaders. We are investing in the north. We are building wells and schools, with our American partners. That is also why the malaria campaign is so important. But we still have a bandit problem."

"What about smuggling?"

"There has always been smuggling in the north, Dr. Ryker. I am certain you already know this. It is part of the culture of the Sahara. Our military is trying their best to keep things under control, but it is very difficult." Maiga turned around. "General Idrissa is here. He is in charge of the northern sector. Everything from Timbuktu to the border with Algeria. He can tell you."

"Thank you, sir," responded Idrissa, still standing firmly at attention. "The president is correct. We are working hard to prevent insecurity, but it is difficult. Security. Yes. We must maintain security. My zone, Zone Six, is very large and we have few vehicles or radios. The bandits have many trucks and are well armed."

"We have provided special forces training for a camel corps that patrols the border," interjected the ambassador. "The training has been going very well. We have also trained and equipped counterterrorism strike teams, the Scorpions."

"Yes, we are very grateful for American help," replied Idrissa, a little too disingenuously.

"What about the helicopters? I saw one at the airport. It's a Russian HIND attack gunship, yes?" asked Judd. *I may be a liberal arts professor from New England, but I know my attack choppers.*

"Correct, Dr. Ryker," answered General Idrissa. "We call them crocodiles. But they are from Ukraine. The Soviets used them to fight terrorists in Afghanistan. We are using them to fight terrorists in the Sahara."

Judd nodded.

"And, General, how are things in Timbuktu?" asked Judd, drawing a puzzled look from Larissa that he ignored.

Before Idrissa could answer, Maiga interjected, "Timbuktu is very well. No problems there. General Idrissa has everything under control."

"That's very good to hear. And what about terrorist cells infiltrating the north? Are they a growing threat?"

"Yes, we have them. But they are not Malian," replied Maiga firmly. "They are foreigners who have come from Libya and Algeria into Mali to take advantage of our open and welcoming country. They will never take root here since our religion

82

rejects extremism, and our culture accepts all people. Going back to the Songhai Empire and the merchant center at Timbuktu, Mali has always been a place of many peoples. For a thousand years we have been a place for people of all cultures to meet and trade. We will never accept violence."

"What about jihadists from the Middle East?"

"I don't think we have any. But we would welcome more cooperation. We must work together to keep the radicals from poisoning our youth and harming Africa."

Idrissa nodded slowly and added, deadpan, "We need more intelligence sharing to prevent insecurity."

Maiga nodded in solemn agreement, before adding, "You know, Dr. Ryker, we are working hard together, but the Tuareg have a saying. 'No one rules the desert. The desert rules you.' " The president then took tight hold of one of Judd's hands. "My friend . . ." He leaned in close. So close Judd could smell his peppermint breath. The president looked right into Judd's eyes. ". . . please tell me. Oh, how I miss summer nights at Shea Stadium. How are my New York Mets?"

Safely back in the car, the ambassador

seemed buoyant and relaxed. "I think that went well," she said. "You do need to work on your press statements, Judd. But otherwise that went very well. The president likes you."

"Yeah, I'm still new at this. The cameras caught me off guard."

The Suburban, still led by a security escort, passed out of the gates and raced onto the wide access road back toward the city center. Judd held the handle above the window and rested his chin in the crook of his arm to watch the city go by.

They passed a bus depot, a flock of multi-colored minibuses buzzing around a crowd of commuters. He could hear the taxi touts, hanging precariously off the back of the vehicles, calling out destinations around the capital.

"You'll get used to it," she said. "I should have warned you about his obsession with the New York Mets. He's not just indulging a visiting American. He really loves . . ."

Everything went silent for a moment, a whoosh of air, and then KA-BOOM! The explosion felt like it went off inside Judd's head. The vehicle jerked violently to the right and Judd white-knuckled the handle and shut his eyes. "Hold on!" shouted the security agent in the front seat. The heavily armored SUV skidded hard, paused for a moment, and then slowly toppled over, coming to a stop on its right side. Judd's hand slipped and he spilled down the now-vertical back seat, sprawling onto the ambassador's lap.

"IED!" shouted the agent into his radio. "Eagle One, Code Alpha!" Through a cloud of dust and the spiderweb of a cracked, but still intact, ballistic windshield, Judd could see the legs of uniforms running around. His ears were ringing, but he could make out lots of shouting, much of it in the local Bambara language.

The agent, still buckled firmly in his front seat, turned around and, with steely calm, asked, "Ambassador, are you hurt?"

She coughed and covered her ears. "Shit, I don't know. I think I'm okay," came the muffled reply from Larissa, now pinned below Judd.

"Dr. Ryker, how about you, sir?"

It took Judd a second to understand the question. *He's talking to me? Am I okay? I can't feel anything.* Then finally, a nod. "Uh-huh, I think so. I'm alive. I'm not sure I can move my legs."

The agent turned back to the radio. "IED explosion, Eagle One, Code Alpha. Both principals with me. I repeat, two of two alive. But the nest has been penetrated. We need medical response."

Then, to the back seat: "Ma'am, security and medical backups are both on the way. I'm going to assess the perimeter. Don't move. Stay in the vehicle no matter what happens."

"Okay, Frank, we won't go anywhere. Judd, you're staying here with me."

"Yes, of course." *Hell yeah, I'm staying here.*

"Are you really hurt? Can you feel your legs?"

But Judd didn't reply. All he could think about was Jessica.

8.

Judd speedwalked down the hallway. When he arrived back at his office, Serena was standing guard again. Judd didn't slow down as she opened and held the door.

"Ambassador James is wired up and ready to go," she said.

"Good. Is she alone?"

"Yes, sir."

"And we are secure?"

"Yes, sir."

"Thanks, Serena. No calls while I'm on the Tandberg."

On his desk was a dark gray videophone with a ten-inch screen: the Tandberg. *Straight out of* The Jetsons. On the screen was Larissa James, sitting in her office in

Bamako. The defense attaché and the CIA station chief were gone. In the upper left corner flashed TS/SCI. TOP SECRET/SENSITIVE COMPARTMENTALIZED INFORMATION. The call was scrambled and secure. They could talk freely on this line.

Judd hit the button.

"Hey, Larissa. Jesus, what is going on there?"

"Judd, this is definitely a coup. I've seen it before. Sorry to have to pull you off the beach. What a mess."

"This is why I'm here. This is why I gave up tenure track at Amherst and almost got killed visiting you. I'm supposed to be the rescue guy, right?"

"Lucky you."

"Yeah. I thought I'd be, you know, making U.S. policy during crises, but I see I'm now the designated babysitter for the task force."

"You'll have to keep them busy and feed the beast upstairs with regular reports. That's the only way to keep control. You know that, right, Judd?"

"Sure. I'm going to need your help to figure out what's really going on if we are ever going to fix this."

"I'm ready." Larissa smiled for the first time.

"You and I are going to reverse this one if I have to come down there and walk Idrissa out of the palace myself. It's got to be Idrissa, right?"

"Colonel Houston and Cyrus, the station chief, say they don't really know for sure, but that's our assumption, too. Cyrus should know more later today after he gets back from making the rounds. We've asked NSA what chatter they are picking up, too."

"If it is Idrissa, could he be in league with Oumar Diallo? Could this be General Diallo's second bite at the cherry?"

"Could be." Larissa nodded gently. "I'll talk to the British high commissioner here and see what the Brits think. I assume they are tailing him in London. Maybe you can double back with your counterpart at the Foreign Office and see what they know, too."

"Who else is really a player in Bamako?"

"The French still have eyes and ears here. I'll talk to them, too, but their ambassador is old-school foreign ministry. I'm not sure he'll have anything I can't pick up myself on the cocktail circuit. You'll have to find a contact in Paris that you can trust."

"What about the neighbors?"

"They will stay quiet for a few days. I expect the United Nations and the African Union will both issue blanket condemna-

89

tions of the coup, but no one will even start thinking seriously about next steps for at least a week. A strategy, much less a special envoy, is at least two weeks away. Maybe three."

"That's too long," said Judd. "We are already more than ten hours into this. You and I need to figure out the pressure points. Can you feed the local press, make sure they know we won't accept the coup, despite what they start hearing from the palace? What about leaking stories that the Americans are pissed off?"

"Sure. I can do that. I can reach out to local Imams, too. They are the real power brokers."

"Good. What about the army? Can your defense attaché call the other military leaders and take their temperature? See who might still be loyal to Maiga? See if there's a whiff of a countercoup brewing. That would be a lucky break. That's Plan A."

"I will ask Colonel Houston. He seems to have good access. The Malians love him."

"We also need to keep Washington happy. Eventually you are going to have to give the counterterrorism guys more than what you gave the task force. I've been back in the office for twenty minutes and they're already breathing down my neck. All right?"

"Yes."

"Anything else that you're not telling me, Larissa?"

"Keep this to yourself for now, Judd. There's a breakaway jihadist cell here calling itself Ansar al-Sahra. They are small, but showing similar patterns to the early Afghan Taliban, so Cyrus is tracking them. The Malians are extremely concerned because they appear even more extremist and dangerous than the other armed groups in the area. We don't believe Ansar al-Sahra could have more than a couple dozen active members, likely all Libyans or Algerians, but Malian intelligence has been watching the mosques closely for recruitment footprints, especially around Timbuktu."

"I can't imagine that a group like that would find many recruits in Mali."

"I agree, Judd. Islam in Mali has always been very moderate. But the remote areas up north are impossible to patrol. Terrorist groups copycatting al-Qaeda are looking for safe havens, out of sight and beyond the reach of the Algerian and Malian militaries. Ansar is probably one of them, but worse because, if we believe the intelligence reporting, their ambition is to attack big targets like Timbuktu. Maybe even Bamako."

"And the Tuareg? Any signs of a rebellion brewing?"

"Not that we can see. The Tuareg are nomads who have been trading across the Sahara Desert for the past two thousand years. Today they are shuttling more cigarettes and guns than salt and gold, but they still just want to do their trade in peace. No one's ever been able to control that area. Not the French and not the government in Bamako."

"Any links to this Ansar al-Sahra?"

"We really don't know. Mali's had five Tuareg rebellions over the past fifty years, so the risk of it spinning out of control is always high. Every time the government overreaches, the Tuareg fight back. There are still half a dozen loosely affiliated separatist groups that want independence from the south, but we don't think they represent a majority. They are, however, operating in the same physical area as the real terrorist groups. But the Tuareg should have no good reason to want to draw unwanted attention and force the Malian military to get involved."

"Or us," Judd added.

"Right. Or us."

"Okay, Larissa. But you know that's not how our counterterrorism guys will see it.

They will see smugglers and ungoverned spaces and want to start dropping large exploding things from planes onto camels to make sure al-Qaeda doesn't find anywhere to hide."

"Ansar knows this, too," said Larissa. "They will probably try to integrate into civilian Tuareg society. So they can blend in. Maybe gain a foothold for the long jihad."

"Then our goal has to be to drive a wedge between them. We can't let our goals of fighting terrorism get conflated with local Tuareg politics."

Larissa nodded in agreement.

"What about our uniformed guys? Do they get this? Colonel Houston said something about Special Forces embedded with the antiterrorism unit. Have you got them corralled, Larissa?"

"Yeah, we've got our people placed with Mali's counterterrorist strike forces as part of Operation Sand Scorpion. Houston has positioned his guys all over the country."

"Is that a good idea?"

"I'm having him pull them all back to Bamako until we know what's going on with the coup. Those guys are still running around up in Timbuktu, Kidal, Mopti, and Gao."

"Jesus, Larissa. That sounds like a mess. We've got a coup by the Malian military and they've got boots in every corner of the country. DoD must be having a fit."

"That's why I'm pulling them back."

"You better do it quick. The Senate is going to have some difficult questions for the Pentagon if we don't get this coup turned around right now. Wait until the Senate Foreign Relations Committee gets wind of this. Chairman McCall wants some scalps over our secret CT programs that don't seem to be bearing the fruit he wants. And now this. McCall is going to have an absolute fit."

"Judd, Bryce McCall is going to have other concerns when he hears of the coup. His daughter is one of our Peace Corps volunteers. In a village up north. Near Timbuktu."

Judd hunched over his desk examining satellite photos of the Mali-Algeria border. Across the top of each threatened a SECRET label. The photos, date-stamped that morning, were light brown, almost sepia, pictures of sand dunes, in succession of increasing amplification.

The last photo showed a cluster of darker-brown squares, with what were clearly three pickup trucks parked in a straight line. A bright red circle surrounded the encampment and vehicles, with a helpful arrow pointing to the center and a label: POSSIBLE TERRORIST CAMP. It looked like many other similar photos Judd had seen of mobile camps in the desert. It could have been Ansar al-Sahra. Or Tuareg. Or Malian military. *It could be terrorists. Or nothing at all.*

Serena interrupted, "Dr. Ryker, I have the other Dr. Ryker on line four."

Push. "Hey, Jess, how's it going? I've been meaning to call you. Sorry, it's just gotten crazy."

"I'm sure it is. What's the news? Is it a coup?"

"Still trying to figure that out. Are you at the beach?"

"Sure. The kids are trying out those boogie boards you got them. You still don't know what's going on in Bamako? How is that possible? What did the embassy say?"

"They're working on it, too. Look, it's starting to get complicated. I don't think I'm going to be back today. I'm sorry this is ruining our vacation."

"I blame Mamadou Idrissa, not you, Judd."

"Well, we don't even know yet who is behind the coup. Or if it's really a coup at all. Is it hot on the beach?" Judd imagined Jessica, lying on a towel, simple black bikini, hair up, dark sunglasses, reading the *African Crop Science Journal.*

"Yeah, but the breeze is keeping us cool. Come on. It's gotta be Idrissa. What did Papa tell you?"

Uh-oh, thought Judd.

"I'll take your silence as an indication you haven't called him yet. Come on, Judd. You have no idea what's going on and you haven't called Papa Toure? No wonder. He'll know the story even before the CIA will. He should have been your *first* call."

"Yeah," was Judd's sheepish reply.

"Your guys should probably put him on the payroll."

"Uh-huh. I'll suggest that," he said with a tinge of sarcasm.

"You know why Henry Kissinger was so powerful, Judd?"

"I have a feeling you are going to tell me."

"Because he built his own private network to solve problems. He had his own parallel communications and intelligence systems. Diplomatic theater is one thing, but he did the real work away from the headlines and behind the scenes. Scheming is done in the shadows, Judd. Didn't you read Kissinger's *Diplomacy?*"

"You're right, Jess. Of course. I know. I will call Papa. I just haven't had the chance yet."

"Judd, I'm sure you feel like you are drinking from a fire hose today. You must use what you have. Don't let the rest distract you. What do I always tell you? 'Until the desert knows that water grows, his sands suffice.' It fits here. You can do this."

"Yeah, I remember. Emily Dickinson. I will try to use what I have. I won't let the Sahara die on me. Thanks, Jess. Um, what are you doing later? How late can I call you?"

Serena poked her head in with a look of urgency on her face. Judd cupped the handset and raised his eyebrows at Serena.

"Idrissa," she whispered.

"What?"

"It is Idrissa. Ops just called. Idrissa is on Malian television right now. They are piping it into your screen in ten seconds."

Judd nodded and uncupped the phone. Jessica was shouting at one of the boys. "No, put that down!" He could hear crying in the background.

"Uh, sorry, Jess. I have an urgent call. Let me take this and I'll call you later. Give a hug to the boys."

"I have to go, too. All hell is breaking loose

on the beach," she said. "Get cracking and fix this thing, Judd. And then get back here already."

Jessica's voice projected neither irritation nor disappointment. *No read yet.*

Judd hung up and pushed the button on his computer screen.

". . . today, my people, Mali takes another step forward in its glorious history as a leader of Africa and a crossroads of the Sahara." General Mamadou Idrissa was behind a large wooden desk with the Malian flag behind him. *He's sitting in President Maiga's office. Jessica was dead right.*

"We have had a long journey, from the Songhai Empire to the terrible suffering of our people under French exploitation, to the splendor of our hard-fought independence. The arrival of democracy to the republic in 1992 was a triumph of the people and set us on the course for peace and development." Idrissa was in full military regalia. He appeared calm and spoke straight into the camera.

"But, my people, we all know, things have gone astray. Yes. The greed and corruption of the elite have stolen from the people and threatened our magnificent democracy. The gains from the blood and sweat of our fathers were on the verge of being lost to the gluttony of those who would sell us to foreigners and would eat food from the mouths of our children. We could not allow this to continue. No. We could not allow our democracy to be weakened by those who would steal from our own nation. No. We had no choice but to act against those enemies from within in order to save the nation. We must have security. Yes. We must have security," said Idrissa. The words were bold, but the general's fingers were twitching.

"As of today, parliament and the cabinet are hereby dissolved. The president has been relieved of his duties. The Council for the Restoration of Democracy has taken over the responsibilities of government. I, as commander in chief of the Malian Armed Forces, will chair the Council until we can organize new elections at an appropriate time." Idrissa picked his cuticles as he spoke. "Security, security," he repeated.

"This is not a step I take lightly, nor a role I want for myself. No. I am responding to the demands of the people as a humble servant of the nation. I accept their demands. The people can no longer be expected to merely accept the immoral ways of the past. This day has been thrust upon me, and the Council, and the people, by the fate of our history. I have no choice but to embrace this role, even if I did not seek it. I accept the demands of the people to lead us back to democracy and salvation." More fidgeting. *There is still time.*

"Like Charles de Gaulle and Thomas Jefferson before me, I accept this mantle of history with a heavy heart and clear intentions. The burden of history can instead become wind at our backs." Judd shook his head in disbelief.

"To our many friends in Africa and partners around the world, do not be alarmed. No. Do not be swayed by the naïve claims of the previous government and the minions of corruption. We ask for your understanding of the situation and why this action today was unavoidable. This will become even clearer over coming days. As commander in chief, I have appointed a new attorney general whose first task will be to unveil and correct the errors of the past.

"To my fellow Malians and our friends around the world, our beloved Mali was on a path to crisis and depravity. The global threats to civilization were on our doorstep, and the previous government was holding that door open. I tell you today, that we are firmly closing that door and restoring security. We are putting Mali back on the path of the righteous and the good. Long live the Republic."

The screen went black.

"Serena! Get me public affairs and our statement right now. Call the Africa Issue team at CIA and tell them I'll be at Langley in thirty minutes. I need to find out what the hell is really going on. Tell them I need the full briefing, no filters. And forget motor pool. I'm driving myself."

My moment.

9.

Judd cruised up the George Washington Parkway. Flashes of the Potomac River could be seen through the trees off to his right. The Potomac was calm and navigable all the way from the Chesapeake Bay . . . until Washington, D.C. Heading upstream, it was all smooth waters past Fort McNair, Ronald Reagan National Airport, the Kennedy Center, even the Watergate. But once past the Georgetown University boathouse, nestled under the Key Bridge, the serenity ended. The Potomac quickly, and unexpectedly, became treacherous white water.

Judd's car, an aging silver Honda Accord that he'd bought off one of his Amherst College students, pulled off the parkway at an exit marked GEORGE BUSH CENTER FOR INTELLIGENCE and wound its way to the front security gates.

The first layer was an unmanned barrier. Judd recited his name and Social Security number into a large black bubble beside the gate. The barrier elevated and the vehicle rolled up to the guardhouse. An officer in an unmarked uniform stepped out from behind a blackened glass booth. "ID," he said, more as a statement than a request. Judd handed over his government identification card, and the officer disappeared back behind the dark glass.

After a few seconds, he reappeared and returned the ID along with a large yellow VIP parking card, which brought Judd a small tinge of relief. The last visit to CIA headquarters left him driving around for twenty minutes looking for parking. *Who knew CIA headquarters had a shortage of parking?*

As the steel barriers sank into the ground and the Honda revved forward, Judd's BlackBerry rang. A Washington number he didn't recognize. Judd pushed the button. "This is Ryker."

"Hello, Judd. This is Mariana. Mariana Leibowitz. You remember we met at the Council breakfast on post-transition reconstruction a few months ago. I'm sure you remember. We talked about the Kennedy Center gala for Congo."

"Ah, yes, Mariana. Of course." Judd couldn't have forgotten Mariana Leibowitz. "The Congo gala. And also the McCall Drug Kingpin Amendment that was a problem for your client."

A staple of the Washington disaster set, Mariana had a reputation for always popping up just when a crisis hit. The archetypal Washington player, she used smarts, connections, and beauty to dominate complicated situations. And, Judd had quickly learned, to pry information from the weak.

However, Mariana's real skills seemed to be bringing people together and, for a hefty price, problem-solving for unusual clients. In her late forties, she was still able to turn the heads of younger men. And she knew it. But it wasn't only her physical looks that attracted men like Judd. She appeared, from the first time he met her, to be oh so very good at her job.

"I understand you are working the Bamako situation and Rogerson is tied up in Africa somewhere," she said. *Yes, Mariana is very good.*

"If you say so."

"Well, that's what my sources tell me. I want to make sure you have all the information you need. Also, I hear you are a hard-data man, so you should know there is a lot of terrible misinformation coming your way. I just hate rumor and insinuation."

"Since when are you involved in West Africa, Mariana? What's your interest?"

"Oh, Judd, darling, you haven't done your homework. Boubacar Maiga has been a longtime client. I helped him when he was still an idealistic banker who wanted to return home as president and save his country. Those were some crazy days. He didn't know the first thing about running a presidential campaign!"

"I see."

"Today I have a new client, too. So new that I'm not obligated to reveal any names yet. But I'll share this with you since I know you can be trusted, Judd. President Maiga's daughter, Tata, called me this morning and I'm now advising her. She's a senior at Georgetown University, you know."

"Yes, I'm aware," lied Judd.

"Tata is an extraordinary young woman with a bright career ahead of her. She has received word from Bamako that her father is being held at an army barracks on the outskirts of town. So far, the army is treating him well, but they have threatened him and his family if he doesn't resign. She insists her father will never resign. So I now expect stories, awful lies, to start coming

105

out about the president."

"I see."

"Don't believe the lies, Judd. I'm sure you know that General Idrissa is a snake. And involved in all kinds of naughty business beyond his day job."

"Mariana, I really can't talk to lobbyists right now."

"I know, darling. Idrissa hasn't secured power just yet, and the political circles in Bamako are looking for signs from the United States before they line up on one side or the other. They are all looking to you, Judd. We are all looking to you. It's critical that you send the right signals. You can't abandon President Maiga. You can't abandon Mali's democracy."

"Mariana, the only reason I haven't hung up yet is because I know what great work you did with prodemocracy activists in Zimbabwe. I respect you for that. Most lobbyists just cash their checks, but I know you produce for your clients. So if you have information, you can send it to me. But I can't discuss anything more with you. Especially on the phone."

"I know. But, Judd, a seasoned scholar like you also realizes how useful friends can be. How useful *I* can be. I shall be in touch."

"I am certain you will, Mariana." Judd

pulled into a parking space at the front of CIA headquarters. "I've got to go."

"Don't believe what you are about to hear."

Click.

The main entrance of the original CIA headquarters looked and felt more like a college campus in the 1950s than the modern epicenter of America's global intelligence-gathering and operations network. A pack of young women in identical gray tracksuits ran by, ponytails bobbing in sync.

Judd stepped inside the lobby and walked across the marble insignia on the floor, an eagle head and shield with a sixteen-point compass. Around the outside ring read CENTRAL INTELLIGENCE AGENCY, UNITED STATES OF AMERICA. On the wall to one side was a stone engraving with the agency's motto: AND YE SHALL KNOW THE TRUTH AND THE TRUTH SHALL SET YOU FREE.

Judd approached the security desk, flashed his ID again and waited for his escort. There were clusters of young people, all casually dressed, rushing around.

Across the lobby, Judd eyed a statue honoring General William "Wild Bill" Donovan, founder of the original Office of

Strategic Services, or OSS, the precursor to the CIA, during World War II.

After a few minutes, a stoic young man in khaki slacks and a button-down shirt appeared. Judd had never seen him before. "Dr. Ryker? I can take you up."

Judd was led silently through a series of corridors and up an elevator. After another long corridor, they arrived at a door marked AFRICA ISSUE. Inside, rows of cubicles were stacked high with paper, the walls covered with maps, political posters, and head shots of African leaders. Their destination was a windowless conference room with several twentysomethings seated patiently around a table. The analysts. *They could be my students.*

As Judd entered the room, a woman stood up. Judd guessed that she was maybe thirty years old. "Good to have you here, Dr. Ryker. I'm Zoe, the new regional team leader." Judd shook her hand and turned around to thank the escort and confirm that visitor custody had been transferred, but he was already gone. Judd would never see him again.

"Let's get started." Zoe was all business. "I've rallied all hands on deck. Political analyst, economist, military watcher, and a leadership profiler. But we haven't had time

108

to prepare a formal briefing. What would you like to know first, Dr. Ryker?"

"Thanks. I appreciate you pulling the team together on short notice. Let's get an update of what we know."

"Okay, politics. Sunday here is our lead Mali analyst." She gestured to a young black man with a closely cropped goatee sitting next to her. "Sunday, go."

"Roger." Sunday looked directly into Judd's eyes. "This morning, about twelve hours ago, we had a classic coup d'état. It is a break in the data pattern, however. Aaay, yes, Africa has seen a steep decline in coups in recent decades. More specifically, my cross-country statistical analysis shows a zero-point-eight percentage-point drop per year in annual risk prediction metrics since 1985. Despite this trend, Mali's risk metrics remain high relative to both its income and regional peer groups." *I like this kid.*

Sunday continued, "Turning to this morning's events, General Mamadou Idrissa arrested the president and has him in detention. Idrissa had been consolidating his power base for years, building loyalty among his special guard that operate in the Timbuktu zone number six against Tuareg insurgents. He recruited these elite forces mostly from his home area, near Dogon

Country in the eastern belt along the border with Burkina Faso. The Scorpions are well trained and highly motivated."

"Trained by us," interjected Judd.

"Aaay. Trained by U.S. Special Forces. We suspect that Idrissa pays the Scorpions extra to maintain loyalty. He is now using sizable cash offers to secure the support for the junta of other military brass and members of parliament."

"He's not doing that on his army salary, so he has to be dirty. What's his racket? Is he in mining? Running drugs?" asked Judd.

"Not clear. He's certainly got access to funds and he associates with some known negative elements. There are cocaine pipelines running up from the towns all along the coast into the northern stretches of the Timbuktu zone. They are all operated by Colombian cartels that have bought their way into the region and tried to buy almost every army general in West Africa. It's possible Idrissa is in their pocket."

"Not good," said Judd shaking his head.

"Heroin is also a problem. The Taliban in Afghanistan run opium into the tribal zones of Pakistan, convert it into heroin, then find ways to transit the drugs into Europe through weak states. A recent influx of Pakistani traders into northern Mali might signal that heroin has arrived here, too."

"And that would mean direct involvement in financing attacks against American forces in Afghanistan and the Middle East," added Zoe.

"The Taliban? Really?" asked Judd. "There's an Afghan heroin connection to Mali?"

"It would represent a major escalation. But there are some markers. We just don't know the scale."

"So, is this Idrissa's secret income source?" asked Judd. "Today's coup maker is running drugs for Colombian cartels or maybe even the Taliban?"

"It's all circumstantial at this stage. Right now, we have no direct intel. We just don't have many resources dedicated to this part of the world."

"Is Mali cooperating on counternarcotics? What about their annual scorecard for the McCall Kingpin Amendment?"

"Inconclusive. So far they've only gotten green lights."

"Which means what exactly?"

"Not much. McCall's vetting is based on embassy reporting, not empirical data."

"I see."

"It's not just drugs, Dr. Ryker. Idrissa is from a small village about an hour's drive from Bandiagara. His home area along the border with Burkina Faso is a favorite transit point for smugglers. We have a report from a European intelligence source that Viktor Chelenkov is using that route. We know Chelenkov has been running light weaponry to insurgents in Chad and Niger. There could be a connection to Idrissa, but we don't have it yet."

"Chelenkov, the Russian arms dealer arrested in Dubai last year?"

"The very one. He's awaiting extradition to the international court in The Hague for war crimes."

"Since when have there been Russians involved in Mali?" asked Judd, aware that he was probably showing too much unease.

A young female analyst took her cue. "Russian activity has accelerated recently. There is also a geology team from Moscow in-country right now. They told the Malians they are conducting early-stage seismic studies. Supposedly hunting for oil in the zone between Kidal and Timbuktu. The station reports that the equipment patterns are more consistent with mining than oil. We suspect the oil team may be a cover for uranium exploration."

Judd raised his eyebrows in an expression of worry.

"Uranium?"

"Yes, sir. It's a possibility."

"Okay, so you say Idrissa has been building up power internally and probably building a war chest for himself and the junta, possibly funded by links to Russian mafia or mining companies."

"Or drugs," she added.

"Right. Or drugs," responded Judd, revealing his growing annoyance. "So, whatever the income source, why does Idrissa move now against Maiga? Was Maiga about to clamp down on him or threaten his business?"

"That's plausible," said Sunday.

Judd turned to Zoe. "What motivates Idrissa?"

She nodded to another analyst, who took the cue and began, "General Idrissa is clearly ambitious, and rose quickly through the ranks of the military. He headed Zone Six around Timbuktu for many years but was passed over as Chief of Staff twice, which we know was a source of anger. We believe that's when he started building a separate power base. Maiga appears to have recognized this and promoted him to army Chief of Staff only a few months ago. Idrissa has packed the new counterterrorism strike teams, the ones we are training and equipping as part of Operation Sand Scorpion, with people from his home area. It's a standard consolidation move. Perhaps Maiga feared Idrissa's growing power base; perhaps he was trying to placate him. We suspect Idrissa moved against Maiga because he learned the president was getting ready to cut him down."

"Do we know that Maiga was planning to fire Idrissa?"

"Yes."

"I see. What about Idrissa's health? He looked very gaunt on television. He's definitely thinner than when I met him eight months ago."

"Idrissa is rumored to have early-stage colon cancer, but we don't see any pattern to confirm this. He has not traveled for medical treatment outside the country and is not known to be on any specific medication. We can check on this."

"Okay, so where is Maiga? Do we know?"

"No, sir," replied another analyst. "We don't yet have eyes on him. There is a lot of activity at the main barracks on the east side of Bamako, so it's highly probable he is being held there. And we have confirmed Red Berets manning the approaches."

Judd turned back to Sunday. "What about Diallo? Does he have a role here?"

"Aaay, good question. General Oumar Diallo has a pattern of opportunism. He had spent years building up a network of allies with an eye to becoming king one day. Idrissa was, at one time, a protégé of Diallo's. Not long ago, Idrissa was a principal lieutenant and likely a key part of his plan for seizing political power. Even though that's all gone awry, he still has a healthy view of himself. We expect him to make a push to return to Mali at some point. We just don't know if that point is now."

"Where is he now?"

"We believe he is still in London."

"And what's he doing?"

"MI6 reports he is in contact with senior military personnel in Mali, but they don't have anything more, at least not that they are sharing with us. So it's not clear if Diallo is giving orders or just gathering information. We have to assume he is plugged in, but we can't characterize his current relationship with Idrissa."

"Could Idrissa be fronting for Diallo? Just clearing the way for him to return to the country?"

"Possible but unconfirmed. They have historically been both allies and rivals."

"Desperate times can make unusual bedfellows. And I've been told Diallo is the

115

cousin of the First Lady, Mrs. Maiga? Is this correct?"

"Yes, sir."

"Okay, so how does that figure into this morning's coup?"

"It might be nothing. The political class in Mali is actually very small. Everyone knows each other."

"And this new group, Ansar al-Sahra? Are they relevant to the events of today?"

"Glad you asked," responded yet another analyst. "Our counterterrorism team is gathering evidence on all new active cells in Mali. Ansar al-Sahra, loosely translated as 'defenders of the desert,' is the latest variant and does appear connected to extremist jihadist elements in the region."

"What do we know?"

"High probability that Ansar is a splinter group from al-Qaeda in the Islamic Maghreb. AQIM began as an opposition movement in Algeria but soon disappeared underground and then spread into neighboring countries, including northern Mali. AQIM commanders have been trying to project the impression they are the local affiliate of the global movement built by Osama bin Laden and now run by Ayman al-Zawahiri. AQIM is known to be recruiting across West Africa, so we would expect

Ansar to follow similar tactics."

"Is there any evidence?"

"Last month our counterterrorism unit tracked two known Libyan jihadists who came down into Mali with cash and attempted to infiltrate mosques in Timbuktu and Djenne. They were picked up by Malian security. The Scorpion unit under the direct command of General Idrissa provided both the initial intel and executed the snatch-and-grab."

The analyst pulled a small remote control from his pocket and pointed it at a screen. "We've also got this." A video monitor on the wall sprang to life. "Taken by cell phone and smuggled out within the past seventy-two hours."

A short video clip ran for about fifteen seconds. It was mostly out of focus and moved too quickly to see clearly, but there were glimpses of a line of men, faces covered with black scarves, aiming automatic weapons at targets offscreen. The sound was mostly of wind, some shouting, and the rat-tat-tat of short firing bursts.

"The yelling is Tamasheq, the Tuareg language. We think he's saying something about killing infidels and to aim for the heart. We can't ID anyone because of their head coverings. But the source that provided the video claims it came from a mobile camp in the far north of Mali, near the Algerian border. And that it's Ansar al-Sahra."

"Who is the source?" asked Judd.

"You know we can't say."

"Okay, but is it an American source or does it come from the Malians? Is it Idrissa's guy or ours?"

"It's an insider who penetrated this cell and took great risk to shoot this clip. That's all I can say."

"So what exactly does it mean?"

"Still being assessed. It's another data point that new armed groups are sprouting in northern Mali. We'll send it over to NSA to analyze and see if they can cross-reference the voice with any known terrorists."

"So what's next?"

"We now expect Ansar will take advantage of the turmoil in Bamako to exploit the situation. Both Malian and U.S. personnel have been put on a higher security status. That's mostly where we are now."

"But Idrissa hinted in his television address that Maiga was going soft on radicals. What is your assessment?"

"There is no consensus on that, sir," said one analyst. "Our counterterrorism team had been hoping Maiga would take a harder line. We were approached by Idrissa for additional train-and-equip of another camel corps for the border. He has repeatedly asked for a consignment of night vision equipment and satellite photos. Maiga was sitting on all of these requests. I'm sure Idrissa was frustrated."

"The political assessment is much more nuanced, sir," interrupted Sunday. "Maiga was reaching out to moderates to keep the extremists from gaining a foothold. He is very close to the religious leader of the whole north, the Grand Imam of Timbuktu, and periodically seeks his political and spiritual advice. We have no indication that Maiga was reducing the pressure on dangerous elements or trying to make a bargain with Ansar al-Sahra. I've been looking at these patterns for months. Maiga was certainly aware of Idrissa's ambitions, suspicious of his growing influence, and skeptical of his leveraging our terrorism concerns for his own gain. Maiga is smart enough to know that."

"Okay," inserted Judd, who tucked his notepad into his pocket as a signal that the briefing was coming to a close. "Where are the French on all of this?"

"We are in touch. They are intensely

interested, Dr. Ryker," said Zoe, the team leader.

"What do the French really have at stake? Is this a colonial hangover or something new?"

"Aaay, they feel some historical responsibility, but their main angle is regional spillover," said Sunday. "The French economy runs on nuclear power, and French nuclear power runs mostly on —"

"Uranium," interrupted Judd.

"Yes, sir. Uranium. Especially from Niger, which is right next to Mali."

"And Niger has a northern rebellion problem, too, right?" asked Judd.

"Correct. The French can't have terrorists disrupting the whole region. It could mean no more lights on in Paris."

"So, yes, Dr. Ryker, the French government has a stake here," added Zoe. "They are interested. Deeply interested."

"I appreciate the insights from your team. Please keep me updated. I'll be working on the Mali situation full-time, and will need the Agency's resources."

"That's what we are here for. You'll have to excuse me, Dr. Ryker," said Zoe, standing up, "but I'm late for another meeting, so I'm going to ask Sunday to escort you out."

"Okay, but one last question. Has your team ever figured out who set off that roadside bomb in Bamako that nearly killed Ambassador James and me?"

"No idea, sir. That's gone cold. It's still a mystery."

CIA headquarters is a labyrinth. Sunday led Judd back through the maze, past the paintings of early surveillance planes and the entrance to the gift shop. *Maybe I should get the boys real CIA spy pens?*

"So, Sunday, how long have you been the Mali political analyst?"

"Just eight months. Aaay, good timing, I guess. No one cared too much until this morning."

"Well, good fortune for you."

"I'm still learning about the Sahara, Dr. Ryker. I started out working on Mexico and was on the Western Hemisphere desk, but I have always been drawn back to Africa. My parents are from Nigeria. I was born there but raised in California. The family ties keep pulling me in. Aaay. I've got the Africa bug."

Judd nodded politely. Sunday continued, "My Ph.D. was on the exploitation of technology to organize political violence. I referenced a lot of your work, especially your surveys of Rwandan refugees during the 1994 genocide. You were the first to bring data to a series of anecdotes. When I read that paper, a lightbulb went on. It's an honor to be working with you."

"Well, I'm glad to hear that it was useful for someone, Sunday."

"You probably don't remember, but we met once when I came to Amherst to hear you give a talk on applied statistics in conflict research. I was working under Professor BJ van Hollen at the time."

"I'm sorry, I don't. But of course I knew Professor van Hollen. He was my supervisor, too. I owe my career to BJ."

"Aaay, so do I. We are all part of the van Hollen diaspora, I guess. The CIA's current station chief in Bamako is also one of his protégés."

"Small world."

Judd paused for a moment to ponder the connection. *Small world indeed.* BJ van Hollen trained the CIA's Bamako station chief and the Mali analyst. And me. Papa, too. *Who is CIA? How can you ever know?*

"You know the professor died last year?" asked Judd, bowing his head.

"Yes, I heard. I was so very sorry. He was a great man." They both nodded solemnly.

"So you know BJ van Hollen and now me. That's all good. But you still don't really know what's happening this morning in Bamako or the motivation behind the coup?" Judd added a small smile, a sign that the line of questioning may have taken a turn back to the serious matters at hand, but was still friendly.

"I'm trying to figure it out, Dr. Ryker. This part of the world has always been confusing for outsiders. The Arabs, the Scottish explorers, the French, and now us."

"The Scots didn't have satellites."

"I'll keep digging and let you know what I come up with," he said, handing over a folded piece of paper to Judd as they broke their grip. "This is my personal e-mail and my encrypted cell phone with secure SMS. In case you ever need it. To chase a data point. Or run down a phone hit. To find someone that no one else can find. I don't want to just write reports out here. I want to help you connect the dots."

"Look, Sunday, I know you're trying to be a solid analyst." Judd said, slipping the paper into his pocket. "But look at it from my standpoint for a second. There has been a coup and the first step to turning it around is understanding what the hell is going on and who the players are. So I drive out here to find out. What does the CIA give me to work with? Narco trafficking, arms trafficking, Russians looking for oil, the French worried about uranium. Mali may be the next front in the war against global jihadist terrorists. Then again it could just be a petty squabble among a small Malian family for control of the country. Diallo, sitting in London, could be behind Idrissa. Or he may be trying to help Maiga as a way to get back in power. Or this could all be nonsense. You are just giving me a laundry list of possibilities, not hard information. There's no data here."

"Aaay. You're right. The numbers can't tell us."

They arrived back at the lobby. "And to make matters worse, the more information thrown at me, the murkier things become."

Judd handed his ID card to the security guard and firmly shook Sunday's hand.

"Roger. I get it. I understand," said Sunday. "And that's not all."

Sunday lowered his voice to a whisper. "No one will admit this outside this building, but the community is split on Ansar al-Sahra. Not everyone is convinced it actually exists."

Back in the car, Judd impatiently dialed a long telephone number. The line crackled and beeped. After a long pause and several clicks, Judd heard a deep *"Oui?"*

"Papa, it's Judd."

"Ah, Judd my friend, I've been expecting your call today. How are Jessica and the family?"

"They are fine, thank you. It's been quite a day in Bamako, I hear."

"Yes. Yes, it has been quite a day for us. Especially for your friend Maiga. How are Noah and Toby? I'm sure they are getting very big now."

"Yes, sure. They are fine. Jessica is with them at the beach. But I'm calling to make sure you are safe. And to see what you are hearing."

"Ah, the beach is good. I'm sure the boys will like that. Their father should be with them, no?"

"I was with them until Idrissa pulled his stunt this morning. What are you hearing, Papa?"

"Miriam and I used to love to go to the beach in Dakar. Funny thing for a man born in a landlocked country to love the ocean so much. Ah, don't you think, Judd?"

"Papa, I need to know what you know." This is no time for prolonged African greetings.

"Judd, you have been away from Africa for far too long."

"Tell me about it, Papa. I'd love to catch up. But right now, I'm trying to put the pieces together."

"Yes, yes. I'm glad you called me, Judd. I was thinking about you, too. You know about the Harmattan, yes?"

"The sandstorms? Of course I do. But it's not Harmattan season, is it?"

"When the Harmattan blows, it is difficult, often impossible, to see clearly. Yes, you are right, my friend, the sandstorms are usually in the winter. But the Harmattan, the force of the Sahara Desert that blows down from the north, burning the eyes, and blocking the light, is more than just the physical sand. The Harmattan can obscure the truth at any time. Do you understand, Judd?"

"Yes, Papa," lied Judd. "Well, um, maybe. What exactly do you mean?"

"Did your people tell you about the north? About Timbuktu? You remember when you were here last year and we spoke on the phone? I told you to watch out for Timbuktu. I told you to go there."

"Yes, Papa, I remember. You told me," said Judd, looking out the car window at the grand edifice of CIA headquarters. "You were right. Of course."

"So if you knew, Judd, why are the Americans so confused about today?"

"I haven't been getting the whole picture, Papa? I need your help to get Maiga back."

"Are you sure that's what you want?"

"Of course we do," responded Judd, perhaps a little too quickly. "Why wouldn't we?"

"If you say so, *mon ami*."

"I do. But I need help from my friends."

"Don't we all, Judd. That's a lesson I learned early on from BJ van Hollen. Today, I think you may need new friends. We all have to use what we have. Make the best of what we know. Just like that poem Jessica always recites."

"Yeah, I know, Dickinson."

"*Oui,* Emily Dickinson! I can still remember it, Judd. 'Until the desert knows that water grows, his sands suffice. But let him once suspect that Caspian fact . . .'"

" 'Sahara dies,' " added Judd, finishing the poem. "I know it well."

"Precisely. I have someone in Paris who you should know. You must make contact with the president's office, the Élysée. Ask for Luc. He is a big man today. He is the one. He can help you get back to the beach." And Papa slowly reads out a Parisian cell phone number.

"Thank you, Papa. What about Diallo?

127

Should he be a new friend?"

"Call Luc."

"Okay, I will. *Merci,* Papa."

"And come back to Mali soon. You are missed."

"Yes, Papa."

10.

Three pickup trucks rolled along desert tracks, meticulously weaving their way through the sand dunes. Each truck was packed with armed men pointing their AK-47s menacingly at the desert. Heavy guns were mounted on tripods in the truck bays of the lead and trailing vehicles. The gunners swept the barrels side to side, searching for targets among the dunes.

The trucks paused when they reached a high sand peak and rested for several minutes. Then the vehicles roared to life again, driving in separate directions this time before taking positions along a ridge. Once the trucks halted, the men silently climbed down and fanned out in a well-scripted dance. They appeared alert, yet also to be guarding nothing more than a valley of sand.

A tall man exited the cab of the lead truck, his face covered by a scarf and sunglasses. He pulled a clunky satellite phone out from underneath his robe and used it to block the sun as he scanned the cloudless sky. Nothing.

After a moment, a faint buzz could be heard in the distance and the men pivoted their necks, searching for the direction of the sound. The buzz slowly grew louder, then faded. Then, like an explosion over their heads, a huge airplane swooped over the ridge, casting a dark shadow over the men. The plane banked hard to one side and then circled around before landing gently on the hidden airstrip.

11.

Serena was standing sentry at the front door to Judd's office. "You have calls in from the Treasury, the State counterterrorism co-ordinator, and the refugee people. I've got Embassy London on hold. Our Africa watcher there has a name for you inside the Foreign Office. A Simon Kenny-Waddington." *Of course.*

"Thank you, Serena. Is that all?"

"A Mrs. Valentine, from something called Global Child Relief and Rescue, is also here for you. She's been squatting outside your office for the past hour."

"Right now? A drop-in?"

"Yes, sir. I checked with the legislative affairs office and they strongly recommend you take the meeting. Mrs. Valentine has

131

clout on Capitol Hill."

"Christ." Judd shook his head. *I've got a coup to fix and I need to meet with every do-gooder with a project in Mali who knows some congressman?* "What kind of clout?"

"I don't want to say."

"Does she play golf with the Speaker of the House or something?"

"Yoga. With Senator McCall's wife."

"You're kidding, right?"

"Legislative affairs doesn't joke."

"Do I have a choice?"

"No, not really."

"Fine. Drop London, tell them we'll get back to them in ten. Give me five minutes for a call, then send in the yoga lady, and interrupt after ten. No, make that five."

Serena nodded.

"And I need you to check out a lobbyist named Mariana Leibowitz. Find out any information you can."

"If she's an agent for foreign interests, she'll be registered with the Justice Department. I'll start there."

"Good." Judd leaned in close and lowered his voice further. "I need another favor. It's important."

Serena leaned in, too.

"I need you to find out where Bill Rogerson is and when he's coming back." Serena backed away with a nod.

Judd mouthed a silent thank-you, then turned and walked briskly into the office, averting his eyes from the seating area. He settled down into his black leather high-backed chair behind his desk with a deep breath. Out of his pocket he fished a small scrap of crumpled paper, placed it on the desk, and attempted to smooth it out with his fingers. He squinted at the scrawl on the scrap, then dialed the phone.

Almost immediately came an answer. *"Allo?"*

"This is Judd Ryker in Washington. Is this Luc?"

"Oui."

"Papa Toure gave me your number."

"Yes, I know."

"I am working the Mali situation for the United States. I'm calling you from the State Department."

"*Oui,* I know that, too."

"Papa said that we should be friends. He also said that you may have some useful information about what is really happening in Bamako."

"What happened is Maiga fucked up. We told him this was coming. He didn't want to listen. They never want to hear the truth, these presidents. Always think they are invincible. Now that bastard Idrissa is in Koulouba and Maiga is a prisoner at Wangara barracks."

"What is the real issue? Is it drugs or guns or jihad?"

"It is none of those high-minded things, Judd. You Americans are overthinking this."

"Is it uranium?"

"You give Idrissa and his coterie too much credit. This, it is a family squabble, *une lutte familiale.* Idrissa is still furious over what happened after the Diallo coup attempt. It was a debacle. His promotion to Chief of Staff wasn't enough. Now he wants to be boss. Idrissa, he thinks he is *l'grand homme,* the big man."

"So now what happens?"

"We will tell Idrissa that we understand Maiga fucked up, but that now he has fucked up, too. He must go. He will understand that soon. I think perhaps tomorrow."

"Your ambassador in Bamako is reaching out to Idrissa tomorrow? To tell him to step down?"

"Ah, no. Our ambassador is useless. A useless bastard. The Élysée will do that. We will tell him."

"You have confidence that will work?"

"We will make it work."

"The United States also wants to get Idrissa out and Maiga back in the seat. What can I do to help you move this along?"

"We will be talking to him. Give us time."

"I'm glad to hear the Élysée is engaged and we are all on the same page. But we need to act fast, before Idrissa consolidates power and gets too comfortable in the palace."

"I know all about your *l'heure d'or,* the Golden Hour, Dr. Ryker. Don't be impatient. There are other actors in play. Not just impatient Americans."

"Who? The British?"

"Ha! No. The British are not paying attention, Judd. There are others. And our own. You also need to get all your own people on board. You have work to do, too."

"What?" asked Judd, slightly confused. "What are you hearing?"

"We all have our interagency issues, *mon ami.* We all have our own internal rivalries that we must fight. You work yours and I'll work mine. Then we can crush Idrissa."

"And get Maiga back in power," added Judd.

"Perhaps. *Peut-être.*"

Serena appeared at the door. Judd nodded his head. "Thank you, Luc. Let's speak again tomorrow. *Au revoir.*"

Judd put down the phone, brushed both

shoulders of his jacket, and stood up to greet his guest. He walked into the waiting area and spotted a late-middle-aged white woman with long graying hair, wearing an earth-toned pantsuit and large beads around her neck. *Peasant jewelry.*

"Ah, Mrs. Valentine, what a great pleasure to meet you. I understand Global Child Relief and Rescue has a pressing interest in Mali. Please do come in. . . ."

12.

David Durham's heart should have been racing. Through the tall grass, he made out the shadows of his pursuers. Even at seventy-five meters away and the sun sitting low, Durham could easily identify the stocky outlines of the Special Operations Forces combat assault rifles slung low on the front of the six soldiers hunting him. *They're carrying light 5.56mm versions, not like mine with the enhanced grenade launcher.* As the long shadows moved in formation to the east, he crawled silently in a sweep to the northwest. *Rookies.*

After several minutes snaking his way through the grasses, he reached the edge of a small creek. Coiled and ready to strike. A quick look left, then right, and he jumped across with unexpected grace for a man of forty-two years, 220 pounds, known to most simply as "Bull." On all fours, he was quickly back into the safety of the grasses on the other side. He stopped to take his pulse, still a steady sixty beats per minute.

From this spot he could just make out his target, a yellow fluorescent disk nailed to a post, about four meters high, at the northern tree line, the face of Osama bin Laden squarely in the center. Durham lay flat in the grass and lifted his torso to rest on his elbows. Up came the barrel of his gun. Left eye closed. Focused on the target. Steadied his hands. Focus. Slowed down breathing. Focus. Felt the trigger. Ready . . .

"Waaaaaaahhhhh!" interrupted a loud siren. Bull sat up straight like a prairie dog, dropping the assault rifle in his lap. "What the fuck?"

Over the monotone loudspeaker: "Colonel Durham, report to base. Team Zebra, restart at checkpoint Beta." *What now?*

Bull pulled a small towel out from his rucksack and wiped the sweat off his bald head. The towel turned immediately green and black from the smeared camouflage paint.

He trudged back to the makeshift base, a small tent with a table and an overeager soldier, no more than eighteen years old, with bad teeth and worse acne. "Special reassignment message from the Pentagon, sir." Then he whispered, "Office of the Secretary of Defense."

"Thank you, Corporal." Durham grabbed the folded sheet of paper from his hands. *What kind of special assignment? I'm not due to rotate back to Afghanistan for six more months.*

He unfolded the paper:

CONFIDENTIAL — DELIVER IMMEDIATELY

TO: Colonel David Durham/Special Operations Command/Stuttgart

FROM: Office of the Secretary of Defense/Washington, D.C.

MSG: Urgent reassignment for military liaison mission in Mali. Report to Patch barracks for full briefing at 20:00.

"Christ! That's in half an hour," he said out loud to no one. The teenager pretended not to be listening. "What goddamn part of Afghanistan is Mali, anyway?"

"Er, sir," interrupted the corporal. Bull shot him a glare of disgust. "Mali's not in Afghanistan. It's West Africa."

Durham blinked. *Africa?* He stood there

for a few moments, hands on his hips, staring ahead. Then he read the paper again.

Africa? Who the hell did I piss off?

13.

Serena poked her head into Judd's office and glared seriously at him. She was holding up a two-fingered victory sign. "Task force, two minutes."

Judd stood at his desk, a phone cradled between his shoulder and his ear. He paced back and forth as far as the headset cord will allow him. A huge map of West Africa was rolled out on his desk. On top was a tall stack of classified CIA reports, bright red SECRET — NO FOREIGN DISTRIBUTION stamped on the covers. A half-eaten sandwich rested precariously on the desk's edge.

Judd nodded gently, if dismissively, at Serena's reminder.

". . . yes, Simon, I understand London isn't consumed by events in Mali and you've

141

got problems elsewhere, but surely Her Majesty's government is worried about spillover. The domino effect across West Africa could be devastating if we allow this coup to stand. We know what's going on in Sierra Leone and Nigeria. We know the Foreign Office is watching that."

"Indeed, Judd," said Simon Kenny-Waddington, the West African diplomatic chief for the British government. "We are terribly concerned about this morning's events. Dreadful business. We shall certainly put out a firm statement of condemnation once we understand exactly what has happened. All in good time."

"We'll look forward to that. I've got to run, Simon. At least tell me what your boys are hearing."

"Our assessment is Libya."

"Libya, really?" Judd shook his head.

"Yes, Libya. Those cheeky buggers from Libyan intelligence are trying to insert themselves into the Tuareg situation. Be the king makers, just like Khaddafi used to, we reckon."

"Okay, Simon. I'd love to see your side's full assessment. Can you ask your friends to pass anything through intel channels ASAP?"

"Very well. Might take a few days."

"And what about General Oumar Diallo? I hope your people have eyes on him."

"I'll have to check on that one," said Simon.

"Yes, please do. If you hear anything new, anything at all, give me a shout, Simon."

"Cheers, Judd. Good luck with this one. Shame this had to happen. But that's Africa, you know."

Judd set down the phone and slumped into his chair.

Serena returned, unhappy. "Now you're late. Task Force Mali is ready for you."

"You find out anything about Rogerson?"

"Not much. Here are Mariana Leibowitz's clients," she said, handing him a one-page list. "I got it from DoJ's Foreign Agents registry."

Without reading it, Judd folded the paper in half and slipped it into his jacket pocket. "What about Rogerson? You at least have a location?"

"All I know is that he's mediating peace negotiations. But I don't know where. Apparently it's sensitive, so they aren't sharing any details."

"What peace negotiations?"

"I don't know."

"And where is it?"

"I just told you I don't know, Dr. Ryker.

It's all close hold. No one is talking about it. I also don't know when he's supposed to be back."

"You don't know or you don't know *yet*?"

"Now you are *really* late. Let's go."

Judd slipped into the conference room and strode up to the sole chair at the head of the table. It felt cramped. Every seat was taken and several staff were standing along one wall. Task Force Mali was growing. *It was starting.*

Judd began, "Okay, everyone, thanks for coming back for Task Force Mali. This is meeting two and it's eight o'clock in Bamako. I assume everyone has seen Idrissa's statement. Before we go to Bamako, any updates from around the building?"

"The region isn't saying anything yet, Dr. Ryker," said one staffer sitting at the table. This sparked paper shuffling around the outer ring.

"Okay, thank you, Regional Affairs," responded Judd, then turned to the long table. "Let's keep feet to the fire for all our ambassadors in Ethiopia and Nigeria, and let's see if our UN team in New York has anything to add. Probably too early, but if we don't push them, no one will pay attention to Mali."

"Dakar and Accra are reporting that the border is open and traffic is flowing as normal," said another.

"Drugs and Thugs is picking up accelerated chatter," added one staffer from the law enforcement bureau, using their nickname. *They weren't here before.* "We have indications of a large shipment of narcotics moving across northern Niger and heading toward Mali. Might be Russians or Colombians, probably working with Nigerians out of Katsina State. The traditional smuggling channels are all showing signs of accelerated traffic. Our conclusion is that something big is brewing."

"Not good," added Judd, shaking his head. "What else have we got on a narcotics link?"

"Nothing."

"Any connection to Idrissa?"

"Don't know yet."

"Any link to arms trafficking?"

"Don't know yet."

"Okay, six hours later and we're still in the dark. Everything is speculation right now. Press the intel community for anything concrete. Anyone else?"

"Legal has called about pulling the plug on our aid program."

"Already?" asked Judd.

"Yes. We need to make a declaration about the coup. Once it's declared, the congressional provision kicks in and all the accounts are frozen."

"Well, things are still in flux, so we aren't declaring anything yet. It's not a coup until we say so," replied Judd, perhaps a bit too firmly. "Any views?"

Silence.

"Anyone here from North Africa? Anything out of Libya?"

Silence.

"Anything else before we turn to Embassy Bamako?"

"This is public affairs. We still need the Secretary's statement of condemnation cleared."

"It's not out yet?" asked Judd, holding up his palms in frustration.

"Not yet. We've got twenty-three clearances, but one holdout. One of the regional bureaus had a question on precedent and wants more time to review the language."

"This should have been done hours ago," said Judd, suppressing rising anger. "Who've I got to call to get this done?"

"We'll follow up with your office."

"Fine. Anything else?"

"Counterterrorism is confirming our contacts, and ensuring that lines are being kept open with Malian military."

"Who is here from CT?" asked Judd. Two hands went up at the table, four more in the outer ring. *Six people, for one little African task force?*

"Is that all?" he asked no one in particular.

"CT wants to ensure that our policy doesn't disrupt ongoing security operations in the Sahara Desert. We have concerns about potential negative spillover effects of premature overreaction."

"Well, so does everyone sitting around this table. We need everyone to sit tight until we have a better handle on the situation. Every bureau, including CT, should stand down until further notice. Make sure your people in the field understand this. That's direct from Landon Parker."

Without waiting for a reaction, he turned to the video screen. "Embassy Bamako, we are ready for your update. Ambassador James?"

The whole table turned to look at the big screen. Larissa James was square in the center, joined only by Colonel Randy Houston, the defense attaché.

"Thank you, Dr. Ryker. During his national address, General Idrissa confirmed that he has deposed President Maiga and has declared himself head of state and chairman of the Council for the Restoration of Democracy. They are already using the acronym CRD. Most of the cabinet is in hiding, but we know that Idrissa is trying to reach out to key ministers with offers for them to stay, plus large envelopes of cash. The foreign minister is still in China and is unlikely to return. Would be helpful to have Embassy Beijing send someone to track him down."

Judd turned to the group. "Can someone chase East Asia to make that happen?" And then back to the screen. "What else, Bamako?"

"Idrissa is already trying to dress this up as a seamless transition. I expect that he'll convene the diplomatic corps in the morning to justify the coup, probably using the same script we heard on TV. Media is back on, but other than Idrissa's address, the national television is just playing reruns of *Dynasty* dubbed into French. Colonel Houston is here to give you a security update."

"Thank you, ma'am. The streets are currently quiet. Sundown was eighteen forty, about ninety minutes ago. The authorities have not, I repeat not, issued a curfew, although there remains a heavy security presence on the streets. The regional security officer and I were able to move through sectors of the city about one hour ago. Roadblocks are mostly down, with the exception of those up to the palace and airport. The black-hatted Gendarmerie have disappeared and we have troops in army regulars along the key avenues. Red Berets remain along the palace road."

"Idrissa is clearly trying to show the city, and us, that things are normal," added the ambassador.

"Yes, ma'am," confirmed Houston. "At least in the capital. Kidal, Mopti, and Gao are also reporting ordinary traffic and market activity. Timbuktu is a different story. We have a very heavy military presence on all the major thoroughfares into the city. The governor's office and the Great Mosque are each surrounded by a full Special Forces squad. Our embedded advisors have been asked to stay in barracks, but they are still reporting."

"What about the Scorpions?"

"The Scorpion counterterrorism strike force based up in Timbuktu remains AWOL. We are trying to get a bead on their location and status, but we have conflicting reports. They may be heading north in an offensive column, or possibly they are moving southwest, toward the border with

Burkina. It is unclear if the Scorpions have split into two units or if we have mistaken intel. A cost of having our guys pulled out."

"Thank you, Bamako," said Judd, noticing that Serena had slipped in the door and was beelining for him. "What about American citizens?"

"We still have no reports of any problems with AmCits, and no reason to believe they will be targeted," said the ambassador.

"White House Situation Room, fifteen minutes," whispered Serena into Judd's ear. He gave her a look of query. She shrugged. "They didn't say. Must be something big."

"The embassy has formally issued a travel advisory, but we're not recommending anything other than vigilance for American citizens already here," continued the ambassador.

"You have to wrap this up and leave. Right now," Serena said at full volume.

"All official personnel are accounted for. Peace Corps is activating its emergency tracking system and they have contact with almost all of their eighty-five volunteers. A few are off grid, but they'll let us know if anyone is missing."

Judd looked back to the assembled staff. "Okay. Thank you, Ambassador. I know that we have more questions for you from the different bureaus, but I'm going to ask them to hold off until our next meeting, tomorrow morning at oh six hundred, our time." Judd stood up. "Thank you, everybody."

Judd stared at Larissa through the screen, and gave her a little nod. *She can see me, right?*

14.

Papa Toure was heartily greeted at the door of the Farka Music Club with an elaborate handshake that ended with a loud snap. The bouncer was a plump African man wearing a tight black suit and, despite the late hour and low light inside the club, aviator sunglasses.

Papa was escorted to his usual table, where he rocked back to let the chair take his weight. The creaking seat reminded him that he was no longer the scrawny village boy of his youth. The extra pounds around his waist, along with the gray hairs in his scraggly beard, provided an aura of sage authority.

It had been a stressful day and he was relieved to escape the web of phone calls. So many calls: Mopti, Gao, Timbuktu, Paris, Lagos, Johannesburg, and Washington. It was exhausting to manage so many expectations.

He waved casually at the barman, a signal for a cool Castel beer.

Papa Toure was a man who loved the blues. Growing up in a village several days' walk from Bamako, he would run home from school every day to finish his chores and schoolwork in time to listen to his grandfather play traditional music on the kora, a twenty-one-string harp made with cowhide pulled over half a calabash. The old man would sing about family history and their ancestors and, increasingly over time, about amazing changes going on in the country. Papa was still a young boy, but remembered the day his grandfather sang about independence, when it finally came in September 1960. It was his first hint of big-city politics.

Around that time, traveling musicians began to pass through his village with guitars instead of traditional instruments. It opened a whole new world: the sounds of Cuba, France, and Mississippi. *Especially Mississippi.* Papa was instantaneously drawn to the cadence and sensation of the American blues.

But neither Papa nor his grandfather was born into the *jeliya,* the caste of professional musicians. *Jeliya* were no mere buskers, but more like local historians, mediators, and preachers of morality all wrapped into one.

Papa's ambitions for a life as a guitarist were not to be. His hopes were squashed in the end, not by social strictures, but by an early, and mature, realization that his talent did not match his passion.

Instead, he became a bookworm. His father saved his small profits from selling cassava to send his most promising son to school and to buy him dog-eared books for his studies. Papa, rising above his modest lot, secured a scholarship at a private school in Bamako and then another to attend the prestigious University of Ibadan in southern Nigeria. At the time, it seemed like the other side of the world.

What to study for a boy from the village on the edge of the world's largest desert? *Hydrology, of course.* Papa became obsessed — and expert — in the study of water, how to find and manage it in a place where such a commodity was chronically, and too often fatally, scarce. It was ironic, but at once practical.

Papa soon learned that water in Africa was not really about the science. It can be found and stored even in the driest of places. Water was really about politics. So the studious village boy became a reluctant and accidental student of the men who ran Africa and their motivations. And what better place for the lessons of power than Nigeria?

In Africa's version of Texas, everything is big, brash, and fueled by a noxious combination of easy oil money and human greed. During Papa's ten years in Nigeria, he witnessed two coups, saw governors grabbing oil contracts for themselves, and watched top generals amass billions of dollars. Papa could see how Nigeria earned $400 billion from its oil yet had almost nothing to show for it. The average man on the street had actually become poorer since the black gold began pumping.

Papa secretly planned for the day his 3-D seismology studies might inadvertently hint at an oil reservoir rather than an aquifer. He decided he would do the only sensible thing: delete the data.

It was also easy for an African hydrologist to return home, triumphant with his Ph.D. in hand, ready to help develop his own country. But the time in Nigeria had given Papa a keen sense of suspicion for the motives of powerful men, and a belief that the human impulse for greed was infinite, even in a dirt-poor country.

The sad events of this morning only

confirmed in his mind that this was true, even in his own nation. To survive, one had to make many friends like Luc Bosquet and Judd Ryker. Like Professor BJ van Hollen, the man who befriended him in Nigeria and introduced him to so many important people. Rest his soul, *Allah yarhamu*. And, of course, the beautiful Jessica Ryker. You had to maintain these friends in order to keep moving forward in this uncertain world. To keep your options open.

He would, of course, help Judd, his friend. But deep down he also knew he was going to point Judd in the right direction to help his country, too. And to help himself.

The lights came down and the crowd hollered. Everyone craned their necks, waiting for the musician to appear. Just then the barman silently arrived and set down a tray to clear away the empty beer bottles nudging each other for space on the small table. When the tray was lifted away and the barman departed, a brown envelope was left behind, the rectangular bulge of a stack of banknotes barely visible. Without averting his eyes from the stage, Papa slid the envelope off the table and into his jacket pocket.

Onto the stage ambled an African man, barely twenty years old, holding a guitar tightly by the neck. He sat on a lone stool and began to play. A bluesy rhythm, the lyrics extolled the glories of the thirteenth-century Mande Empire and the legend of its founder, the warrior Sundiata Keita, the king of kings.

Listening to the history of a lost empire beneath his feet, Papa felt Mali's future weighing on his shoulders. He knew that tomorrow he was back on the road, back to work. But tonight he leaned back, shut his eyes, and drank in the sounds. Tonight was for the blues.

15.

Judd jumped out of the black sedan that drove him the five blocks from State headquarters to the side of the White House. Since the Secret Service had closed Pennsylvania Avenue between Seventeenth and Fifteenth streets for security and turned it into part of Lafayette Square, he had to walk the last block.

On the corner was a tourist T-shirt stand. TERRORIST HUNTING LICENSE and a drawing of a camel in crosshairs were on one shirt, flapping in the breeze. Judd weaved through a school group of loud teens in matching fluorescent green-and-pink T-shirts.

At the West gate, he flashed his badge through the bars and tinted plate glass. A loud buzz, the gate opened, and then slammed loudly behind him. He was now inside the White House grounds.

Straight ahead was the driveway up to the West Wing. Back to his left he could see crowds of tourists, their faces pressed to the security fence. To his right sat a field of television cameras and equipment covered in dark green tarps where the press corps reported. Today it lay abandoned and silent.

Rather than follow the path straight up to the West Wing main entrance, where two marines were standing at attention, Judd took a short flight of stairs down to the right and underneath to a canopied entrance. Here was where the National Security Council staff — the president's personal foreign policy team — entered the West Wing from their offices next door in the Eisenhower Executive Office Building.

Judd arrived at another security desk. On the walls were huge photos of the president walking his dog, speaking at a UN podium, looking stern and serious at his desk. There was one of the First Lady, standing on the bow of a sailboat, wind blowing her hair. Judd's ID was silently checked and he was then cleared to enter a hallway that led down to the Situation Room.

Judd paused briefly at the deserted maître d' desk at the White House dining room and smoothly pocketed two boxes of M&M's

with the White House seal. *For the boys.*

Judd descended another level and opened an unimposing walnut-paneled door that led into the Situation Room complex. He deposited his BlackBerry into a nook in the wall and double-checked his pockets.

To his left, he peered into a control room, with large mounted video screens and a small army of bright-eyed staffers wearing headsets. White House Operations. The Nerve Center. *One of those punks woke me up this morning,* he thought. Digital clocks read WASHINGTON, BAGHDAD, BEIJING, MANILA. *Something must be going on in the Philippines today.*

"Dr. Ryker, you are in Sit Room One. They are starting," said a woman suddenly blocking his path.

"Er, thank you," said Judd and turned to open the door for the room labeled one. He pulled on the door handle and felt the air valve seal release. He stepped inside.

The Situation Room was shockingly small. From the movies, Judd had expected something grand and imposing, but instead he found the ceiling uncomfortably low. Compounding the cramped feel, bulky leather chairs circled the main table, tightly hugged by another ring of seats around the outside. Along one wall was a bank of six flat-panel televisions, each with a large head on-screen, several in military uniform. The clock, reminding the participants why exactly they were here, read WASHINGTON and BAMAKO. Judd took the lone empty seat at the main table and sat quietly.

The Washington clock ticked from 4:29 to 4:30, and in from a side door entered a short, stocky man with thinning, slicked-back hair. He was wearing a shiny designer suit, but it looked like he had slept in it. He nodded to no one in particular and began without sitting down. "Okay, people. Everyone here?"

No answer.

Judd recognized no one. *Asking who is here is admitting I don't belong.*

"We're activating an emergency inter-agency group to deal with a special situation. Have we got FBI here? How about the counterterrorism center? You guys here, too?"

Several nods around the table.

"As most of you know, Africa is a new area of concern." One of the screens sprang to life, displaying a high-resolution map of Africa.

"Al-Qaeda is on the run. We've killed bin Laden, and Ayman al-Zawahiri is feeling our pressure. The core al-Qaeda has turned

161

to regional franchising by co-opting local grievances to advance their agenda. Al-Zawahiri's radicals from the Middle East have been penetrating the Horn of Africa, using Somalia as an operations base, and working through the Somali al-Shabaab." Somalia was highlighted in yellow on the map, with red explosion icons dotting the coast.

He continued, pointing to the map. "Our counterterrorism operations in the Horn have been highly successful against al-Shabaab. Maybe too successful. We've decapitated or disrupted nearly all cells operating across East Africa, so radicals are now seeking new entry points in the western part of Africa. The Sahara Desert region is their new target." The map flashed a vast yellow blob covering most of West Africa. The speaker swept his arm across the screen with a flourish.

"Al-Qaeda in the Islamic Maghreb or AQIM was born out of the conflict in Algeria. We have been working with local partners, especially the military and intelligence services in Mali, to inhibit further penetration. But extremists have continued to try to pierce our defenses by exploiting local conflicts for their own jihadist aims." Thick black arrows appeared on the map, swooping down from Algeria, into northern Mali, and spreading across the whole region. "We've been keeping a close eye on developments. Over the past few days, the Sahara region has taken a major turn for the worse."

More nodding around the table.

"We've got an emerging situation now in northern Mali. Ansar al-Sahra, a previously dormant group of jihadists based in southern Libya, have successfully recruited disaffected Tuaregs in Mali and are now active. This is an extremist splinter group, and let me be very clear: They present an imminent threat to U.S. interests. Everyone got that? The Sahara is now hot. We have chatter indicating a developing threat to our people in West Africa. An Ansar cell is moving from the northern border area in the direction of Timbuktu with hostile intentions. This came in today."

Projected on another screen were satellite photos. They were light brown, highlighted with bright red circles and arrows. Familiar satellite photos. *I saw these already.*

"We have a series of camps and convoys along the border. We now have confirmed information from eyes on the ground that these are Ansar, and the pattern of movements suggests purposeful migration in a

163

southwestern direction, toward the population center of Timbuktu."

Several more nods around the table. Judd raised his eyebrows in disbelief. *What eyes on the ground?*

"The local authorities have agreed to allow accelerated reconnaissance overflight, and they have several strike teams, trained by us and with embedded advisors, positioned in strategic garrisons. A complicating factor is a coup in the capital early this morning that deposed the president. The terrorists may be taking advantage of the political uncertainty to strike now. The coup does not, however, appear to be impacting our counterterrorism operations. We are being assured, through confidential channels, of continuity of cooperation across the board."

Judd's stomach twisted into a knot. *What channels?*

The suit continued, "This includes Operation Sand Scorpion, our search-and-destroy elite strike force teams based in Timbuktu. The embassy is confident that we can continue counterterrorism operations, even as State works the diplomatic angles on the coup. Is State here?"

Judd sat up straight. "State is here." *Goddamn right.* "We've got State Task Force

Mali activated. We are in constant contact with the embassy and still establishing the facts. But it is confirmed that President Maiga was arrested and detained this morning and that General Idrissa, who had recently been promoted to army Chief of Staff, is claiming power and in the process of installing a junta. As with all coups, things are still very much in flux and the information can change quickly. Once we have a better idea what exactly has happened and why, then we will be formulating a strategy. The Secretary's instructions are to reverse the coup and reestablish President Maiga's authority as soon as possible. Once we have a plan, we'll come back to the interagency for execution."

"Thank you for joining us," the still-nameless chair responded, with no attempt to hide his condescension. "Our priority today is Ansar al-Sahra and to keep our people safe. There is a grand arc of terrorism growing that starts in Yemen and sweeps across Somalia, through the center of Africa, then up across the Sahara Desert. It's a dagger pointing through Europe and into the United States. Smack in the middle of this arc of terror, the heart of this thing, is Mali. I will not allow Mali to become a new front in the global war on terror on my watch. We are going to kill this baby in the cradle."

"State agrees. We have to stop the spread of al-Qaeda or AQIM, if that's what this is. As a close ally, Mali is the locus of our strategy to contain extremists across West Africa," responded Judd, trying to stay cool. "Reinstating President Maiga as soon as possible is the best means to keeping our people safe. That's how we keep this thing from spreading."

Judd noticed eyes around the table averted. His stomach knotted again.

"And State has reports that elements of the Scorpions may be missing," Judd added.

"Who is chairing the State Task Force? Bill Rogerson? Where the hell is Bill?"

"No, I am."

"Okay, well not everyone shares State's enthusiasm for Maiga. We've got credible reports that he is going soft. And possibly getting in bed with some very dangerous individuals." The rumpled suit turned away from Judd, toward the group.

"We have another complication, people. Our CIA station chief in Tripoli received this via e-mail. Go ahead and run it."

One of the screens lit up and a fuzzy still photo appeared showing a pale young woman, on her knees, blindfolded and hands bound behind her back. She was wearing a simple white T-shirt and her head was loosely covered with a scarf, but a crescent of fire-red hair was still visible. *American.*

Standing over her were three tall men, all in black robes, their faces covered. Behind them was a black flag with white Arabic lettering. The two men on either side of the girl held AK-47s across their chests. The one in the middle, directly behind her, held a long sword.

Oh, shit.

The video began.

"Uh, hello?" said the young woman. She was sniffling. "My name is Katherine Mc-Call. I am a Peace Corps volunteer in Bangoro. I am being held . . ." The sound crackled and the wind thumped. Her voice was trembling. She was terrified. The man with the sword reached down and grabbed her head. A collective gasp swept across the Situation Room.

The man removed the girl's blindfold. She squinted and blinked, adjusting to the light. She continued, "Immoral American crusaders are not welcome in the Great Sahara. They must leave." She spoke slowly and haltingly, obviously reading off something to the side of the camera. The three men stood motionless as she spoke. "I will not be released until all imperialist infidels leave Mali and Niger, and . . . and Pakistan. They will send further instructions." More crackles and wind, then the screen went blank.

"Okay, people. That's the whole clip. The National Security Agency confirms the voiceprint and the image are that of Kate McCall. For those of you not paying attention, she is not just anybody. The woman kidnapped by radical jihadists is the daughter of Senator Bryce McCall, chairman of the Senate Foreign Relations Committee. Diplomatic security is informing him now. We should all expect a mother lode of pressure to get her back."

Judd instinctively grabbed for his Black-Berry, which was still sitting in a cubbyhole outside the Situation Room.

"I want CIA liaising with Special Operations Command in Stuttgart on possible rescue scenarios in the next fifteen minutes. Make that ten minutes. I want a full intel team on this up and running by the end of today. And tell Langley I want their best crisis manager running this. I want the Purple Cell team leader. I won't accept anyone else."

"Sir, CIA has already activated the Purple Cell. She is aware and mobilized."

"Good. Let's get ahead of this, people. Let's go."

16.

Larissa James pushed down with both hands on the crutches and took a deep breath. She knocked on the open door and tentatively peeked inside. "I'm not waking you, am I?"

Judd slowly opened his eyes and squinted. He was staring straight up at the dull fluorescent lights of his hospital room, which smelled of Lysol and chicken soup. Not the comforting nostalgic scent of his grandmother's house, but the sour chicken–like odor of his grade school cafeteria. His stomach twisted.

"Oh, I did wake you, Judd. I'm so sorry."

"I'm not really sleeping," he said, his voice still froggy. "I can't sleep."

"Come in, Larissa," said Jessica, sitting in a hard-backed chair next to Judd's bed. "Judd's doing much better. Wonderful to

170

see you up and around." She set her book down in her lap and removed her reading glasses.

Judd groaned as he arched his back and squirmed in the bed.

"Thank you, yes. I came to tell you both that today's the day. My medical clearance just came through," said Larissa. "Judd, I'm going back."

"Already? You sure you're up to it?" he asked, smoothing his gown as Jessica tucks the sheet under his legs.

"What else can I do? I can't stay here. If I'm ready to go, I'll go."

"You don't want to take medical leave and go home? To see your family?"

"No. I'd rather not. Plus, Embassy Bamako needs me."

"They'll be fine," said Judd. "The beast will run without you."

"Okay, so maybe I need to get back for me," said Larissa. "I am going crazy sitting in this damn hospital. I haven't read my classified e-mail for three weeks."

Judd nodded, more a gesture in solidarity than in agreement.

"What are the doctors telling you, Judd? What's your timeline?"

"As soon as possible," answered Jessica. "Once he's cleared for medevac, we'll transfer to Georgetown Medical. We've got to get him home."

"They keep saying soon," added Judd.

"Good. I'm sure you're anxious to see your kids, too."

"And Grandma is ready for us to get back."

"Madam Ambassador," interrupted a gruff voice. A balding man in an ill-fitting suit appeared in the doorway, holding both handles of an empty wheelchair. "I've been cleared to take you down to discharge."

"Thank you, Cyrus. You didn't have to come all the way to Germany to get me."

"I wanted to make sure you get back safely, ma'am."

"Cyrus, this is Judd Ryker," said Larissa, gesturing to the hospital bed. "He was the other casualty."

"Hello, sir. I'm sorry about the incident. How are you feeling?"

"Better."

"And, this is Jessica Ryker, Dr. Ryker's wife. She's come from Washington to help nurse Judd back onto his feet. Jessica, this is Cyrus. He works with me at the embassy in Mali."

"Hello, ma'am," said Cyrus coldly to Jessica, who returned the gesture with a minimal nod. "The car is waiting, Madam

Ambassador. I've already gathered your things."

"Well, I need to give Judd a hug good-bye first," she said, hobbling over to the bed and bending down for an embrace. "We almost died together. That means we are tied to each other for life." She wiped a tear on Judd's shoulder. "I can't just leave without a real good-bye."

As Larissa settled into the wheelchair and gathered herself, Judd turned to Cyrus. "Is there any progress in the investigation? Any news on who set that bomb and why?"

"There is some new information, but no hard answers yet."

"What new information, Cyrus?" asked Larissa, snapping back to her work persona.

"I can't share that here."

Larissa looked confused, then looked at Jessica. "Because she's here?"

Cyrus didn't reply.

"I need to know," said Judd, sitting up in bed.

"For fuck's sake, Cyrus. She's his wife. Just tell us," insisted Larissa.

Cyrus turned, closed the door, and then faced the three of them. "The bomb material is the same type that Malian security forces recovered when they raided a terrorist safe house outside Timbuktu a few months ago. The trigger also suggests professionals with access to military-grade equipment. This was no accident, and these were no amateurs."

"But were they targeting us?" asked Judd.

"We still don't know, but we can't rule it out."

"How would they know we were going to be on that road at that time?" asked Larissa.

"Good question, ma'am."

"Maybe the terrorists have a mole inside Idrissa's Red Berets?" proposed Jessica, drawing startled looks from Judd and Larissa.

"Yes, maybe," replied an unfazed Cyrus.

"Anything else, Cyrus?" asked Larissa.

"There is one more thing, but it's sensitive," he said, turning again to Jessica. "I'm sorry, ma'am."

"Fine, I'll step out," she said, turning to leave the room.

"Sorry, sweets," offered Judd.

Once the door had closed again, Cyrus, in a low voice, reported, "We now know that Idrissa had a Scorpion unit ready to raid a terrorist safe house in Bamako, not far from the palace road. They are almost certainly the group that planted the bomb. But, without explanation, President Maiga ordered the operation canceled and Idrissa was forced to stand down."

"When was that?"

"One day before the bombing."

17.

In front of Judd sat three tall, empty coffee cups. Stacks of papers mounted the edges of the desk like the defensive walls of a castle. Well-thumbed copies of CIA leadership profiles on Maiga, Idrissa, and Diallo laid open with key passages highlighted in fluorescent yellow. Sitting on top of the mess was a one-page fresh-off-the-presses assessment of Ansar al-Sahra that was decidedly, irritatingly noncommittal. Several maps, with suspected extremist camp locations circled in bright red, were taped on the wall behind him.

Judd leaned forward, elbow on the desk, with his forehead resting in his open outstretched palm. It was a pose — Jessica called it *Judd's Thinker* — that he used to

176

keep working during all-nighters. Positioned like this, in the middle of the night immersed in reading material and his head swirling with data, had been how he came up with the Golden Hour.

Tonight was starting to smell like an all-nighter, too.

Judd turned his attention to a diplomatic security report on kidnapping patterns. Kidnapping risk was high in Latin America, where it had become big business to seize, and to protect, wealthy businessmen. Colombia used to be the epicenter for ransom seekers, but Mexico became the world leader of kidnapping for cash. The Middle East was where political hostage takings occurred most often, with Iraq still the most dangerous.

But Africa had been relatively quiet. Other than swashbuckling Somalis off the coast of East Africa, the report sitting on Judd's lap suggested kidnapping had not yet taken off as a full-scale venture industry in Africa. Al-Qaeda terrorists operating out of Algeria had kidnapped a few European tourists, and one Australian diplomat. But these hadn't yet fit into a pattern. There was no evidence that Ansar al-Sahra had ever kidnapped anyone. The numbers couldn't explain if the McCall kidnapping was for money or notoriety. There was no way to know. Why target an American senator's daughter in the midst of a coup? Were they even connected?

Judd's thoughts were interrupted by Serena. "Dr. Ryker, you've got a call from London. You're going to want to take this."

"Simon Kenny-Waddington? Awfully late for the Brits to be in the office."

"Not the Foreign Office. An Oumar Diallo is on the line."

Judd dropped the report in his lap. *Diallo?*

"Have him hold for one minute, then put him through."

"This is Ryker."

"Hello, Dr. Ryker, this is General Oumar Diallo. You know me, yes?"

Judd paused. Make him wonder.

"How can I help you, General?"

"Actually, Dr. Ryker, I am calling because I can help *you.*"

Judd said nothing.

Diallo, undeterred, continued, "I am very concerned about the events in Mali today. I have been watching with dismay from my home in London. I am disappointed that our democracy turned out to be so fragile. I am disappointed with Mamadou. What he did today was not proper. I want to help you resolve this problem."

"What can you tell me about what happened this morning, General?"

"Dr. Ryker, I am retired from military service. I'm a civilian now. A private citizen. I am here in London working on my next career."

"Very well. What do you think happened?"

"Maiga made a mistake. Mamadou Idrissa is very powerful and has many friends. You cannot just fire a man like that and expect him to go quietly."

"Are you suggesting President Maiga is to blame for bringing today's coup on himself?" asked Judd as calmly as he could.

"No, no, Dr. Ryker," said Diallo. "Democracy is a beautiful thing. It is a flower. It must be watered. It must be protected. Idrissa stomped on that flower with his unacceptable actions. I'm only saying this to you to help you understand. Maiga was too rash. There are proper ways to handle these problems. Perhaps Boubacar learned too much from New York City. Perhaps my sister was unable to make him see the right path."

"Your sister? You mean Mrs. Maiga?"

"Yes, she is my sister. We grew up together. I love her dearly, but she was not able to control her husband's foolishness. She is now in trouble, too. Safe, but in trouble."

"What about General Idrissa?"

"Ah, he was my deputy. I trained him. He is like a brother. He is a hard worker and a patriot. But he got greedy. He was a good man but also petty and insecure, you know. He has become corrupted by outsiders. Very corrupted."

"So why exactly are you calling me, General?"

"I want to help. I am told you are a clever man. I am told you are the big man for the Americans. Is this true?"

"What precisely are you offering?" asked Judd.

"Whatever you need from me," said Diallo.

"And what do you want in return?"

"I only want to restore democracy to my beloved country. I want nothing for myself."

"Okay," said Judd. *And?*

Pause. Pause.

"If the people of Mali call me back, I would, of course, be willing to serve my country again. In whatever capacity." *There it is.* "We will soon need a neutral party to step in to fill the void. I know your friends, our friends, in Paris and here in London are welcoming my assistance. All of you will need me, if not today, then very soon."

"Are you suggesting you have official support from the French and British governments to negotiate an end to the coup?" asked Judd. *Let's see how bold you are.*

"Oh, Dr. Ryker. It's much too early for anything like that. These things come with time." *He's got nothing.*

"Well, thank you, General, for your call. We'll take your offer of assistance under advisement."

"I know we will speak again soon. Godspeed, Dr. Ryker."

"*Inshallah*, General."

18.

Judd was sitting alone at a bar, overlooking the Potomac River, nursing a tall beer. *Just one to clear my head, then back to the office.* The usual mix of lawyers and tourists had already cleared out, leaving the real drinkers at the riverfront bar. Mostly college students and middle-aged drunks.

An open-bow speedboat pulled up to the dock and spilled out half a dozen boisterous young women who had obviously already been partying. "Wooo, wooo!" yelled one with pale-blue GEORGETOWN LABELED across the back of her tiny pink gym shorts.

The Sahara Desert couldn't have felt farther away.

Maybe two beers.

"Judd?" interrupted a voice that he recognized.

182

He spun around on the barstool to find Mariana Leibowitz, holding a martini delicately in one hand. "What a wonderful coincidence, darling. I was hoping to come see you tomorrow, but here you are. Here *we* are."

"Hello, Mariana." She was wearing a trim red pantsuit, with a large butterfly brooch on the lapel. "How fortunate."

Several feet behind Mariana stood a tall, striking black woman, dressed in a power business suit, her braids pulled tightly back into a ponytail. Although her clothes screamed confidence, her eyes were submissively averted to the floor. Mariana followed Judd's vision line and saw him eyeing the woman.

"Okay, Judd," she said, sliding onto the stool next to him and dropping the bubbly mask. "We know each other, so no need for bullshit. This is no coincidence, of course. I won't patronize you. I have information. I know you can't tell me anything, but you can listen."

Mariana leaned in, close enough that Judd could detect hints of vanilla and jasmine in her perfume. "Point one, I hope that your friends at Langley have told you about Idrissa's smuggling business. I told you about this before, but it's even worse than I thought. The place is now flooded with heroin and cocaine, and Idrissa has been running the whole north of the country. Nothing happens up there without Idrissa's blessing. You do the math. The president was finally building up the support to fire him. That's the real precipitator of the coup, Judd. Don't believe all that other nonsense."

Judd gave her a slight nod that said, *I'm listening but not confirming anything.* Not that he knew the truth, either.

"Point number two, I have it on good authority that Antonov cargo planes landed at a remote airstrip north of Timbuktu within hours of the coup. This happened even though all of Mali's airports were supposedly shut down and the airspace closed. I don't know what was on those planes, but it's damn suspicious. I don't believe in accidents. Someone needed those planes to land in secret and out of sight of the Americans. And there's no way anyone could be operating in the north without Idrissa's knowledge or permission. You need to assume that the general is deeply involved."

Another poker-face nod. *Christ, she knows more than I do.*

"Okay, and point three, Judd, is that you've got to watch your back. I know you are still new to politics here in Washington, but you need to learn fast." She scanned the room for dramatic effect. "Our military is under tremendous pressure to be more aggressive in West Africa and not allow safe havens. After years of training special units and millions of dollars, Capitol Hill is pushing the Pentagon and the White House to show some results. Congress doesn't like to spend all that money chasing ghosts. Senate Foreign Relations, especially Chairman McCall, has been calling for more scalps." *She doesn't know everything.*

"And we all know Rogerson has been in the Foreign Service too long. He's not going to roll anybody. I mean, who do you think got President Maiga that seat next to the Secretary at the Jakarta Democracy Summit? Rogerson? No, that was me. Rogerson doesn't even know how it happened. The military guys will eat him alive on this. So will the French. It's lucky for us he's tied up in South Africa. We're lucky we have you, Judd."

The news broke Judd's poker face.

"You didn't know? You didn't know Rogerson was in South Africa?"

Judd paused then, realizing he'd been outed, shook his head.

"Well, then I'd say you are lucky to have me, too." Mariana leaned in closer and

185

whispered, "Rogerson is locked up in the InterContinental Hotel in Johannesburg, trying to get the Congolese rebels to agree to a peace deal. One of the faction leaders is Bolotanga. He's an old friend. Bolo's a real teddy bear once you get to know him."

"Isn't Bolotanga the warlord famous for recruiting child soldiers and playing Xbox from his hideout in the jungle?"

" 'Warlord' is an ugly word, Judd. Bolo and I prefer 'freedom fighter.' He would have been president if the last elections hadn't been stolen."

Judd shot her a skeptical eye.

"Don't be so cynical, Judd. Having Bolo there in Jo-burg will be useful. You'll see."

"Thank you for the insight," said Judd, anxious to shift the conversation. "I appreciate it. I do. If you have more information, you know how to reach me."

"You're fighting a lonely battle, Judd. Right now no one in this town gives two shits about President Maiga and democracy. Don't be naïve. They aren't going to just abandon the fight because of a political squabble a million miles away in some palace in a country that no one here's ever heard of. You're on your own here. But now you've got me."

Judd looked blankly back at her, unsure

how to respond to this apparent offer of an alliance.

"I know, I know, you can't say anything to a lobbyist," she said, feigning insult. "I'm not looking for any official comment. Just know that I'm working behind the scenes with you on this. You don't need to reciprocate. Just know it."

Judd gave her a subtle nod and smile.

"And I know when it comes to crunch time that you'll do the right thing."

"You seem to think you know me pretty well, Mariana."

"Oh, I *do* know you, darling. I know you are from Vermont and you were raised by your grandmother. I know you love the Boston Red Sox and became an academic after becoming obsessed with baseball statistics. Your work on civil war metrics won the Trombley Innovation Prize, which set you up for a professorship at Amherst. And then a year ago you took extended leave to move to Washington, D.C., to start the Crisis Reaction Unit. And I know you've been struggling at S/CRU and you need a big win. That's why I'm here."

"Impressive, Mariana. And a bit frightening. Are you investigating me?"

"Of course not. I'm just a professional. I know what I need to know. It's adorable that you think knowledge is threatening. It's nothing of the sort. It's *Washington,* Judd." She paused, unsatisfied with Judd's non-reaction. "Okay, fine. If it makes you feel better. Mariana Katrina Leibowitz. I was born and raised in Miami, my parents were lawyers, now both retired and still living in south Florida. I'm forty-nine years old, twice divorced, probably have at least one more marriage in me. I have one daughter, lives in Los Angeles and doesn't speak to me. Anything else you want to know?"

"No," said Judd, holding up his hands in surrender, a soft smile signaling acceptance of her olive branch. "I really don't."

"Good. One last thing before I leave you to your beer, darling." She broke into a wide grin and nodded to the attractive woman standing at the nearby table who had caught Judd's attention. "Dr. Ryker, I want you to meet Tata Maiga, the president's daughter."

19.

The beer and the barrage of information were churning inside Judd's head. Too hyper to go home to bed, he returned to the office for another attempt to unravel the threads.

On a giant whiteboard in front of him, he sketched out a map linking all the main players: Idrissa, Maiga, Diallo, the Red Berets, the Gendarmerie, the Scorpions, parliament, local media, Tuareg separatists, al-Qaeda, Ansar al-Sahra, drug traffickers, Russians, Nigeria, France, and Britain. The United States was drawn in a large box to the side. Arrows and lines connected many of them. But there were big red question marks. It was a jumble. It didn't make sense.

A knock on the door. "Dr. Ryker, can I

get you anything?"

"Serena, what are you still doing here? You should go home."

"I'll go when you go," she said.

"I'm going soon. Give me ten more minutes."

He looked at his clock. Still too early to call Larissa James. *Must call her before the next task force.*

Judd made a list on a lime-green Post-it: Larissa, Papa, Luc, Simon, Sunday. He thought for a moment, then reached into his pocket and pulled out a folded piece of paper.

FOREIGN AGENTS REGISTRATION ACT (FARA)
DEPARTMENT OF JUSTICE

Active Registrant:

Leibowitz Associates International, Mariana Leibowitz, President, 1599 K Street NW, Washington, D.C.

Active Foreign Principals:

BPO Industrial, Rio de Janeiro, Brazil
Caribbean First Holdings, Cayman Islands
Kingdom of Bahrain, Manama, Bahrain
People's Party of Latvia, Riga, Latvia
Republic of Mali, Bamako, Mali
Sumayata Corporation, Jakarta, Indonesia
SunCity Bank, Geneva, Switzerland

Previous Foreign Principals:

AKZ Energy, Lille, France
BamakoSun Bank, Bamako, Mali
Democracy Union of Zimbabwe, Harare, Zimbabwe
Movement for a Free Congo, Lubumbashi, Congo
Republic of Haiti, Port-au-Prince, Haiti
Republic of Nigeria, Abuja, Nigeria
Sanderson Ogata Farah, Nassau, Bahamas
ZBR International, Vienna, Austria

Judd turned his attention back to his call list. He crossed out Simon and added Mariana.

Judd's planning for the next day was interrupted by another knock on the door and, before he could say anything, in walked

Landon Parker.

"Ryker? Good. You're still here."

"Hello, Mr. Parker."

"Listen, Ryker, I know you are working hard on this Mali thing. The Secretary, the whole seventh floor, is taking a big interest in this Mali business. The Secretary is concerned. *Very* concerned. She is giving a big speech on democracy in Mexico City tomorrow and doesn't like what she's hearing about Africa. She just spoke with Assistant Secretary Rogerson. Bill is going to be tied up for a while longer than we thought. That means Mali is yours. The Secretary wants you to stay on point and work it to resolution."

"Thank you, sir. Absolutely."

"You'll have to go to Bamako. You can't sit here in Washington and fix real problems. You can't do this from our bubble. You've got to get out there."

"Yes, of course."

"You need to find out what the hell is going on. Meet with this General Idrissa and see what the fucker wants. The Secretary is worried. This is the goddamn twenty-first century. We can't have coups rolling across Africa again. It's not the fucking *Dogs of War* anymore. Did you read the Secretary's Senate testimony last week? She said no

192

dominos on her watch. Ryker, you got it?"

"Yes, sir. No dominos."

"Her speech tomorrow is going to announce a new zero-tolerance policy for coups. No compromise on democracy."

"Yes, sir. No compromise."

"We have too much at stake here to have a setback in Mali."

"I've got it."

"And, Ryker?"

"Yes?"

"Don't think that because it's Africa no one's paying attention. This time, the spotlight is on, Ryker. The White House is calling over here; they're pissed off. Senator McCall is pissed off. He's already called the Secretary on her private line about his daughter. He's pressing hard. You've got to get us something for McCall, too. The Secretary assured him that his daughter's disappearance would be a top priority. No resources spared and all that bullshit. I'm sure he's called to press the FBI, CIA, and the Pentagon, too. It's your game now, Ryker."

"I understand."

"If I were you, Ryker, I'd be wheels up ASAP."

"Yes, sir, I'm on it," he said, standing up.

"Get a plan together and then execute.

You've got to fix this cluster quickly."

He's telling me *about the urgency?* "I'll be on the first flight in the morning."

"There're still flights to Paris and London tonight that haven't left yet. My office will call Dulles Airport and have them hold the last plane. Ryker, you are good to go, right?"

"Absolutely."

"One more thing. We're not sending you in there alone, Ryker. The Pentagon has assigned a special liaison to accompany you."

"I don't need an escort."

"Good instinct, Ryker. I like it. You keep the military guy in line. But it's always useful to have a big motherfucker in a uniform standing next to you. No offense, but we're not sending in a lone civilian professor to talk tough to a general. Ryker, he's your muscle. Let's hope he's big and ugly. Stuttgart says his name is Durham. Colonel David Durham from Special Ops. Plenty of experience from Afghanistan. So he knows a thing or two about thugs and warlords. Durham is standing by in Germany waiting to meet you at your layover in Europe."

"Yes, sir."

"But it's still your mission. It's a State Department delegation. DoD is only along for the ride to help you. That means it's your show. Make sure Durham understands this from the get-go."

"Uh-huh."

"You never know what kind of orders he is really getting. Use him. But don't let him use you."

"No, no, I won't. Is CIA sending anyone?"

"No. You'll have the station chief in Bamako. You don't need anyone from headquarters."

"What about the Purple Cell? What are they doing?"

Parker paused slightly. His face revealed nothing.

"I don't know anything about any Purple Cells. I wouldn't worry about it, Ryker. They'll tell you if you need to know anything. Stay focused on your task. That's Idrissa."

"I will. Thank you. And thank the Secretary. I appreciate her confidence. I won't let her down."

"Here's your chance to put your Golden Hour theory to the test. Good luck, Ryker. The United States still stands for democracy, you know."

Parker ducked out before Judd had a chance to reply.

"Serena! Grab my go bag. I need a car to Dulles right now. I'm going to Bamako."

"I'll call Air France."

195

He paused. "Not Paris this time. London. Give me at least four hours on the ground. I need to see someone. And call over to Special Operations Command in Stuttgart to tell them when I land in London. That's where I will meet up with this Colonel Durham. Tell them he can't be late."

Judd glanced again at the clock. *Shit.* He looked down at his call list. *Have to make these tomorrow.*

At the very top of the list, he added one more name: Jessica.

■ ■ ■ ■

PART TWO:
TUESDAY-WEDNESDAY

■ ■ ■ ■

20.

The flight attendant was wearing the navy blue uniform of British Airways, but had added a ruby-red scarf tied tightly around her neck. She leaned over, reaching toward Judd with a glass of champagne. The rising bubbles drew his attention from the flute up to her eyes. "Would you like anything, sir?" she asked with a slightly mischievous smile and a hint of East London cockney.

Judd sat up straight. He gazed again at the champagne, then past it to the scarf choker and then back up to meet her eyes again. She was still smiling, her head playfully askew. Judd pursed his lips and shook his head slowly.

"You let me know if you change your mind, love." *Back to work.*

Out came the BlackBerry. Judd rolled his thumb over the side of the phone, scrolling for the cell phone number for Sunday, the CIA analyst. He typed:

En route 2 BKO. R u avail?

Send. Judd then leaned into the aisle, searching for the attendant. *I should have accepted that drink.*

Over the loudspeaker, "Welcome to British Airways flight two zero eight to Heathrow Airport. We apologize for the late departure this evening. We had an unexpected delay due to administrative procedures here at Dulles International Airport, but that is now resolved. Please turn off any electronic devices . . ." Judd blocked out the chatter so he could make a mental list of his plan on arrival in London. Just then, his phone bonged with a text message.

Sunday: Roger. How can I help?

That was quick. *Good man.*

Judd: Stopping in London to see OD. Need update on his intentions, advice on pressure pts.
Sunday: Ambitious. Wants 2 return 2b king

Judd: Behind MI?
Sunday: Maybe
Judd: In touch with MI now?
Sunday: Yes
Judd: OD is Paris favorite?
Sunday: Probably
Judd: Who else?

"Sir, we need you to turn off your phone now." Judd looked up, ready to charm his way to a few more minutes. But it wasn't the same attendant. Instead, an older woman, heavyset with a navy apron and her gray hair pulled tight in a bun, was scowling. "Our departure has already been held up for Lord knows what. You are making us even later," she snarled.

Judd nodded politely, said, "Yes, ma'am," and turned his attention back to his phone.

Sunday: Us

Fuck.

Judd: Who = us?

"Sir?" Judd didn't look up. "Sir, you are holding up takeoff. I need you to turn your phone off immediately."

Sunday: DOD

201

Fuck. Fuck.

Sunday: MI may be theirs too.

"Fuck!" said Judd aloud.

"Sir! Do I have to call the captain?"

"Okay. Sorry. I'm turning it off."

Judd shook his head, pushed the power button, and threw the phone into his lap in disgust. He sank back in his seat, the weight of the news pulling his shoulders down.

Once the plane was up in the air and had leveled off, Judd stretched up and pressed the call button. The girl in the choker glided down the aisle toward him. She was still smiling.

"You ready for that drink now?"

21.

BAMAKO, MALI
TUESDAY, 8:05 A.M. GMT

"Ahmed, can I get out *here*?" pleaded Larissa James.

"No, ma'am. Not here. Not yet," was the reply from the front seat of the ambassador's black SUV.

"Well, then *when*? I don't like being trapped like this. It's undignified."

"Yes, ma'am."

"The goddamn ambassador of the United States of America does not hide in the car. That's not what I've been sent here to do."

"Yes, ma'am."

"That's why we are on this drive in the first place. I'm here to see for myself what's going on. To meet the people. To get the mood on the street. We've got to see what's really going on."

"Yes, ma'am."

"Don't 'Yes, ma'am' me, Ahmed. I know

what you're doing."

"Just doing my job, Madam Ambassador."

"This is not what a superpower does! We don't just sit scared inside an armored car! We don't just live inside a bunker! I've served in Honduras and El Salvador and Congo. Even when things got really ugly, we were still out in the streets. If I'm going to be locked in the embassy, I might as well stay in Washington . . ." She trailed off, watching the bustling street scenes of Bamako.

It may have appeared like utter chaos, but Larissa's experienced eye could see the system outside was working in its own organic way. Cars and trucks dominated the middle lanes of the road. Motorcycles, two or three riders each, weaved in between. The next layer, the outer lanes of the road, was for pedestrians, jammed mostly with young men selling small items and women in bright multicolored dresses carrying large bundles on their heads. The final outer edge of the road, where an American might have expected a sidewalk, was stuffed densely with makeshift market stalls. Women lined the street, seated in long rows, showing their wares in woven baskets resting before them: tomatoes, mangoes, dried fish, onions, plastic buckets, batteries, red fleshy meat,

Manchester United calendars.

"Yes, ma'am," said the front seat again.

After a few minutes, the crowds of people and minibuses grew thicker.

"How about *here*? Let's stop at the market."

"I'm sorry, ma'am. Not yet."

"Goddammit, Randy. Let's get out of here," she said, turning her attention to the defense attaché, sitting in the seat next to her.

Colonel Randy Houston had been quiet so far, staring out the window, scanning the passing crowds for anything suspicious. He was wearing a pale-blue golf shirt tucked tightly into freshly pressed khaki trousers. The logo on his shirt displayed a circular insignia with an eagle and UNITED STATES MARINE GUARD, EMBASSY BAGHDAD. Oakleys hugged his shaved head, the arms of the sunglasses digging parallel creases into his scalp above his ears.

"Not yet, ma'am," he said, turning to face her. "Too dangerous. Ahmed will tell us when it's safe."

Larissa exhaled in frustration.

After a few more minutes, the ambassador's vehicle slowed to a crawl. "Sorry, ma'am, traffic ahead. Bus depot."

As her car came to a complete halt, street

vendors converged at the window, holding up boiled eggs, fried donuts, phone cards.

The truck's door clicked open and Larissa stepped out. "I'm going to walk for a few minutes. You can come with me or you can wait here," she said, slamming the door without waiting for a response.

Randy Houston muttered, "Shit," under his breath, then, "Ahmed, I'll go. You stay with the car!"

Larissa tiptoed back along the side of the road, navigating the crowd and a trail of slimy brown water. She stepped over a pile of trash on the street and then darted into the market. Houston rushed over to catch up.

"How is business?" she asked in perfect Parisian French to a young woman sitting on the ground nursing a small baby and tending a meticulously arranged pyramid of bright red chili peppers. The woman stared at the ground and did not answer.

"How is business, madam?" Larissa asked again.

The woman looked up and said softly, "No good."

"Was it better last week?"

The woman did not answer.

"Because of the coup? Are things worse this week because of the problems in the palace? Are the police harassing you? Soldiers?"

No answer.

"How about if I buy some peppers?" asked Larissa, pulling out a roll of local bills. "How much?"

The woman was staring at Larissa's shoes.

"Randy, how much are peppers these days? A thousand francs? Is that enough?"

"I don't know, ma'am. This is a bad idea. You should put your money away. We should return to the vehicle."

Turning back to the woman, "Okay, here, one thousand," she said and handed her the money. The woman grabbed the bill, folded it up tightly, and stuffed it into her bra on the opposite side of where the baby was still nursing.

"Merci," said Larissa, accepting a small plastic bag filled with chili peppers. She handed the bag to Colonel Houston. "Let's try someone else."

She turned and darted deeper into the market.

22.

Judd stepped off the plane, go bag in one hand, the other thumbing through his BlackBerry. His in-box churned like a slot machine as it downloaded hundreds of new messages coming in from all corners of the State Department.

Once off the jetway, he ducked out of the foot traffic and behind a pillar. He took a deep breath and dialed a number.

"Hello?" said a deep male voice.

"General Diallo, this is Judd Ryker, U.S. Department of State. We spoke last night."

"Dr. Ryker. Yes, I knew you would soon be calling. Jolly good to hear from you." *So English.*

"I'm in London, General. Just for a few hours. Should we meet?"

"Ah, yes, very well. I agree. Brilliant idea.

208

Brilliant. May I suggest Marble Arch? I will be at the Bull and Bear in the Cromwell Mews, just off the Edgware Road. Shall we say half one, Dr. Ryker?"

"I'll be there at one thirty, General." Click. *Too confident.*

Judd scanned the airport. Crowds of loud Italian tourists were swelling in the hallways. He receded farther behind the pillar and dialed another number.

"Hi, sweets," answered Jessica. She was still groggy. *Her sexy morning voice.*

"Hey, Jess."

"Glad you called. Everything okay?"

"Yeah, sorry I didn't call last night. It got crazy and then it was too late. The boys all right?"

"Yes, sure. Except they got up at dawn. You can't wake them for dead on a school day, but on vacation they're up with the sun. Always the same. How are things in Mali? What's happening?"

"About that, Jess. I'm on my way to Bamako now. I'm already at Heathrow. I'm calling you from London."

"Now?" she said, with less surprise than Judd expected.

"Yeah. Don't ask. The Secretary's office is pushing for quick action, so I flew out on the last flight to Europe late last night."

"Isn't this exactly what you've been wanting? Rapid response, right? Isn't this why you are at the State Department in the first place?"

"Um, yes. Of course it is."

"Judd, what's the hesitation? This is your chance. This is *your* Golden Hour."

"Right. I know."

"So what's the plan?"

"What do you mean?"

"What is your game plan, Judd? First step is obviously to neutralize Idrissa's moves to consolidate support. He's probably already bribed the legislature and the newspapers. So, what's your countermove?"

"We are working on it."

"I sure hope so. You obviously need to scare him a bit. Threaten Idrissa with sanctions and maybe criminal charges and asset seizures. But you also need to give him an out. What's the out?"

"We're working on that, too," said Judd unconvincingly.

"Good. I've got confidence in you. Obviously, so does the Secretary. It's exciting that she's asked you. Just do it quickly and then get back here to the beach. We miss you."

"Thanks for the pep talk, Jess. I'll try."

"Sure."

"You were right about Idrissa."

"I know. You have a DoD ride-along, right?"

"A what?"

"A DoD ride-along," Jessica repeats. Then, slowly, "Who is the Pentagon sending with you?"

"Why do you ask that?"

"They don't just send a civilian professor to confront a junta. Everyone knows that."

"Uh-huh. They have some colonel meeting me here in London."

"Is he from public affairs?"

"Special Operations. Durham's his name."

"That's good news. Use him. And let's hope he's big. It'll help with Idrissa. He always struck me as a thug. An insecure thug. Which is the worst kind."

"Uh-huh," said Judd, slightly puzzled. "Have you ever met General Idrissa?"

"Me? Oh, no. Just what I've read. You must send my love to Papa. Make sure you see him this time."

"I will. Hug the boys for me, okay?"

"Don't forget you are in Africa, Judd. Even when you are talking to friends like Papa."

"What do you mean by that?"

"You are going to have to scratch below the surface to figure out what's really going on. It's never what it seems. And no one will want to tell you."

"Yeah, I know."

"You are still an outsider."

"Uh-huh."

"Everyone will tell you yes, even when they mean no."

"I remember. I'm actually looking forward to being back."

"Are you nervous?"

"I don't think so."

"Honey, it's your first time back in Mali since . . . you know. The bomb."

"I know. I . . . I'll be fine."

"And, Judd . . ." she said, switching to her deep, serious voice.

"Yeah, Jess?"

"Keep a close eye on Rogerson. Don't play the rookie."

"I know."

"You better watch your back this time. Don't let him cut you out again."

Judd nodded to himself. "Love you."

"You too."

Click.

23.

Papa Toure pushed his way out of the overcrowded minibus onto the street.

"S'il vous plait! S'il vous plait, grand-père!" implored a young boy, propping up an elderly blind man with one arm and extending a begging hand with the other. Papa, revealing neither annoyance nor sympathy, dropped a coin in the boy's hand.

Papa weaved his way through the mass of people and darted in between two market stalls selling pineapples and mangoes. He cut through a narrow alley and, after several more deliberate turns, emerged into a large courtyard filled with stalls.

"Good afternoon, madam," Papa greeted a young woman, sitting behind a tarp and tall piles of fabric typically used to make wraparound skirts. Lying on top was a traditional West African pattern with ovals where the president's face was usually shown. As Papa stared down at this particular pattern, he recognized the face staring back: Mamadou Idrissa.

"Your wares are very beautiful today," he said in the local Bambara language.

"Thank you," she replied with a wide smile.

"This must be very new. I have never seen this pattern before. When did it arrive?" asked Papa.

"The price is very good," she said, erasing her smile.

"Yes, I'm sure it is. Where did this cloth come from? Mopti? Timbuktu?"

"Special price for you," she insisted with a serious look on her face.

"Yes, okay, how much?"

"Twenty thousand francs."

"Ah, no!" said Papa, starting a familiar ritual. "That is too much! You think I am from France? That is too much! I do not even know where it comes from. How can I buy cloth if I don't know who made it or where it is from?"

"Ten thousand," she said.

"Still too much! How about four thousand, and you tell me who brought it and when it arrived?"

The woman shook her head and stared

intently just over his shoulder.

"You think I am a rich man, that I can buy all these clothes?" Papa continued gesturing wildly, swinging his arms around and turning his head. Away from the woman, he identified the target of her attention. A tall, thin man in a cheap gray suit and dark sunglasses was smoking a cigarette and watching over the market, closely eyeing their transaction.

Papa turned back to the woman, nodding vigorously. "Yes, yes. I can see. I can see now why the cloth is so expensive. It is very good. Yes." He handed her several bills and she folded the cloth and placed it into a black plastic bag. As he reached to accept the bag, he whispered to her, "Soldiers? Are they coming to the market?"

She nodded ever so slightly.

"Please, you hold the cloth for me. I will be back tomorrow to get it," he said, passing the bag back to her.

She shook her head. "No, no."

"I will come tomorrow. You keep the money."

"No!" she cried, standing up. Shouting could be heard in the distance, followed by screams. The market woman started to frantically gather her fabric. The noise grew louder. Suddenly soldiers flooded into the square, wielding batons over their heads and overturning tables, sending fruit tumbling across the alleys. The other women scrambled to collect their goods and run. An elderly woman at the far end of the square shouted, "No! No! No!" as a soldier cracked her on the head with a nightstick. She crumpled to the ground.

The man in the gray suit, ignoring the developing chaos in the courtyard, discarded his cigarette and walked directly toward Papa, who dropped the bag and scooted into a side alley. Papa quickened his pace but did not run. He turned crisply through the narrow alleys, following a pattern he knew well. Abruptly, he opened a blue door, slipped inside, and locked the door behind him.

A few moments later, Papa calmly exited the front door of a small café and emerged back onto the main street. He glanced left and right, then he slid on aviator sunglasses and melted back into the crowd.

24.

The road was lined on both sides by shops and cafés with signs in Arabic. The cafés were all full with Arab men — only men — sitting at small tables in groups of three or four; sipping thick, sugary tea; and arguing loudly. Many were smoking through tall, ornate glass-and-bronze *shishas*, sucking on the snakelike hoses.

Judd turned a corner and stepped from what felt like bustling contemporary Cairo back in time into quiet Dickensian England. Cromwell Mews was a mere cobblestone path of narrow Victorian town houses, marked only by a small black-and-white sign. Tucked tightly at the dead end of the mews was a small wooden door. A hanging sign above announced, with a whisper of local exclusivity, that the visitor had arrived at the BULL AND BEAR.

Judd opened the door and ducked his head to enter the pub. Once inside, he could see diminutive elderly men sipping on large pints of coffee-colored ale. No one looked up or made eye contact with Judd. Scanning the dark room, he spied, perched on a stool behind a small table in one corner, incongruously, a husky African man in a houndstooth jacket. *Diallo is positioned to watch the door.* Judd approached him.

"General," Judd said flatly, extending a hand for a firm, formal handshake and trying his best to suppress his face's natural instinct to smile.

"Dr. Ryker! Very good to finally meet you," Diallo responded with a wide grin and vigorous nod. "I have taken the liberty of buying you a pint of Irish stout," he gestured toward the glass filled with thick chocolate beer and a creamy foam top.

"Thank you, General. Guinness is my drink. How did you know?" Judd took his seat.

"It is good to meet our American friend. I know you have been a good friend of Mali for many years. You and your wife, Jessica," he said, still smiling.

He was trying to impress Judd with his intel. *Or is that a threat?*

"And Africa needs many friends, Dr.

218

Ryker. Especially when we are going through difficult times, like Mali is experiencing today."

"And you want to help, I am sure, General."

"Of course. But there is time to come to that. The priority must be security. We cannot have insecurity. Mali and America are under great threat. There are forces that want to tear apart our partnership. To bring bloodshed and mayhem to our peace-loving peoples. We cannot allow that to happen, Dr. Ryker. *You* cannot allow that to happen."

"What exactly are you saying, General? Do you have specific information?"

"I only know that there are bad men with ill intentions, and they are on the move. The threat is imminent and we cannot be weak. I do know this."

"I thought you were now a private citizen, General. How can you be so sure, sitting here in London?"

"Check with your people, Dr. Ryker. They know, too. They can explain. I am just a helpful servant of the Malian people. Trying to save us both from a new crisis."

"My people? Who do you mean?"

"I am a military man, Dr. Ryker. I have been in the army my entire adult life. It is natural for associates to get together. To have a beer like we are doing here in the Bull and Bear. It is very natural for friends to watch a Saturday football match together. Like my side Chelsea over Crystal Palace. And to help one another. To share information about weakness and vanity. To work together to fix problems. To overcome weakness with strength. To defeat the enemy together."

Judd squinted and took a large gulp of beer to try to hide his confusion.

"Your man called it soccer, of course," Diallo added.

Judd's mind was racing, trying to put the pieces together. He took another drink to buy time. Had Diallo just revealed covert contacts here in London with American officials? Why was he disclosing this? Was he suggesting Americans had prior knowledge of the coup? *Did we give him a green light?*

Switching tacks, Judd set down the glass and brightened his face, allowing a small smile to appear. "I see, General. Let's look forward. Let us talk about how we can best overcome the current situation. I know you do not want any harm to come to President Maiga. And the First Lady, your sister. Have you heard from her? Is she safe?"

Diallo reacted, as Judd hoped, with a wide

grin and an exaggerated nod. "Yes, yes, my sister. Very good. You have done your homework, Dr. Ryker. She is safe, of course. She was unable to stiffen the backbone of her husband and get him to see clearly. That is why he is no longer president. Boubacar was too weak." He was now shaking his head and tsking. "Shame, such a shame."

"The United States government still considers President Maiga to be the rightful and legitimate head of state. That has not changed."

"I am aware. We can find a resolution. That is why we are talking here now. Yes, Dr. Ryker?"

"I'm going to Bamako today to meet with General Idrissa. The United States cannot recognize an illegal coup, of course. It would be helpful if he heard from his mentor that our position is set in stone. It cannot be changed."

"I see."

"But we do want to find a safe and honorable way out for all."

"I agree. Yes. I am glad to hear you say this. Mamadou needs advice. And a path. He has become greedy, but I can speak with him. I am still his elder. I am willing to talk to him. But he will need assurances about the future."

The general paused to ponder how to say what came next.

"Dr. Ryker, you know we cannot allow Mali to fall back into the hands of the irresponsible. The dangers of insecurity are still too great to permit that. We must find a strong and experienced leader for the nation at this critical juncture."

Their eyes locked for a moment, broken by Judd's wooden reply: "That is something we can discuss when the time is right, General."

"Ask your British and French colleagues. I know they would all welcome my help. I am certain of it, Dr. Ryker. But we do not have much time. Every moment increases the risks."

"Yes, General. I agree. We must be swift but also patient." Judd drained the last of his beer and slammed the empty pint glass onto the table. "I'll be in touch."

Once safely in a black cab, Judd dialed the number for Simon Kenny-Waddington.

"Simon, it's Judd Ryker from State."

"Judd, nice to hear from you. What's the news from Bamako?"

"Heading there now. I'm in London as I speak. Have you got a tail on General Oumar Diallo yet?"

"Not that I know of."

"Well, I just saw him ten minutes ago at a pub off the Edgware Road and he said that London is backing him to return as the compromise replacement to Maiga. You know anything about that?"

"I'll have to check."

"When I get to Bamako, I'm going to tell Mamadou Idrissa that his time is up, so it would be helpful if he was hearing the same thing from London. Can you make that happen?"

"I'll pass that message to our high commissioner."

"Thanks, Simon. And one more favor. Are you a Chelsea football fan?"

"No, no," responded Simon with a slightly derisive chuckle. "Rugby is my game. I played at school and never miss a match at Twickenham. You know football is a gentlemen's game played by hooligans, but rugby is a hooligans' game played by gentlemen."

"My mistake, Simon. We are soccer, I mean football, fans in my family. My son really loves Chelsea, but I'm a Crystal Palace man myself. Do you have any idea when Chelsea next plays Crystal Palace?"

Judd could hear low mumbling on the line, followed by. "Judd, you still there? The chaps here say you just missed it. Two-one

Chelsea, I'm afraid. Maybe next time."

"When was that?"

"Just last Saturday."

Two days before the coup.

25.

Bazu Ag Ali's camp had only been in place for one day, but he was already feeling jumpy. It was time to move again.

He stepped outside the three-sided tent, the same kind his ancestors had used when they trekked up and down these very same desert tracks by camel to trade salt and gold across the Sahara. Today, trucks had replaced the camels and the cargo was mostly cigarettes and guns. Counterfeit Marlboros and knockoff Eastern European AK-47s.

Bazu, like any respectable smuggler, wouldn't think of going anywhere without his own AK companion. He'd acquired his eleven years ago, traded for two sacks of rice and a crate of Coca-Cola. The AK was his closest friend and they depended on each other. Bazu stripped and meticulously

225

cleaned the gun every day. In return, the AK provided him with both protection and an honorable living.

Bazu looked to the north for any sign of the Harmattan, the seasonal sandstorm that turned the sky into a milky haze. All clear. He gazed toward the sun, scanning the sky. Nothing, no clouds, no birds. *No planes.*

Time to move. Quick check, three vehicles, all Toyota Hilux pickups stolen from the Malian military. Originally provided by the American government. Two of Bazu's trucks were outfitted with mounted heavy guns in the back. The third was empty to allow for more cargo.

This day his twelve-man crew, mostly boys he had known since they were children, was hauling unopened crates, stamped with Russian words he couldn't read. Bazu assumed they were filled with guns, but the price was good enough that he knew better than to ask.

Russians paid well. But they also would hunt you down if you failed to deliver. Knowing this had shaken Bazu's usual confidence.

He checked the sky again, then called out to his men to load up and prepare to move. Their course was due north today, toward the Algerian border.

Just then his Thuraya satellite phone rang. It was a familiar number from the United Kingdom. He marched off to a far sand dune, out of earshot of the other men.

"Yes," he answered in formal Arabic. On the line, a voice he recognized asked him about the weather and the direction of the wind. Instructions in code. Bazu listened intently to the series of questions, replied, "As you wish. . . . *Wa Alaikum As-Salaam,*" and then hung up.

Bazu stared off into the distance. It was a rolling sea of white sand. No choice but to obey. He jogged back to the convoy, idling and ready to go. All the men's eyes were on him.

Switching back into the native Tamasheq language, he announced, "New plan. Today, we will all earn extra!" Nods and smiles all around. "Yallah, let's go!"

And they rolled off over the dunes, heading due south. Toward Timbuktu.

26.

TERMINAL 5, HEATHROW AIRPORT,
 LONDON
TUESDAY, 3:15 P.M. GMT+1

Judd was now running late, but slowed his speedwalking to double-check his flight number up on the screen. As Judd neared the gate, boarding was still under way, so he slowed down and relaxed his shoulders. Standing off to one side and watching over the passengers was a burly and completely bald man in jeans and a tight golf shirt. He had a small navy blue gym bag by his feet. Judd approached him.

"Colonel Durham?"

"Yes, sir. Dr. Ryker, I presume?"

"Glad I found you. Thanks for flying up from Stuttgart."

"Those were my orders, sir."

"Well, I'm still glad the Pentagon sent someone."

"Yes, sir."

"If we are boarding, then I assume this means the Bamako airport is open again?"

"Yes, sir. Our flight will be the first one allowed into the country after they shut it down at oh six hundred yesterday. Lucky timing for us."

"Yes, lucky. We can talk about the game plan on the plane. General Idrissa is a real scoundrel, but this is going to be fun. You've been to Mali before, Colonel?"

"No, sir. I have been fully briefed by the Africa Command in Stuttgart. I am aware of the situation and our objective."

"Well, I'll be interested to hear what they've told you."

"Not here, sir," he said while tilting his head toward the other passengers. "So far, I've ID'd three groups. In the northern chairs facing the window are Eastern Europeans, probably Ukrainian or maybe Russian. Definitely ex-military and they know each other. They absolutely work together. I'll try to get a visual on their passports when they board."

Judd just nodded and noticed, for the first time, that all the passengers waiting to board were men. They were clustered in small groups and were unusually quiet. Of course. *Who flies into an African country the day after a coup?*

Durham continued, "The group of men boarding now are British. They also know each other and, based on their rapport, I am confident they are Special Air Services. That is, British Special Forces, Dr. Ryker. Likely working private security now."

"Mercenaries?"

"Contractors, sir."

Judd nodded.

"The other group sitting in those chairs" — Durham was now looking to his left with his eyes but kept his head steady — "are Americans."

Judd leaned in close. "Colonel Durham, what Americans would be flying into Bamako today?"

"You mean other than us, sir?" said Durham, with a toothy smile.

A sense of humor.

"They don't have official passports. Also likely private security. Contractors. Maybe for the mining companies."

"Could they be undercover?"

"Not based on their tattoos. Recognizable body marks like theirs aren't permitted in U.S. Special Forces."

"Of course."

"Dr. Ryker, if I may, I suggest we hang back, wait for last call, and board once all the others are already on. Keep your passport shielded from view. Last thing we need is to broadcast an American diplomat on the plane."

Judd nodded, with a touch of satisfaction. Durham appeared calm and cool, but also emitted a hint of suppressed violence.

"You've been in Germany long, Colonel?"

"No, only a couple of weeks. Just in between Afghan tours."

"Where were you stationed?"

"Bagram Airfield, sir."

"Based on this assignment, I assume you are a special liaison and experienced negotiator with warlords?"

"No, sir," responded Durham. "I'm a career Green Beret. I have no idea why I was selected for this. I've been running aviation teams on counternarcotics campaigns."

"Airplanes?"

"No, sir. Helicopters. We use Black Hawks and Little Birds to disrupt the Taliban's opium trade. The poppy fields are their main source of financing, so we patrol the trade routes by air and attack their couriers when we can."

"Well, this is a very different kind of assignment. I don't expect much action."

"Yes, sir."

"You know, I hear the soccer team down in Stuttgart is pretty good. You a soccer fan,

Colonel? You ever get to a match?"

"No, sir. No time for that kind of thing. Not my game anyway. I grew up in rural Minnesota. A Twins fan before I could walk. I'm a baseball man."

27.

"Who needs a triple cinnamon latte with extra whipped?" asked Serena, holding two tall coffee cups.

"Oh, you spoil me!" said the overweight secretary, squeezed into her chair. Sitting on her desk were a bouquet of plastic flowers, photos of three pudgy children, and a sign declaring YOUR LACK OF PLANNING IS NOT MY EMERGENCY. Behind her, on the wall, was a discreet engraving that read OFFICE OF THE CHIEF OF STAFF.

"I was on my way up here to the seventh floor anyway."

"That's a lie, Serena, and you know it! But thank you anyway."

"How is your mother doing?"

"Oh, she's doin' good. Real good. The

stitches are supposed to come out next week."

"That's wonderful news. So hard to recover from a fall at that age. It's terrible getting old."

"Don't I know it!"

"Are you able to get home at a decent hour and help her?"

"You think the State Department cares about my mother? Mr. Parker always said the right things. It's all 'Yes, dear, you go home and take care of your momma.' But as soon as he's workin' late, I've got to stay, too."

"Yep, that's how it is in this building. Is Parker working late every night?"

"Uh-huh. And most Saturdays, too," she said, pulling out a tissue and loudly blowing her nose.

"I'm so sorry. That's just not right." Serena added a sympathetic shake of the head. Then, quietly, "You hear anything new about Rogerson?"

"I already told you he keeps calling Mr. Parker from South Africa."

"Has he called again?"

"Early this mornin'."

"Right. Did he say how it's going?"

"Doesn't sound like it's goin' too well. That man's always a grouch. But he was especially snappy today. He's prob'ly been talkin' all night."

"Is he almost done? Is he ready to come home?"

"They keep gettin' close, but then there's always a last-minute hitch. I think he's booked his return flight twice already and had to cancel both times. I don't have a new return plan."

"I see."

"Rogerson sure is popular 'round here."

"What do you mean?"

"You're not the only one asking about him. Lots of people calling up here, asking when Rogerson's coming back."

"What people?"

"All kinds. Regional security, political, military. The terrorism people musta called five times. The White House even called over here last night asking about him."

"Will you keep an ear out for me?" asked Serena.

"Don't I always?" she replied.

"Yes, you do. Can I ask you about something else?"

"Of course. Shoot."

Serena lowered her voice. "You know anything about a Purple Cell?"

The secretary's smile disappeared. "No. I do not know anything about that. And you really should not be asking. You should know better."

"Oh, okay. I'm sorry I asked. Never mind. I must have heard wrong. Let's forget it."

"That's a good idea. You don't want to be asking around about that. It doesn't exist."

28.

As Judd stepped out of the plane onto the roll-up staircase, a familiar wall of heat hit him square in the face. It was nearly midnight, but the gentle breeze offered no relief. *Welcome back to Mali.*

His stomach twisted as it sank in that Jessica was right. It was the first time he'd been back to Africa in eight months. *The first time since the bombing.*

The sky was jet-black, but the airport's low concrete buildings were illuminated under large spotlights. *Looks the same.* The mobile-phone billboard and the handsome young man with the blue suit and sparkling white teeth were, comfortingly, still there, too. Judd squinted toward the grasses behind the sign. It was pitch-black over where the prefab white building should have been. No attack helicopter anywhere to be

237

seen this time.

At the bottom of the steps was another familiar sight: Larissa James. She was surrounded by a crowd of beefy security men in dark suits. Behind them hummed a three-car train: Peugeot police car with lights ablaze, white Toyota paramilitary pickup truck, and the ambassador's black Suburban behemoth. The bumper flags were mercifully sheathed. *Low-profile protest or security measure?*

Judd, trailed closely by Colonel Durham, descended the stairs.

"Dr. Ryker. Great pleasure to have you back in Bamako," said Larissa loudly over the jet engines. Her hand was outstretched for a formal handshake. She was all business.

"Thank you, Ambassador," he responded, trying not to yell.

She took Judd's hand and pulled him in close, then into his ear said, "Judd, really good to see you. We will talk later. Just go along and smile. Tonight is all theater."

Judd nodded emphatically, and then, loudly again, "This is Colonel Durham, our special liaison from the Office of the Secretary of Defense."

Durham stepped forward, handshakes, polite nodding, and then everyone piled into

238

the vehicles for the quick ride over to the lounge.

As they passed through the door, Judd leaned over to Durham. "Hope you're wearing your long johns, Colonel." Just as Durham crinkled his forehead in confusion, they were hit by a blast of arctic air. Judd gave Durham a satisfied nod, then turned back to the lounge.

Larissa was already working the greeting line of officials in white and blue boubous. Judd and Durham joined her for a succession of warm welcomes. *"Merci, merci.* So nice to have you back in Mali, Dr. Ryker. . . ."

Once they reached the end, the men withdrew to the sofas and their mobile phones. *Déjà vu.* The only thing different from his previous visit was the missing picture of President Maiga. In its place was a studio photo of General Idrissa, in full military regalia but clearly straining for his most paternal pose. *That was quick.*

"Time to move, gentlemen," interjected Larissa. "Ahmed will take your passports and bring your bags to the residence. You need to get a few hours' rest, because we'll be starting very early in the morning. Let's go."

■ ■ ■ ■

Back at the ambassador's residence, Judd closed the door to his room and dialed a number on his phone.

"Papa, it's Judd. Sorry to wake you. I'm here."

"You are welcome, Judd. You have come back to Mali at the right time."

"I still need your help, Papa. I spoke with Luc and I have been pushing my people for information, but things are not getting clearer. Just the opposite. They are getting murkier."

"Timbuktu. Judd, I have been telling you about Timbuktu since you were last here. You remember, yes?"

"Of course I remember, but I still don't know what you mean. I'm trying to figure it out, but I need more clues. Papa, my friend, just tell me, what in the name of Allah is going on in Timbuktu?"

"Judd, we cannot speak of such things on the phone. You must go there to find out. I will send a message to the Grand Imam to expect you. He is very wise. He has tales to share."

"The Grand Imam?"

"Go to Timbuktu. See the Imam. Listen

240

to him. All will become clearer and the way forward will come to you."

"I know we are old friends and I need your help, but I can't just drop everything and rush off to Timbuktu on a whim. That would be crazy."

" 'Love all, trust a few.' "

"What's that? Are you quoting Emily Dickinson again? I don't understand, Papa."

"Shakespeare. Judd, you disappoint me. *All's Well That Ends Well.* You should know that!"

"I still don't get it."

"I'm asking you to trust me on this. You have come to me for assistance and I'm advising you to go to Timbuktu."

"Now? Are you saying I need to go to Timbuktu now?"

"Rest, my friend. Tomorrow. You go to-morrow."

"Why don't you come with me? I'll come get you. We can go together."

"I am not in Bamako, I am in Bandiagara, near the border with Burkina Faso."

"In Dogon Country? Why?"

"I came today to inspect Haverford's water projects. It is very beautiful here. You remember?"

"Now? To check on your projects? Mali's in the middle of a coup, Bamako is a fiasco,

241

and you choose now to tour the country-side? Come on, Papa. You are asking me to trust an old friend, and I do trust you. But I don't buy that story for a second."

"See, Judd, you understand more than you think. Van Hollen always had a good eye for talent. He was right about you."

"What does that mean? What does BJ have to do with this?"

"Go see the Grand Imam in Timbuktu and then you will know what to do next."

"I don't know. I'm here to meet Idrissa. I don't have much time."

"Go to Timbuktu."

"I'll think about it, Papa."

"Sleep well, *mon ami.* You have a lot on your shoulders. You have a big day tomorrow."

29.

The line of gray trucks sent scattering a flock of vultures feasting on the rotten remains of a bushrat. As the convoy rolled up to the border post, it fell dead silent as the drivers simultaneously cut the engines. The roadblock was no more than two dented oil barrels filled with rocks and a board of exposed two-inch nails laid on the road.

The post commander woke up from a nap in the small guardhouse and, as he emerged, annoyed to be roused, wiped his face with his hand and slipped on a black beret. Another soldier asleep under a tree jumped to attention and snatched his rifle that had been lying in the dust. They circled the half-dozen dark green GAZ-66 off-road trucks with OKTYABRSKY SUPPORT SERVICES printed on the side in small white letters.

The commander was excited to see them but didn't show it. This was the third day in a row that Russian trucks had appeared at the border. The drivers were all Indian, or maybe Arabs? But it was always the same. After completing a full circle, he approached the driver of the lead vehicle.

"What are you hauling?" he demanded as the other soldier pointed his gun menacingly at the cab.

"Mining equipment," responded the driver in a thick accent with a bored look on his face.

"Where are your passports and import papers?"

"Right here," said the driver, handing over a fat roll of CFA francs, the local currency, bound by a rubber band.

He exchanged glances with his partner, then accepted the money and deposited the roll into his breast pocket.

"*Oui.* Everything seems to be in order. On your way. *Bon voyage.*"

The soldier set down his gun, slid the nail board off the road, and rolled one of the barrels out of the way. The trucks roared back to life, belching muddy clouds of smoke into the air.

The two soldiers stood in the middle of

the road and watched the convoy rumble away. Once the trucks were out of sight, they lazily replaced the barrel and nail board. The commander took off his beret and returned to the guardhouse. The other sauntered back to his tree, dropped the gun in the dirt, and lay down to return to his nap.

The vultures, abandoning their roadkill, took off into the air and followed the convoy of trucks, high above in wide sweeping circles.

30.

Judd Ryker and Bull Durham woke early,
but Larissa James was already dressed and
ready to go by the time they came down-
stairs.

"We can have coffee at the embassy. The
briefers are waiting for you. You are here to
hit the ground running, right?" She didn't
bother to look up from her BlackBerry to
see them both nod. "The car is ready. Let's
go. Yallah!"

Security at the embassy was tighter than
normal. At one hundred yards from the
fence was the first perimeter. A contract
guard checked the underside of the SUV
with a mirror on a long pole. Another
inspected under the hood, while a third led
sniffing dogs around the vehicle.

Once they were through inspection and
the first gate closed behind them, IDs were

checked. Then a second gate opened to the compound. Inside were manicured lawns, colorful tropical plants, and men with automatic weapons.

As the party of three passed through the embassy's main foyer, Larissa acknowledged the staff with a noble nod but no introduction of the visitors. No explanation. At the end of the lobby, they ascended a set of stairs to an unmarked door.

"You'll need to remove the batteries from your cell phones."

"What?"

"Your battery. For security. If you want to bring your cell phone in here, you'll need to take it out."

Judd shrugged, then he and Durham removed the cases from the back of their phones. They placed the battery in one suit pocket and the rest of the phone in the other.

Satisfied, Larissa inserted her ID card into a slot next to the door and punched in an eight-digit PIN. The door opened with a release of air.

"This is the secure classified area of the embassy. Americans with top secret clearance only."

They stepped through the door, leaving Mali behind and entering the sterile inner sanctum of U.S. national security.

"Coffee?"

"Hell yes, Larissa," answered Judd. "A strong one."

"Yes, ma'am," said Durham.

"Someone will bring it to you," said Larissa, now pointing down a long hallway. "At the end is the office of the station chief, Cyrus. Judd, you met him at the hospital in Germany, remember? The defense attaché, Colonel Randy Houston, should be in there, too. It's the black door. They will give you a briefing. Judd, I'm going to make some phone calls. When you are done with Cyrus and Randy, come back to my office so we can chat and catch up. I want to hear about Jessica and the boys."

Once they were alone, Durham asked, "You two know each other?"

"We survived a car bomb last time I was in Bamako, eight months ago. I guess that makes us lifelong friends."

"Yes, it does," said Durham, in a way that suggested Judd wasn't the only one with that particular experience.

Judd knocked on the black door. He was greeted stiffly by Colonel Houston, whom Judd recognized from the video briefing. "Dr. Ryker. Welcome back to Mali," he said, deadpan.

Inside, Cyrus was wedged behind a large desk crammed into a tiny office. Tall piles of papers surrounded him. The office walls were floor-to-ceiling with photographs. Most were satellite pictures of desert camps, shots of crowds of young men, or of mosques with labels of the major towns around Mali: Bamako, Segou, Kidal, Mopti, Gao, and Timbuktu. Cyrus was wearing the same rumpled tan suit from yesterday.

"Gentlemen," said Cyrus. "Please shut the door, Colonel."

"Thanks for getting to the office so early to meet with us," said Judd, trying to break the ice and squeezing himself down into a chair.

"I'm here every day at oh five hundred, Dr. Ryker."

"Okay, so what can you tell us?" said Judd, shooting a look at Durham.

"We are tracking several active hostiles moving through the northern sector and along the border with Algeria," said Cyrus, pointing to one of the photos. "The chatter is accelerated and likely indicating some kind of attack on Malian installations, with a nontrivial probability of targeting U.S. interests and personnel. We have reports that an Ansar al-Sahra cell crossed over from Algeria late last week and is seeking a rendezvous with another element that will provide instructions and explosives for an attack. We've got the birds keeping an eye out for new movement, but we expect with a high degree of probability some kind of assault within the next twenty-four to forty-eight hours. Colonel?"

Houston began, "DoD elements in-country have additional monitoring capacity. We have eyes on the border, Dr. Ryker. Russian trucks have been transshipping material up from Nigeria, from the swamps of the Niger Delta, into Burkina Faso, and then across the border into northern Mali, up past Timbuktu. The Russians are disclaiming any official knowledge of this, but quietly they are acknowledging an oil exploration project that they would rather people didn't know about. They claim they want to keep it low-key to avoid unwanted attention from bandits or terrorists operating in the area. The quantity of goods they are hauling suggests heavy equipment, but this could also be cover. Small arms smuggling is one possibility. Could be anything. Victor Chelenkov has ties to the Russian oil companies as well as the Russian army."

"What about the coup?" asked Judd. "That's why we are here."

"Nothing new since yesterday," answered

Cyrus. "Idrissa has taken charge and is putting his people into place. We do know that Maiga is at the Wangara barracks and he is alive."

"Let's not get distracted with complicated local politics. Not today," broke in Houston. "Idrissa is cooperating. His people are providing intel, and he is ready to countermove Ansar."

"He is supposedly making progress on the missing Peace Corps volunteer, too," added Cyrus. "The Malians know how to make contact, so they currently are our best lead for getting the girl back safely."

"You mean Idrissa is already in direct contact with the kidnappers?" Judd was incredulous, but Cyrus was steely calm.

"I can't reveal any more than I have already. I'm sure you understand."

Durham turned to Houston. "Colonel, what is the status of Operation Sand Scorpion? Where are your men who were embedded with the OSS strike teams?"

"The ambassador ordered a no-exceptions withdrawal from all counterterrorism strike forces until further notice, so they are no longer in barracks with the teams. But she understands that we still need eyes and ears if we are going to know what's happening. So we have left a handful of Special Ops guys in the field. They are on standby in Gao and Timbuktu, just not living with the Malian teams right now or providing advice on their exercises. It might be wise at this critical juncture to consider letting them go back in. At least a temporary lift, until this Ansar thing blows over. For security. We need the Scorpions up and running ASAP."

"What are you hearing about Diallo?" asked Judd, ignoring the attaché's suggestion, and turning back to the station chief. "Is he involved with the coup? Is he planning on coming back?"

"We do not know," replied Cyrus. "Idrissa would like to think that he is asserting himself now and has moved out from under Diallo's shadow."

"But Diallo could very well come back," said Houston. "I'm guessing he may want to return. He's in London, you know."

"Yes, I'm aware," said Judd. "How long have you been the DATT, Colonel?"

"Three years."

"So you were here when Diallo's coup attempt failed?"

"Yes, sir. I was the liaison with the Malian military leadership. General Diallo was our primary contact."

"Diallo was our guy then?"

Houston paused, meeting Judd's gaze.

"Too bad he threw it all away. His mistake. Perhaps he sees the current situation as a chance at redemption."

"What are the pressure points on Idrissa?" asked Judd, changing the subject again.

"Idrissa is looking for American assurances, and some kind of recognition," said Cyrus. "I think he's smart enough to know you won't say anything in public just yet, but he's going to want some signal from you on American acknowledgment."

"Idrissa's fighting for his life and he's got Ansar al-Sahra breathing down his neck," said Houston. "We trained the Malians for just such an encounter. This is his big moment."

No, thought Judd. *This is my moment.*

"Where are the French on all of this?"

"Active. We are in close contact," said Cyrus.

"Is there a connection to Niger here? Are they worried about security of their uranium supplies?"

"You will have to ask them," said Cyrus abruptly. "I wouldn't know anything about that."

"Um, okay," said Judd, taken aback by the change in Cyrus's tone. He turned to Colonel Houston. "After my meeting with Idrissa this morning, I may want to head up

253

north. Can you get me up to Timbuktu if I need to go?"

"Sorry, sir. We have no air assets at this time. Since the coup, they have shut down internal commercial flights. You can drive there in about two days, maybe do it in one day if you really push it. I wouldn't recommend it, but that's the only way to get up there right now."

A knock on the door and in popped a woman's head. "Gentlemen, the ambassador has asked me to pull our visitors. The palace called and General Idrissa is ready. The ambassador asked if Colonel Durham could take the rest of the briefing from Colonel Houston and Cyrus. She needs Dr. Ryker for five minutes before the convoy leaves."

"Yes, ma'am."

On his way out the door, Judd stopped and turned. "Cyrus, I believe we have an old friend in common, Professor BJ van Hollen from Ibadan."

"I am sorry," he responded, giving Judd an expressionless stare, "I have never been to Ibadan. I don't know anyone named van Hollen."

31.

Tucked among the sand dunes and high grasses of the Outer Banks were small holes that were this evening suddenly stirring. There was no wind. The only movement was tiny flippers clawing away the sand. After a moment, several dozen loggerhead baby sea turtles, having squeezed their way out of their spongy shells and wriggled from their underground nest to the surface, began a desperate dash to the sea. Whether they would live for sixty years or sixty seconds was decided by fate, right at that moment. Seagulls, sensing their moment, dove and swooped overhead, squawking in the night.

Resting up on the dune, just behind this struggle of nature, was a modest bungalow, oblivious to the life-and-death action down

255

on the beach. The cottage was entirely dark, except for the soft glow of light in one window up in the top attic room, the master bedroom.

Sitting up in bed, reading glasses low on her nose, scanning her laptop, was Jessica Ryker. She searched the French and Arabic news websites for information on Mali. She wasn't finding much. She clicked again to open a program, logged in as EMILYD.

Jessica sipped lemon tea from a mug on her bedside table, then typed brief messages to several addresses, requesting information. She finished her tea, closed the program, and turned back to the news sites.

"I must have missed something," she mumbled to herself. "Judd, my dear, what are you doing?"

32.

Judd was escorted back down the hallway to the ambassador's office. Larissa was on the phone behind her desk with her back to the door. On either side of her were American and Malian flags resting on tall poles.

One wall of her office was a bank of windows, looking out onto the manicured lawns of the embassy compound. Through the fence, off in the distance, Judd could make out a long snake of people waiting for the consulate to open, waiting for the chance to try their luck at the chess game between themselves and a young Foreign Service officer — usually on their first tour overseas and scared to death of making a mistake — shielded by thick plate glass. The Malians were also anxious, arriving at the American fortress with stacks of neatly folded documents, desperately trying to

257

prove the validity of their claims, hoping to make it through, to win that ultimate lottery prize: a U.S. visa. Young boys were walking up and down the visa line, hawking boxes of gum, hard-boiled eggs, car air fresheners, Chinese-made flip-flops.

The other wall of Larissa's office was a rack of bookshelves, floor-to-ceiling, littered with plaques, statues, and medallions of every shape and size from every ministry and government office in the country. The empty tokens of appreciation of bureaucrats and politicians for a brief meeting with the representative of the president of the United States. *The detritus of diplomacy.*

"That's a lot of courtesy calls, Larissa," said Judd as she hung up the phone.

"Tell me about it. Every one of those tchotchkes is an hour of my life lost," she replied. "But that's the job we all signed up for. Right, Judd?"

"Not me. I didn't give up the sweet life to be a real diplomat. I'm supposed to be the cleanup guy."

"That's right. And we don't have much time, so let's get straight to it. Are you ready for Idrissa?"

"I think so. Wasn't Houston supposed to find soft spots in the junta? Isn't that why we invest in having a defense attaché who is plugged in so he can reach the generals when we need to?"

"Houston tried. But he hasn't gotten anywhere. He said that Idrissa has the whole military hierarchy lined up already. If there are any loyalists to Maiga left in the army, they aren't showing themselves."

"They will. We just need to give them the opportunity. They will bend to the wind if it blows the other way."

"I hope you're right."

"But I'm worried about what the embassy is telling Idrissa. I mean, what they are *really* telling him. Houston and Cyrus are entirely focused on security. They're not vaguely interested in the coup. That's not our message. Don't they realize why I'm here?"

"Of course they do. But they are watching their backs. They have to follow our lead. I've got chief of mission authority, and they work in my embassy. But you know they have other masters back in Washington with their own agendas. They may even be getting mixed signals from other offices inside State."

"Come on, Larissa. You know I can't control all the channels coming out of Washington. I'm just trying to keep the front channel clear."

"I know, Judd. But they are hedging.

That's how the game works."

"I'll deal with State. I need you to help me contain the mixed signals the embassy is sending to Idrissa. I can't go in there and talk tough, and then have your Colonel Houston give him a wink and tell him not to worry about some Girl Scouts from the State Department. We just can't have that."

"I'll make sure he understands."

"Houston already asked me to lift the hold on military engagement, for fuck's sake, Larissa. I've been here less than a day and they're already clamoring to work with Idrissa."

"What did you tell him?"

"Nothing. I ignored the request."

"That won't be the end of it. These guys aren't built to go away just because you ignore them. You should know by now that's not how it works."

"I know. I'm just going to buy as much time as I can. But I need you to be open with me. I'm going to need your help."

"You have it, Judd."

"And what about your station chief?"

"He's prickly, but he gets the job done."

"I asked him about any French connection to uranium in Niger, and his face almost fell off."

"Well, Judd, you stepped on a land mine

there. Cyrus was with the Agency in Niger during the run-up to the Iraq war. You remember yellowcake? Valerie Plame, Joe Wilson, Dick Cheney? He was smack in the middle of all that."

"Holy shit. No wonder he's touchy. What was his role?"

"I don't really know. But it's definitely made him wary of visitors from Washington, D.C. You should tread carefully."

"Good advice. I will."

"And what about your man? That big fella you brought? Durham?"

"He goes by Bull."

"Of course he does. Can you trust him?"

"Too early to tell. So far he seems straight up. Doesn't say much, but he seems efficient."

"Okay, Judd. And . . ." Larissa paused, looking down at her shoes.

"And?"

"How are *you,* Judd? You holding up okay?"

"Of course. Why do you ask?"

"You . . . you need to be careful."

"What do you mean, Larissa?"

"It's more of a hornet's nest down here than you think. Keep things close hold. Especially now, while everything's in flux."

"I'm not getting you."

"Look, Judd," she said. Then she stopped, stuck her head out her door, peered up and down the corridor, then closed her office door and stared hard right into his eyes. "I'm going to be straight with you. There are concerns about some of your . . . acquaintances."

"Mine?"

"I know you have friends here in Mali. We all do. But you need to be careful. Envelopes of money change hands often here in West Africa, as do loyalties. You know that."

"Of course. I know that."

"Idrissa will look for anything to undermine you. You can't give him anything. Don't underestimate him."

"I'll be more careful."

"All right, then. It's showtime. Are you ready?"

"I need three minutes and a quiet office before we go," said Judd.

Larissa leered at him.

"I will be careful."

Larissa hesitated, then stepped out and closed the door behind her, leaving Judd alone in her office.

Judd sat behind Larissa's vast desk and removed his cell phone from his jacket pocket and reinstalled the battery. As he waited for the phone to power up, he noticed a small bust on her bookcase of a woman's head, the kind tourists picked up for a few dollars at the souvenir market in central Bakamo. A small inscription at the bottom read IN APPRECIATION FOR AMERICAN SUPPORT FOR OUR COMMON FIGHT, FROM GENERAL MAMADOU K. R. IDRISSA, COMMANDER OF THE SIXTH NORTHERN ZONE. His irritation was interrupted by an answer on the other line.

"*Allo?*"

"This is Judd. I'm now in Bamako."

"Ah, *très bien.* Very good."

"Do you have anything new, Luc?"

"*Oui.* We have sent word to Mamadou Idrissa that his little game is over. It is *fini.* We understand he was frustrated. But now his time is up."

"And how did he take that?"

"What do you expect? Idrissa is an arrogant bastard. His big head, it is swelling. For now, he is resisting," said Luc.

"Well, I'm about to go see him. The car is running. I'll give him the same message. Maybe it'll help if he hears from the French and the Americans."

"Yes. He will feel cornered. But we have to give him a path. It is too early to make an offer, but you have to give him a way out of this. He must see some escape."

263

"Agreed. Speaking of escape, what are you hearing of General Diallo?"

"I think you should be telling me."

The French were indeed paying attention.

"Yes, Luc, I saw him. Clearly, he wants to return home. Diallo definitely sees himself as the statesman to save the day. He thinks he is Mali's savior. And he thinks Idrissa has given him another chance."

"Yes. It is an option we will need to consider."

"Are you encouraging him? He seems to think he has support from Paris already. What kind of signals are you sending?"

"It is far too early for anything like that."

"Well, I'm not sure Washington is going to be too comfortable with the Diallo option. Replacing one coup plotter with another is not exactly supporting democracy."

"I understand," replied Luc. "But we need to keep all options open. Idrissa must not see any doors closed."

"Are you hearing anything else?" asked Judd.

"Yes. I have the same warnings ringing in my ears that you are receiving, Judd. I am sure of it. My people in Bamako are getting the same stories. We are all hearing the same."

"Do you believe it?"

"It doesn't matter what you and I believe. It doesn't even matter what is real and what is a façade, a mirage in the desert. We just need to control our people. We have to stay in front of this, or it will be lost."

Lost.

That word hung around in Judd's head.

"We can't allow that, Luc."

"Absolument, Judd. Good luck with Idrissa. *Bonne chance."*

33.

She smelled cigarette smoke and sour milk. She tasted dried blood on her lower lip. Her mouth was parched.

Katie was up but not wholly awake. It felt like morning, but she wasn't certain. She couldn't see anything because the burlap sack was back over her head, tied tightly around her neck.

She hadn't gotten much sleep the previous night because the rope holding her wrists was rubbing the skin raw and the pain jolted her awake whenever she moved. The pain and the fear.

Katie's initial terror had receded intermittently and been replaced by the boredom and confusion of long hours in the dark with nothing but her own thoughts. As she opened her eyes and saw nothing, the same questions immediately churned in her head.

266

Who would kidnap me? What could they possibly want? Does anyone even know I'm here? Where is here?

The past hours provided no answers to those mysteries. No clues. She was, in every sense, in the dark.

The questions faded and the dread returned whenever she heard footsteps approaching. Crowding out everything else, *Am I going to die?*

Katie comforted herself with the fact that she was still alive. If they had wanted to kill her, she'd be dead already, she repeated in her head. With the exception of a busted lip from being thrown into the truck — she had stupidly tried to resist — no one had hurt her.

Other than some broken English demanding that she read into a camera a nonsensical statement about U.S. troops leaving Mali and Pakistan, no one had even spoken to her. Would that wind up on CNN? Would that be her fifteen minutes of fame, instead of the life of noblesse oblige she had expected of herself? That her father had expected? How distant those plans now felt, captive, lying on a dirt floor, hands bound. How ludicrous. *C'est ridicule.*

Her thoughts of self-pity were broken again by loud shouting. She couldn't tell what direction it was coming from, but it was definitely getting closer. She didn't recognize the language. It was neither French nor Arabic. Was it Tamasheq, the Tuareg tongue? *That would be better than Arabic.*

Her hands were sweating. The yelling grew louder. Her throat started to burn. Suddenly the shouting stopped, and she exhaled in relief.

Then the door banged open. She was pulled up by her elbow and yanked violently to her feet. She started to scream but quickly realized it was pointless. Flooding back into her head, *Am I going to die now?*

34.

The convoy turned onto the wide road leading up to the palace. On each corner were small groups of soldiers, some appearing no older than sixteen, holding oversized automatic weapons. They were chatting casually and did not appear nervous. As the ambassador's car passed, they jumped to attention and saluted.

Judd scanned the boulevard for armed personnel carriers. He nudged Larissa. "I would have thought the street would be lined with troops and hippos as a show of force. Where is everybody?"

"It's a sign of normalcy. Idrissa is trying to project the image that everything is fine. New president, but it's all business as usual. Nothing to see here."

"So he's not worried about a counter-coup?"

"Apparently not. But you can be sure he has his spies in every unit."

"Those are not elite troops on the outer perimeter," interrupted Durham from the third row of the Suburban. Larissa and Judd turned around in their seats to face him. "It's likely the general is deploying weaker units on an outer ring as a warning mechanism. The crack units will be closer to the palace and out of sight until something goes down. Those kids are just the trip wire. Countercoup fodder."

Larissa gave Judd a little nod of approval, and they both turned back to the front.

As they passed through the final gate, Judd's BlackBerry bonged with an alarm, signifying an urgent message from headquarters. He glanced down to see it was from Serena. *Middle of the night in Washington.*

The car pulled up to the circular driveway at the entrance to the palace. There was a line of dignitaries ready to greet them. Judd turned to Larissa. "I have to read this."

She nodded knowingly and said to the driver, "Hold here." The driver waved away the guards trying to open the doors. They obliged, and suddenly everyone was in pause. The car was idling. The welcome committee was standing in the breeze. All were waiting for Judd.

Serena: Task force screaming. I've held them off by scheduling & canceling to buy u a few hours. But running out of excuses. Others are pushing for new chair. Rogerson called. Still no ETA. Hurry.

Judd suppressed the *Fuck!* in his head. *Jessica was right. Again.*

Judd: Thx. I'll run the TF from the embassy. OK to reschedule. Keep ears open.

Judd pressed send, then turned to Larissa. "We are going to need a Task Force Mali meeting by videoconference later today. Can the embassy handle that?"

"I'll have my people set it up."

"Then let's go." Judd turned to Durham. "Colonel, you ready for the general?"

"Yes, sir. Yallah."

Judd Ryker, Ambassador Larissa James, and Colonel David "Bull" Durham had been sitting in the green waiting room for more than an hour. Judd glared at Larissa with aggravation.

"He's just showing us that he's not in panic mode," she said. "Don't take it per-

271

sonally." Judd nodded back but wasn't convinced. His feet tapped with impatience.

The green sofas, with their dainty lace arm covers, were exactly as Judd remembered from his last visit to this room, eight months ago. He'd found them quaint last time. Now they were irritating.

Durham sat calmly, unfazed by the delay. He was dressed in his formal dark green service uniform, insignias on the shoulders, declaring his attachment to the Third Special Forces Group, and a chest full of badges.

Just then, a petite man arrived and escorted them, with a slight bow of apology, into the next room. "Monsieur President will see you now."

Once inside the presidential office, Judd's sense of uncomfortable déjà vu was immediately reinforced. Idrissa, in a civilian boubou, sat behind the presidential desk. Nothing else seemed to have changed in the office. Idrissa had simply moved in.

The general greeted them with stiff handshakes. Judd met Idrissa's gaze as they gripped each other. "Thank you, General, for seeing us on such short notice."

"It is a great pleasure to have you back in Mali, Dr. Ryker," he said. "We are facing many threats together, so I am so pleased that you have come to see us now at this important time. Yes. Mali and the USA have a strong partnership. We must promote security together."

Judd turned and glared at Larissa. *Is he for real?*

"With all due respect, General, I'm not here to talk about cooperation. I'm here to explain to you, in no uncertain terms, the position of the United States. As you will have seen from our official statement by the Secretary of State, we condemn the coup d'état and are calling for the immediate release and restoration of President Maiga. He is still the recognized president of Mali. This is our firm position. I have been sent here specifically by the president of the United States to tell you this."

Larissa shot Judd a look of displeasure.

"Our aid program to Mali has been suspended," Judd continues, sitting up as straight as he can. "And we have ordered all of our military advisors to return to the embassy. If this isn't resolved in the next few days, then all programs will be terminated, the money will be reassigned to other countries, and our military teams will be sent home. Permanently. It's an outcome we all want to avoid, General."

"Thank you, Dr. Ryker," replied Idrissa,

gently shaking his head. "That is most disappointing, I'm afraid that we do not agree. Security first, yes. Return of the weak and criminal Maiga, no. It is impossible. We cannot allow that. That would be irresponsible. Too dangerous. For Mali, and for the United States. Do not be deceived by propaganda, Dr. Ryker. It would violate the sworn pledge I have taken as chairman of the Council for the Restoration of Democracy. The CRD principles cannot be violated. I am sorry that you do not understand this."

"I think I understand perfectly, General."

"So we are at an impasse? We can live without your aid. We do not need your charity. But there is no reason for our military cooperation to cease. We are working together against common enemies, and the enemy is gaining strength. Even right now as we sit here talking, we are gathering evidence of their plans, and tracking their activities. Our Scorpions, which we built together hand in hand, are ready to defend the country and attack the enemy that lies in wait, set to pounce."

Idrissa paused for dramatic effect. "Dr. Ryker, I know you have personally suffered from this threat. I must tell you that my intelligence service has reported a break in the investigation of the despicable bombing of you and the honorable ambassador. Yes. We have identified the culprits and they have close links to these same terrorists who have stolen the senator's daughter. We are tracking them now and I am certain we will have them apprehended very soon."

Judd eyed Larissa. *Idrissa knows who tried to kill us? He drops this now? I thought he was in contact with the kidnappers.* Larissa returned a slight shrug.

"You see, Maiga was too weak to deal with criminals and terrorists, but I am not," continued Idrissa. "I am confident we can agree to let our brave soldiers work together for our common security. The operation can continue. Yes. I think you will want this, no? I think your people will want this."

"General, we would welcome any information about who is responsible for the bombing and the kidnapping. A team from our FBI is being assembled to assist the case. But that is not the issue today. We have to address our immediate problem. I have Colonel David Durham with me here. He was dispatched by the Department of Defense to join me, so there is no confusion about the position of the United States government. No ambiguity." Judd turned to Durham, sitting in his full uniform, medals

275

across his chest. "Colonel?"

"General, I am here on the direct orders of the Secretary of Defense." Durham stood at attention. "We have appreciated the co-operation with the armed forces of Mali. You have been a close and reliable ally of the United States in our war against the forces of chaos and terror. But the United States can no longer work with you after this illegal and immoral act. You have disgraced your command. You have disgraced our profession, sir." Durham was physically growing larger as his speech reached a crescendo, ending with a booming, "As one proud soldier to another, sir, I urge you to stand down!"

Judd and Larissa were both taken aback, but exchanged looks of satisfaction.

Idrissa was even more shocked, his eyes widening. The room was hushed as Durham took his seat again.

After a few moments, Judd broke the awkward silence. "General, we want to find a graceful and honorable way out of this for everyone. What can we do together?"

Idrissa stared at his shoes, refusing to make eye contact. "When the time is right, we will organize new elections. But we cannot do this tomorrow. No. It will take time. We need to secure the nation first. We must first restore security. Security, yes," he said, lifting his head to finally meet Judd's eyes. "Perhaps elections can be held next year."

"General, you don't want to drag this out for a year. That would be totally unacceptable. We must resolve this immediately. How can we find a way out of this problem right now? We can fix this, perhaps even today."

"There is nothing that can be done now. No."

"I urge you to rethink that. You can contact me through Ambassador James. When you know what you need, you can reach out to her. Let her know what we can do. I am hopeful we can find a way forward that is good for you and for Mali."

Idrissa stared ahead, through Judd. *Does he hear me?*

"General, I also need to be clear on our firm expectations for the treatment of President Maiga. The president of the United States and the Secretary of State are personally concerned about his safety and well-being."

"I can assure you he is safe," interrupted Idrissa.

"Why not take me to see him? Let's go right now. It would be a sign of good faith. Washington would view that as a positive signal of your intentions."

"I'm afraid that is impossible. We will deal with the former president when the time is right."

At that moment a uniformed soldier entered the room and whispered in Idrissa's ear. The general nodded, then turned to Judd. "I apologize, Madam Ambassador, but urgent business of the state demands that I call our meeting to a close. As you are aware, these are precarious times. National security is our top priority. Mali is under attack as we speak. By enemies of the state and enemies of civilization. By criminals and terrorists and kidnappers." Idrissa paused, snapped his fingers at his aide, and motioned for him to come. The aide handed the general a large brown envelope.

"Before you go, Dr. Ryker, I have one more matter to raise with you. I'm afraid that we have detected a foreign plot on our soil." He handed the envelope to Judd, who opened it to find a stack of grainy black-and-white photographs.

On top was a photo of a plump African man with a salt-and-pepper beard, hugging an even larger man wearing a suit and aviator sunglasses. Judd flipped quickly to the second photo, which showed the same man sitting alone in a crowded restaurant, or perhaps a club, bottles of beer crowding a small table. The next photo showed a waiter approaching the man, an envelope clearly visible on the underside of his tray. The final picture was of the man tucking the envelope into his jacket. The man in the photos: Papa Toure.

"These were taken just thirty-six hours ago here in Bamako by my special intelligence unit. We have been tracking this man for years as he has traveled between Mali and Nigeria. We believed he was a courier for Nigerian criminals expanding their business into Mali. But we now know he is in fact working for foreign jihadists based in northern Nigeria. You see the envelope?" Idrissa was pointing to the photo. "It is an envelope of money. The funds are intended for the north of Mali. For extremist Imams trying to radicalize our youth." Idrissa stared straight at Judd. "Dr. Ryker, you know this man, yes?"

Judd glared back at him, then down at his old friend Papa in the photos. He handed the photos back to the general with a shrug. "No. Never seen him before."

"Why don't you pick him up?" asked Colonel Durham.

"We were following him, but this morning he disappeared. We believe the culprit has fled Bamako to the bush. But we will find him. We will get him. Dr. Ryker, you can be very sure we will get him. And his accomplices."

Abruptly, Idrissa rose. "Madam Ambassador, Colonel, Dr. Ryker. You also know how to reach me. Please enjoy the rest of your visit to Mali."

Idrissa turned as the Americans were escorted out. Judd's meeting with the coup maker, the reason for his hasty flight to Africa, was finished. It was over just like that, and he was no closer to resolution.

Empty-handed.

Back in the car, Judd turned to Larissa. "What do you make of that?"

"Well, I think he was genuinely surprised that you threatened to pull our military cooperation. Especially the advisors to his Scorpions. Colonel Durham, you hit him right between the eyes. I can see why they call you Bull."

Durham acknowledged the ambassador's compliment with a slight tip of his hat.

"But will it work?" asked Judd. "He called our bluff."

"Let's wait and see. Let everything simmer. I suspect he'll be in touch one way or another before the end of the day."

"So, what now, Larissa?"

"We wait. I'll ask Cyrus to follow up his claim of a break in our bombing case. And also about this Nigerian courier. Why would he think you know him?"

"No idea. Probably just trying to rattle me. . . . Something's not right."

"Let's just sit tight and see what he does next. We'll go back to the residence and wait."

"I can't just sit."

"Be patient, Judd."

"I can't just sit here on my hands while Idrissa is calling the shots. Why can't we shake things up?"

"Let's wait for Idrissa to move first."

"I don't trust him, Larissa."

"Of course you don't trust Idrissa. We shouldn't trust anyone right now."

" 'Love all, trust a few . . .' "

"What is that?"

"Shakespeare," said Judd, nodding to himself.

"Of course it is," she said, looking away. "I need you to be patient."

"How about Timbuktu? Let's go."

Larissa spun around. "Why in the world would you want to do that, Judd?"

"I've never been."

"Well, now's not the time. I doubt diplomatic security would even let you go. God knows, I can't have another hostage on my hands."

"What if I need to go? Can you make it happen?"

"Absolutely not. They have suspended all internal commercial flights. Colonel Houston has put all his people on lockdown and prohibited travel. How am I supposed to then allow a civilian like you up there? It's far too dangerous, Judd."

"I have a helicopter, Dr. Ryker," interjected Durham.

"What?" Larissa's mouth was agape.

"After we heard from Colonel Houston about the lack of air assets in the country, I thought we might need help, so I called a friend, pulled a few strings. An MH-60K can be here in two hours. The crew is standing by, waiting for the go order."

"You just found a Black Hawk lying around West Africa?" asked Larissa. She was both flummoxed and impressed. "Where on earth is it coming from?"

Durham didn't reply; instead his eyes were locked on Judd. "Two hours, sir. I can have it on the embassy roof for departure for Timbuktu. Are we a go?"

Judd's eyes darted from Larissa to Durham, then back to Larissa. She was shaking her head. Judd smiled.

"Yallah."

35.

Retired General Oumar Diallo had been sitting in a plastic chair at the back of Fiona's Café talking quietly on the phone all morning. The other customers gave the hefty African man a two-table buffer zone, leaving him ample space to conduct his business. Four different cell phones in a variety of shapes and sizes were displayed on the chipped Formica table in front of him. A fifth phone was pressed to his ear. At the end of another call, in a language that none of the other patrons could understand, he set down the phone and stared at cobwebs on the ceiling in contemplation of his next move. He thought to himself, *Yes, after so much that has gone wrong, the pieces are starting to come together. I will soon be back where I belong, my honor restored. I must remain focused. If necessary,* ruthless.

"Sorry, love. Another cuppa?" The waitress had taken the break in calls as her opening. Diallo snapped out of his thoughts to notice he had indeed drained another cup of tea.

"Yes. Extra sugar and plenty of milk. The usual."

"You want a sausage roll? It's lovely with builder's tea."

Diallo turned to the front counter, a greasy glass case held long cylinders of soggy pastry glowing under the red warming light. The thought of eating forbidden pork gave him a slight shudder. No point in explaining, he decided. "No, madam, thank you. Just tea."

He reached for a telephone, a deliberate signal that it was time for the waitress to leave. She took the hint.

Diallo dialed a long number. After five rings he was about to hang up, but finally a click and the raspy voice of a woman who has been asleep. "Uhhh, hello?"

"Tata, we need to talk."

"Uh, Bènkè? Is that you, Uncle?"

"Have I woken you? What time is it in Washington, D.C.?"

"Oh, no, Uncle. I am not sleeping." A lie they both knew was polite and proper to ignore.

"Tata, I have known you even before you

285

were born."

"Yes, Bènkè," she said deferentially, anticipating a line of questioning she had heard many times before.

"Who taught you how to read, sitting under the baobab tree, for so many long, hot days?"

"You, Bènkè."

"Who would take his small, small salary and save to buy for his sister's only daughter her favorite food, fufu and groundnut soup?"

"You, Bènkè."

"Who helped you with your schoolwork when he was home from patrols so that you could become educated and leave the village? So you could go to America, to your Georgetown University?"

"You, Bènkè. I am grateful."

"Who introduced your mother to Boubacar Maiga when he was still a small, small boy working at the American bank?"

"You, Bènkè." Another unacknowledged lie.

"Yes, you have always been a bright girl, Tata. I am very proud of you."

"Thank you, Bènkè. I am very grateful for all you have done for our family. I honor you, Uncle."

"I am worried about your father."

"So am I, Bènkè."

"Yes, I know. That's why I am calling. Your father is now a big man, but he has made mistakes and put his family and our nation at risk. I am sorry to tell you this. I know you are a loyal daughter who loves her father. But you are also a woman now. You need to know the truth. You need to help your mother today. Together, we need to help your mother. Do you understand, Tata?"

"Yes."

"I need you to pass a message to your mother, a very important message."

"Yes, Bènkè."

"Tell her that things in Bamako are becoming very dangerous. But I will look out for her, no matter what happens. Do you understand?"

"Yes, Bènkè. I will tell her."

"Very good, Tata. Do it now."

"Yes, Bènkè. I will call right away."

"I know you will. I am going to send you some money."

"No, Bènkè. I don't need any money. I am fine."

"Don't insult me. What kind of uncle would I be if I didn't send money? I will send it. You will buy something nice."

"Yes, Bènkè. Thank you, Bènkè."

They both hung up.

General Oumar Diallo slumped back in his chair, just as a steaming cup of tea arrived. He was feeling satisfied. Diallo plucked another phone off the table to put the next phase of his plan into action.

Tata Maiga, some 3,600 miles away, was also dialing. After one ring, a voice on the other end answered quickly. "This is Mariana Leibowitz . . ."

36.

Bull was sitting up front with the pilot, speaking to him through a headset. Judd, in the back, had lost the sense of hearing; all noise was obliterated by the whirring of the chopper blades. Encased in white noise, he sat in merciful silence, watching out the window.

The Black Hawk, flying low, lifted sharply over a sand dune to reveal yet another dune. At their high speed, the desert appeared to be nothing more than an endless wasteland of nothingness. A sea of dead sand.

But Judd knew from his experience around the world that there was far more than first appeared. The desert, just beneath the surface, was alive. The struggle for existence by animal and man. The unseen dangers. The ingenuity of survival.

Alone with his thoughts, Judd suddenly had doubts about his decision to fly to Timbuktu. It all seemed so right, flying a phantom attack helicopter to a mythical city on the edge of known civilization. *So adventurous.*

Or, he wondered, *am I becoming a caricature of the outsider in Africa, living out romantic fantasies? Am I risking lives just to try to show that the Golden Hour is right? For the sake of self-validation? Am I playing a self-indulgent game with a foreign country just to prove some arcane academic theory?*

He shook his head to reinforce himself. *Focus. My job is get President Maiga back in power. Timbuktu is the key. Papa told me so, right? Maybe I will learn something about the missing girl, too.* Yes, that justified the trip. The risk. The *mission.*

Before Judd could conclude the debate inside his own head, the helicopter popped over yet another dune to reveal an unexpected sight: water. It was the great Niger River, wandering like a soft brown snake, lost in the desert.

Judd imagined what seeing the river must have felt like for Mungo Park, the Scottish explorer who reached the Niger in 1796 and was shocked to find it flowed eastward, the exact opposite of what he and his philanthropic benefactors had confidently assumed. All the experts had had it exactly backward.

Park returned to Europe with the news a hero, and quickly became a celebrity for his exploits. But, bored with the tedium of seminars back in Britain, he set out on a second expedition down the Niger from which he never returned. Mungo Park, keen to follow the Niger all the way to its mouth, died under mysterious circumstances, probably killed in what would nearly a century later become northern Nigeria.

This part of the world had always been full of surprises for outsiders arriving with big heads and majestic ideas. *Why should I expect to be any different?*

The helicopter pitched hard to one side, Judd suddenly staring straight down at the thick coffee-colored water. The Black Hawk leveled off, and followed the river like a floating highway. *It's the work, not the ego.*

As they approached town, the banks of the river awoke with activity. Fishermen sat in brightly painted dugout canoes, small boys herded scrawny cattle, women washed bright clothes, slapping them on granite rocks. This was the Mali that Judd fell in love with. This was where he and Jessica had fallen in love with each other. *This is the real Mali, right?*

37.

Landon Parker sat in a hard-backed chair, fidgeting with his BlackBerry and trying not to be annoyed that he was there.

The small reception area was full. Beside Parker were several military officers in full uniform. The rest of the chairs were taken by gray men in gray Washington suits. At the desk sat a young blond intern in a tight dress that was just inappropriate enough to make everyone else both pleased and slightly uncomfortable. All the men in the waiting area were pretending not to look at her.

Everyone was also pretending they could not hear the profanity-laced tirade going on behind the closed door.

After a few minutes, the shouting stopped and the door opened. A little man emerged wearing a dark gray pin-striped suit and

293

sheepish face. Parker did not recognize him, but noticed an FBI badge hanging from his belt as the man brushed past.

"Mr. Parker?" asked the intern. He stood without a word. "Senator McCall will see you now."

Parker took a deep breath, then pushed the door open.

"Senator, pleasure to see you again," he started, his hand outstretched.

"Don't give me that shit, Landon. I want to know what the fuck your people are doing to rescue my daughter. And, so help me God, don't you dare give me some bullshit State Department line that 'We're doing everything we can.' I want to know what's going on. I want to know everything. . . ."

38.

YABA VILLAGE, DOGON COUNTRY
WEDNESDAY, 1:04 P.M. GMT

Papa Toure was resting under a tree, taking a break from the Saharan sun. The cheap molded plastic chair wobbled side to side, straining under his girth. Surrounding him, squatting in the sand, were a dozen or so young boys, all barefoot and wearing dirty secondhand American T-shirts: HILTON HEAD, MONROE COUNTY RECREATION DEPARTMENT, HELLO KITTY with butterflies. One of the boys brought Papa a cold beer, which he accepted without eye contact. As he sipped, he spied up the hill to the village, scanning the dotted cliffs.

The Dogon, a minority group in Mali living along the Bandiagara escarpment near the border with Burkina Faso for the past five hundred years, built their homes right into the treacherous sides of the cliffs. Not unlike what BJ van Hollen had taken Judd to see at Mesa Verde in Colorado all those years ago. Just as with their American counterparts, the Dogon cliffs provided protection from attack and the caves built high up into the side of the mountains were ideal for storing — or hiding — food, supplies, weapons, or whatever you needed to keep secret.

As Papa drained the last of his beer, another boy appeared and laid a bowl of meat in chocolate-brown sauce at his feet. As Papa leaned forward with a groan to pick up his lunch, he continued to gaze at the jumble of huts and mud walls of the village. He ate slowly and deliberately. The pack of boys sat quietly watching him. Even though this was his fourth visit to Yaba in the past year, the water man from Bamako was still a spectacle to the children. Once finished, Papa set down the empty bowl and examined his cell phone. Four bars, full coverage, but still no messages.

"*Combien, grand-père?* How many more?" asked the tallest of the boys.

"Two more wells, *petit fils.* Two more," replied Papa.

A buzz came over the boys as the French answer was translated through the group into the local language.

Papa rose out of his chair with a grunt

and the boys scattered like pigeons. He began to trek up the hill, into the heart of the village. The boys followed in his wake, and were joined by more small children. As he approached a well he'd installed last year, he motioned to the tallest boy to walk beside him, an honor the boy eagerly accepted.

"The well near the house of the Hogon," said Papa as he gestured toward a modest mud hut hugging the cliff where the village spiritual leader lives his entire life without leaving. "Is it working?"

The boy nodded.

"Is the village council maintaining the pump as I instructed last month?"

The boy nodded again.

"Are they charging twenty-five francs?"

The boy didn't answer.

"Are they?"

No answer again, then, in a whisper, *"Cinquante.* Fifty."

"Well done, boy," said Papa. "How are your mother and father?" he asked as he handed the boy a coin.

"They are very well." He slipped the coin into a pocket.

"Ah, that is good. Very good. Any other visitors today?"

The boy nodded.

"The soldiers?"

Nod.

"The foreigners again?"

Another nod.

"Good. Very good. Now run along and take this to your mother." Papa handed the boy a rolled-up bill. "I have two more wells to inspect."

39.

Waiting on a sand dune that overlooked the unmarked airstrip was a tall Tuareg man. He was wrapped in a cloak of rich indigo blue, a jet-black cloth coiled around his head, his eyes masked by oversized mirrored aviator sunglasses. He was covering what little of his face might normally be exposed because of the temporary tempest created by the helicopter's landing. Resting behind him was an old nondescript Land Rover, the same color as the sand. Even though the spectacle of an American attack helicopter buzzing over the river announced to all of Timbuktu their imminent arrival, the façade of discretion dictated that their vehicle be low-profile.

As the Black Hawk engines shut down, Bull nudged Judd and pointed to the

Tuareg. "That's our man today."

"Ours?"

"Contractor. Ezekiel."

Judd and Durham ducked their heads and trotted toward the truck. Judd jumped into the back seat, Bull climbed into the passenger seat, slinging a small camouflage rucksack. The Black Hawk lifted off and, in an instant, disappeared over the horizon.

The Land Rover skidded over a roller coaster of sand dunes before finding a flat track and then, eventually, what passed for a real road in this part of the world. As they approached town, the ancient settlement of Timbuktu grew denser. Scattered huts evolved into tightly packed streets. Judd sat up in his seat, anxiously scanning the outside. *Finally, Timbuktu.*

After years of reading about the fabled, romantic city, yearning to be here and see it all with his own eyes, Timbuktu struck Judd as . . . ordinary. Everything was the color of sand: the roads, the houses made of packed mud, the dusty schoolchildren playing soccer in the alleyways.

Once in the heart of the city, the Land Rover pulled into a public square and the driver tucked the vehicle into a shady wedge under a tree. He jumped out and opened the door for Judd, who could now see before him a massive mud building. The thirty-foot walls were topped with pointy peaks and accented by thick wooden logs sticking out along the corners and running across the top. In the middle of the great wall was a huge, fifteen-foot wooden door. *The world's largest sand castle?*

"Is this a fort?" Judd asked Ezekiel.

"Great Mosque of Timbuktu. We are here."

Judd and Bull stared up, sweating in the oppressive heat, but still somewhat in disbelief that what was before them was no desert illusion.

"The Grand Imam, through here. We go."

At the grand front door, the driver slipped off his shoes, removed his head covering, and motioned for Judd and Bull to do the same. They dropped their baseball caps and their boots by the entrance, and stepped barefoot into the mosque. Judd was jolted by the unexpected coolness of the air and floor. He was forced to squint in the dark. A cylinder of light streaked through the main door, revealed straight rows of thick columns every ten feet or so in each direction. Small rugs had been laid in between the pillars, but otherwise everything was made of cool brown mud. As they slowly felt their way down one corridor and Judd's eyes adjusted to the low light, he could see men kneeling on prayer mats and hear them chanting softly.

As they moved deeper into the maze, cutting right and left, and back again, Judd started to lose his direction. Ezekiel was getting farther ahead and then disappeared behind a column. Durham, just behind Judd, poked him and froze. He yanked Judd with him and then pressed his back up against the pillar. Judd instinctively did the same. Bull held one finger in front of his mouth, then two fingers, pointed at his eyes, then down one row of columns. Bull looked up and down the rows, listening. Total silence. Then footsteps.

Ezekiel suddenly appeared. "This way! Quickly!" and he grabbed Judd's hand and led him down one row, Bull trailing behind. They zigzagged through the columns, Ezekiel darting his eyes left to right. Bull was doing the same, their movements suggesting, even to Judd's civilian eyes, that they had similar training. They had done this before. *Situational awareness.*

As they accelerated down one corridor, Judd saw a light ahead, probably a door. *Safety?* A few feet from the exit, they stopped short and Ezekiel pushed Judd behind a column. He felt the cool mud on his skin. Judd, suddenly confused, shrugged his shoulders. "What's happening?"

"Here," Ezekiel whispered. "They are here."

Another shrug. "Who?"

"Ansar."

Before Judd could react, a loud POP! POP! POP! and a suppressed scream broke the silence. "Ahhhh. I'm fucking hit!" Bull was holding his left shoulder, blood already soaking his shirt, as he dragged himself behind a pillar. Judd stared at Bull, frozen for a moment, before Ezekiel yanked Judd's arm to pull him to cover.

"Get down, Ryker!" hissed Durham. He pulled a 9mm pistol from under his jacket, pointing it up to the roof. Then, looking squarely at Ezekiel, he said, "Shots came from the south side. Three-shot burst from an AK." He then pointed off to his left. Ezekiel, who had also drawn an identical gun, nodded knowingly and slipped away into the maze of the mosque.

Durham wrapped his shoulder tightly with a cloth he pulled from his rucksack. He also drew a second 9mm pistol, slid in an ammo bolt, and nodded to Judd, who was crouching one pillar over. *Me?*

After a pause, Judd held out his palms and Bull slid the gun across the floor. Judd snatched it with both hands and quickly pressed his back against the mud, trying to take cover like he'd seen in the movies. Bull raised one hand, showing his palm. *Stay.*

Pinned down behind a mud column, hiding, holding a gun for the first time, his friend shot and bleeding, and a terrorist sniper trying to kill him, Judd was seized — not by the fear he expected would overwhelm him under such stress, but by one dominant thought in his brain that crowded out everything else: *Jessica is going to be pissed.*

Muffled shouting could be heard in the distance. He listened for further gunshots. It seemed quiet inside the mosque. *Could it be over?* The door was just a few feet away, but Durham made no attempt to move, so Judd stayed put.

Abruptly, a tall figure, a silhouette, appeared in the doorway. Bull and Judd both swung toward the shadow and pointed their guns, but the man's hands were high up, his palms open. As the figure stepped inside, Judd could see he had a full gray beard and weathered skin, and was wearing a stark clean white boubou. Around his neck dangled a tether with a bright pink cell phone.

Seemingly oblivious to any potential

danger, the figure, calm and fully upright, approached Bull, helped him up by his good arm and escorted him out the door. Judd, because he couldn't think of what else to do, followed outside, shielding his eyes from the sudden burst of sunlight. They limped through a courtyard and into another door off one side.

Once inside, Judd could see this room was empty except for giant burgundy pillows around the perimeter. An Islamic salon.

The old man gently lowered Bull onto a pillow and gestured for Judd to take a seat, too. Bull grimaced and gripped his shoulder.

Their rescuer lowered himself onto another pillow, meticulously removed the tether around his neck, and softly placed the cell phone next to him.

He gazed directly at Judd. "I'm very sorry about your friend. He will live. The man who did this is now gone. You are safe here."

"Who are you?" asked Judd, bordering on incredulous.

Just then, Ezekiel materialized in the doorway, out of breath. "Dr. Ryker, Colonel Durham." Deep breath. "This is the Grand Imam of Timbuktu."

40.

Serena arrived holding a thirty-two-ounce macchiato quad, the one with four extra shots of espresso. She was anxious to get to her desk and take the first sip, so she removed the plastic lid and blew on the steam. Then she noticed a familiar shape sitting restlessly in a reception chair, elbows out, hunched over, thumbs tapping away on a BlackBerry. A sliver of inappropriate cleavage caught her eye.

"Hello, Ms. Leibowitz," she said, deliberately failing to hide her annoyance.

Ignoring Serena's tone, Mariana said, "Oh, wonderful, you're back! I need to speak to you. It's about our Judd."

"Dr. Ryker is out. I don't know when he will return."

"Oh, I know that, Serena. And please, call me Mariana. I know Judd's gone to Africa. I have tried to reach him, but I just can't seem to get through. That's why I'm here."

"I don't know anything, Ms. Leibowitz. I'm sure you know that."

"I'm not here to get anything. I'm here to *share* with you."

Serena cocked her head with suspicion.

"Not here," said Mariana, scanning the empty foyer. "Is there somewhere more . . . discreet?"

Serena reluctantly led Mariana into Judd's office and closed the door.

"This is secure."

"I know Judd trusts you and that you are in constant touch with him. You must give him this very important message."

Mariana paused to wait for Serena to acknowledge with a nod before continuing: "Judd needs to know that the White House and the Pentagon are coming down hard on State. The White House counterterrorism czar called Landon Parker early this morning and I'm told ripped him a new one. Something about how 'There's no way we are trusting national security to some ivory-tower lab rat.' That's what he said! Isn't it just awful?"

She waited again for a response from Se-

307

rena, but it never came.

"Serena, you know what this means, right? They are coming after Judd."

"And you know about all this . . . how, exactly?"

"That's not the point, Serena. The White House and DoD are about to unleash the dogs. They will order the embassy to back off on Idrissa. They want Judd out of the way. I know Landon should have stood up for Judd, but he didn't. Or couldn't. I love Landon, of course, but sometimes I just don't know what he's really up to."

Serena finally broke her poker face, a hint of anxiety showing through.

Mariana pretended not to notice. "Just this morning, Landon announced to senior staff that Rogerson will soon be en route and taking over Mali policy the minute he lands. Now, can I tell you a secret?"

Serena glared at Mariana. "There's more?"

"You can't even tell Judd, okay?" Without waiting for Serena to agree, she continued, "Bill Rogerson's delays are no accident. My friend Bolotanga is one of the rebel leaders. He's been delaying the talks at my request. As a favor. He's been stalling to help me keep Rogerson at the table."

"Why tell me?"

"Because I can't stall any longer. Bolo is a doll, but he has a greedy streak. It's one of his weaknesses. The bottom line is that negotiations will be wrapping up in a few hours and then Rogerson will be free to return. I expect him in Washington no later than tomorrow morning. We have just twenty-four hours until Bill Rogerson is back and Judd is replaced. You see why I had to come see you right now?"

"Ms. Leibowitz, why exactly are you telling me all this?"

"Serena, darling, I'm coming to you because they are abandoning President Maiga. We are about to *lose*. Judd is almost out of time."

41.

Bull Durham lay in the back of the station-
ary Land Rover. Blood seeped through the
makeshift tourniquet around his shoulder.
He was talking on a small handheld radio,
trying to stay calm but becoming increasingly agitated. Ezekiel hovered over him and
listened intently. Judd paced back and forth,
trying to contain his nervous energy and do
his best to decipher the codes Bull was
shouting into the radio. "Negative, Sand-
stone Blue, negative! You have my co-
ordinates!"

The Imam waited serenely under a mango
tree in the courtyard. He caught Judd's eye
and beckoned for Judd to join him. The
Imam towered over Judd and in a soft
paternal voice said, "It is a shame you came
all this way to leave so quickly, Dr. Judd. We
have not yet had time to speak. We have

many things to discuss."

"You're right. I know. I'm sorry. But Colonel Durham must be evacuated. He's still bleeding and there's a terrorist running around here trying to kill us."

"Your friend will be safe. You are now safe with me."

Durham interrupted with a shout. "The Black Hawk will be back at the extraction LZ in eighteen minutes. They'll probably beat us there. Let's roll."

Judd turned to the Imam. "I have to go. I'm truly sorry."

"Do what you must, *Inshallah.*"

Judd paused, then nodded.

"As-Salamu Alaykum," said the Imam, closing his eyes.

"Wa Alaikum As-Salaam," replied Judd, and then he scurried into the Land Rover.

As they exited the courtyard gate, Judd turned and watched the Imam standing still and alone, receding in the distance. *There goes my best chance to figure out what the hell is going on.*

As the vehicle came up over a sand dune, they were buzzed by the imposing shadow of the American attack helicopter. After landing, two crew members in black uniforms, their faces covered by black helmets and shields, jumped out carrying a stretcher

311

and beelined for the Land Rover. After a brief assessment, they rewrapped Durham's shoulder, hung an IV bag, and prepared to move him.

Judd looked down at Durham. "You're gonna be all right, Bull."

"Yeah, I know. Don't look so nervous. I'm not gonna die. Not my first time getting shot."

"If you say so," said Judd, eyeing the shirt saturated with dark red blood.

"Fucking hell of a way to see Timbuktu."

"Damn shame. We got so close."

"You get anything from the Imam?"

Judd shook his head. "We'll have to figure out another way."

"Fuck."

"Time to go, sir!" barked one of the crew. "We've been on the ground too long. This perimeter is insecure and there is an active hostile in the area."

"Maybe . . . I should stay," said Judd.

Bull's eyes widened in momentary disbelief, then narrowed. "Ambassador James and the station chief?"

"Tell them you were in shock."

Durham nodded, and the two gripped forearms as the crew lifted Bull away.

In a moment, the Black Hawk was up in

the air and then it accelerated, the dark
shadow disappearing over the dunes.

42.

Bryce McCall, the silver-haired four-term United States senator from Pennsylvania and chairman of the Senate Foreign Relations Committee, was resting comfortably in the reclining leather VIP seat at the back of the Air Force Gulfstream C-37B. He was sitting in a top-of-the-line corporate jet that the Pentagon had on standby for just such occasions. On the mahogany side table was a Philadelphia Phillies coffee cup, the senator's preferred mug when he traveled.

The official reason for the secret one-man congressional delegation was a firsthand inspection of counterterrorism cooperation in the Sahara by the Senate's most senior foreign policy leader. At least that's what the flight order listed.

On the senator's lap lay a thick binder, teeming with information about U.S. military and civilian activities designed to contain the threat of violent extremism across West Africa. A red tag highlighted a page about Ansar al-Sahra, the latest jihadist group that U.S. intelligence was actively tracking. The next page explained in short simple sentences the role of a General Mamadou Idrissa and Operation Sand Scorpion, the U.S. train-and-equip program for counterterrorism strike teams. It reported that cooperation had already yielded the interception of several planned attacks and the detention of nineteen probable terrorists. A helpful multicolored bar chart displayed data showing an increase in terrorist disruptions since the beginning of the program. *Results.*

Behind that page was a short summary of the coup d'état against President Boubacar Maiga that had occurred just two days earlier, but Senator McCall, irritable and distracted on the best of days, was already tired of reading.

He leafed through the rest of the pages, pausing on a set of sepia, light-brown satellite photos that caught his eye. Bright red circles and arrows identified trucks and tents, the labels clarifying this as an active terrorist cell. He shook his head. "Bastards," he muttered to himself.

An Air Force escort interrupted. "Sir, we are wheels up in ten minutes. Our flight time to Stuttgart is in eight hours and forty minutes. We'll arrive in time for a quick dinner and some rest. You will have breakfast at oh six hundred with the Africom commander at Kelley Barracks, then receive a briefing from the staff before our flight down to Mali. Our arrival in Bamako will be sixteen hundred local time and the ambassador — her name is Larissa James — will meet you at the airport. We'll have you cleared and on time for your meeting at the Presidential Palace at seventeen hundred. General Idrissa has asked to welcome you personally. Any questions, sir?"

McCall shook his head and waved the escort away. The senator spent the next few minutes mindlessly flipping through the pages. He arrived at a thick section labeled MCCALL DRUG KINGPIN AMENDMENT COMPLIANCE, which detailed in bland noncommittal language the annual assessment of Mali's cooperation on stemming the flow of narcotics. "The GoM is making forward progress in institutional capacity building with the drug enforcement units. . . ."

Despite the section bearing his name, McCall was merely pretending to read, the words rolling through his mind but their meaning not registering. He stopped and closed the file. The senator pulled a small picture of a young girl from his wallet and cradled it in his palm.

The airplane's engines revved up, so McCall tucked the picture into his briefing book and buckled his safety belt. The escort returned to the back to explain safety procedures, but the senator was staring right through her. He clearly had other things, more precious things, on his mind today.

Unexpectedly, the engines then shut down. The door seal popped like the sound of opening a fresh can of tennis balls. A youthful black man in civilian clothes, out of breath, leapt into the cabin and strode down the aisle toward the senator.

"Sir" — deep breath, hands on his knees — "I have been sent by Langley to relay new information."

"Young man, you are delaying my flight. It better be goddamn important."

"Yes, Senator. We have new reports just in from the Agency's station chief in Bamako that indicate a heightened risk of terrorist attack. We have credible information, supported by an increase in electronic chatter, that an attack on U.S. interests may be imminent, possibly within the next twenty-four

317

hours. The embassy therefore recommends against your trip to Mali at this time."

"What kind of information?"

"I can't say, sir. Raw intelligence, backed up by data. The assessment by the station and the embassy concludes it is credible. Or I wouldn't be here."

"Who are you, young man?"

"My name is Sunday, sir. I'm the Mali analyst at the Central Intelligence Agency."

"What kind of name is that?"

"My parents are Nigerian. And I was born on —"

"Sunday. Right, I get it," interrupted the senator. "Well, young Sunday, this plane is mine today, and you can tell Langley, your station, and Ambassador Marisa Jamison, or whatever her name is, thank you for their concern. But I'll be arriving as planned. Tomorrow at four o'clock. You can tell them I told you that directly. And then I threw you off my fucking airplane."

Sunday barked out a quick "Yes, Senator," spun, and headed for the door.

43.

Judd sat in the Imam's salon, alone on a vast ornate pillow, shoes off, a tray of thick black tea and small round lemon biscuits on the floor in front of him. He was trying to be calm, but the events of the past hour were racing through his head. *So many questions. What is going on? How will I get home?*

The room was austere; except for the pillows and a patchwork of carpets, there was no decoration. *No Saudi money pouring in here.*

After a few minutes, the Imam entered, apologizing for having had to attend to another visitor. He gracefully sank onto the pillow beside Judd.

"You are very welcome to Timbuktu. Papa Toure has told me many things about you and your good work. I know you are a friend

319

of Africa and a friend of Mali. You are most welcome here. *As-Salamu Alaykum.*"

"*Wa Alaikum As-Salaam,* Grand Imam. I am happy to be here, and thank you for making time for my visit. I know we have much to discuss. But I must first know about the sniper who shot Colonel Durham. He tried to kill me and he's still out there. How do you know I am safe to be here?"

"I am very sorry about your friend's troubles." The Imam nodded. "But I am very sure that he is now in good hands. You should not be afraid, Dr. Judd. You are safe here with me."

"How do you know? Who was the shooter? Was he trying to stop me from seeing you? Is he Ansar al-Sahra?"

"No true Muslim would fire a weapon inside a mosque. But I will come to that. First, I must know about your family. Are they all well? Papa tells me you have two strong sons. That is very good."

"Yes, thank you. They are well. They are strong." Judd took a deep breath. *Be patient. The ritual matters.* "And how is your family, Grand Imam?"

"They are very good. Thank you. My children are now all in Bamako. Except one daughter, who is studying in Paris."

"Wonderful," replied Judd. "I am sure you

are very proud of her. It's a shame she has to go so far from her father for education, rather than stay here. I know things are difficult here. Can we talk about the situation in Timbuktu?"

"Yes, yes, we will. I first want to thank you and the United States of America."

"You are welcome, but what for?"

"The manuscripts. The ancient library of Timbuktu was once lost, but the manuscripts have been recovered, *Alhamdulillah*. And they are now being restored with the help of America. With the support of the Haverford Foundation. We are very grateful. The manuscripts record Timbuktu's glorious history, our stories, and our advancements in mathematics and astronomy. They are very precious to our culture. To Mali. To the world. We are grateful that they will never be lost again and will live forever, *Inshallah*. They are now quite famous, I believe. Would you like to visit the library?"

"Yes, I would, thank you. I am a student of Mali's history. But I think we need to first discuss the situation in Timbuktu today. Papa Toure assured me that you could illuminate what's going on here. Grand Imam, what can you tell me?"

"Dr. Judd, do you know Anansi?"

"Anansi the spider? From children's folk tales?"

"Yes. Yes, you know Anansi, Dr. Judd. Very good, yes." The Imam chuckled and smiled broadly. Then he became serious again. "But do you know the ancient story of Anansi and the missing yams? That is the important story for us today."

Judd shook his head.

"Very well. Please be patient and allow me to tell you."

Judd nodded and reclined into the large pillow.

"Anansi the spider was feeling strong. He was fat and he was happy. The rains were good and he had plenty of his favorite yams. They were keeping him very satisfied. But one day he noticed that some of his yams were missing. What was happening? he thought. Hyena was watching Anansi and saw that he was looking puzzled.

"Hyena whispered, 'Someone is stealing your yams, I think.'

" 'Are you sure?' asked Anansi. 'Why would anyone steal my yams?'

"Hyena shook his head. 'Yes someone is stealing them and I have a good idea who it might be. You must be very careful.'

"Anansi was now growing angry. 'Who?

Who is stealing my yams?' he demanded to know.

" 'I really shouldn't say,' said Hyena, 'but I did see Monkey eating yams this morning. Perhaps it is Monkey.'

"Anansi thought for a moment and then walked off to search for Monkey. Hyena trailed, out of sight.

"When Anansi found Monkey, he approached him. 'Excuse me, Monkey, have you been eating my yams?'

" 'Why, no, of course not,' replied Monkey.

" 'Someone has been eating my yams. Whoever it is, they should know I will be watching closely,' said Anansi, and he turned and went home.

"The next day, Anansi went out to check on his yams. More were missing. Hyena walked up to him, said, 'Tsk, tsk,' and shook his head at Anansi. 'Monkey was just here eating your yams.'

"Anansi ran off to find Monkey. Hyena came, too, this time trotting just behind Anansi. When Anansi found Monkey, he immediately confronted him. 'My yams are missing, and you have eaten them! I know it is you! If you do it again, I am going to bite you!' Monkey acted surprised by the threat but said nothing.

"As they walked away, Hyena turned to Anansi and said, 'Well done. If he eats your yams tomorrow, I will help you, and we will both bite Monkey.'

"Early the next morning, Hyena woke Anansi. 'Hurry! Monkey has done it again. This time he has stolen *all* your yams! We must get him!'

"Anansi jumped up and ran out to find Monkey, Hyena skipping alongside, urging him on. When Anansi found Monkey resting under a tree, he ran up to him and, without warning, bit him. Monkey yelped in pain and ran off crying.

" 'You have done well,' said Hyena. 'You tried to warn him, but he didn't listen. Monkey won't be stealing anyone's yams now.'

"Anansi nodded.

" 'You can grow more yams, and I will keep watch for you in case anyone else tries to steal them,' said Hyena. 'I will see you tomorrow.'

"Anansi felt proud. He walked home thinking about how he and Hyena had taught Monkey a lesson and how the two of them would protect his yams.

"On his way, a whisper came from behind a tree. 'Anansi . . .' called Tortoise. He was very old and his voice was soft, so Anansi had to come very close to hear."

The Imam was also whispering in this part of the story, so Judd had to sit up and lean in close.

" 'Anansi, I have some very bad news for you, I'm afraid.'

" 'Yes, Tortoise?' answered Anansi.

" 'Monkeys don't eat yams.'

" 'Are you sure?' he asked.

" 'I have lived in the forest for four hundred years, and I have never seen a Monkey eat a yam.'

" 'So . . . who does eat yams?' asked Anansi.

" 'Only two creatures. Spiders . . . and hyenas.' "

44.

Sunday kept typing on his keyboard, but he was getting the same rejection:

Access restricted.

This can't be right, he thought. To clear his head, he exited his cubicle and took a walk down a long corridor. *I'm the CIA analyst for Mali. Who would be denying me access to primary intelligence reports?*

He rode the elevator to one of the CIA's subbasements, arriving with a gentle thud. The doors opened to another long, well-lit hallway. At the end, a receptionist and two security guards were stationed, blocking passage to a heavy steel door.

"Hey, how's it going?" he asked the middle-aged woman sitting at the desk.

"Hello, Sunday," she replied, revealing a

glint of affection.

"This heat wave is making me wish we were back in Mexico City."

"I wouldn't know about the weather. I'm down here," she said, gesturing at the windowless hallway.

Sunday nodded in sympathy. "How's Albert?"

"I wouldn't know about that, either. They've sent him off to Ulan Bator or somewhere like that. He can never tell me."

"Aaay." Sunday nodded again. "Listen, I need a favor," he said, lowering his voice.

"I figured. Why else would you be down here in the tomb?"

"I need to access the primary records for something I'm working on. Can I get in?" he asked, holding up the ID badge around his neck.

"I can't let you in here. You know that. You should be able to see everything you need on the network."

"It's not working. I'm getting the summary reports, but I can't get into all the core files I need. I can't cross-check the sources."

"Well, there's nothing I can do. You know that. You have to call the central network administrator for that. I'm sorry."

"Aaay, I did, but it's going to take a few

hours, and I just need a few minutes to check the sourcing for a handful of reports. It's urgent. I'd really appreciate it."

"I'm really sorry, but I can't help you."

"Listen, I'm not supposed to tell anyone," said Sunday, leaning in closely. "I am doing a special project for Senator Bryce McCall. Very hush-hush. Very urgent. He tasked me to run down some information before he lands in Africa, but his office didn't send the formal request upstairs before his flight took off, and now he's somewhere over the Atlantic Ocean. You know those Hill staffers. Some kid who couldn't care less about intelligence protocol. But if I don't have that data for the senator when he lands, I'm going to be in a heap of trouble."

She looked up at him, a hint of sympathy on her face.

"I can't."

"I'm also not supposed to tell you, but his daughter has been kidnapped. By al-Qaeda."

"How terrible," she stammered, touching a locket around her neck.

"Aaay. You can't tell anyone."

"I won't."

"I just need ten minutes inside."

She took a deep breath, and anguish washed over her face. "You have four."

"Thank you. How do I find the right files quickly?"

"Depends. What exactly are you looking for?"

"I need the raw reporting in from Station Bamako, with source codes. Everything from the last six months."

After a moment and a few swift keystrokes, the woman wrote a code on a piece of paper and handed it to him. "Try this. You can narrow the list by adding keywords in the search field."

She nodded to the two guards, who obediently stepped aside. Sunday positioned his head in front of a small camera in the wall that scanned his face. He widened his eyes, and a green light dropped like a curtain across his iris. A loud buzz, and a clack, and the steel door opened with a rush of air.

Once inside, the all-white room was empty except for a bank of computer terminals, also white. Sunday took a seat in front of one at the far end. He typed in the code and the screen revealed a list of reports, all in from Bamako. The top of the list said "Total Found: 214." He typed "Ansar al-Sahra" into the search field and a new list appeared. "Total Found: 19."

The first report described secret surveillance of a mosque in Gao and a meeting

329

between two suspected terrorists during Friday prayers. The report listed the case officer as "DATT1," which he presumed to be the defense attaché. The contact source was "HOGONSIX."

The second report, on the activities of Pakistani traders in Kidal, also cited DATT1 as the handler and HOGONSIX as the source. The third report detailed money being passed between a Nigerian courier and a known Libyan jihadist at a café in Timbuktu. Also DATT1 and HOGONSIX. Same for the fourth report. And the fifth.

Sunday pushed the chair back from the terminal and scratched his head. He looked over his shoulder toward the door, half expecting someone to be watching him. No one was there.

Sunday checked his watch, then turned his attention back to the screen. He exited back to the full list of reports from Mali. He entered HOGONSIX into the search field and a new list appeared on the screen. On top, the computer flashed, "Total Found: 19."

45.

"I know you're pissed off. Larissa, let me
explain. . . ."

"Do you know what fucking chief of
fucking mission authority means, Judd? I
know you think you can rise above all the
goddamn government bureaucracy, but
chief of mission authority means the ambassador is in charge in her country! That's
me! Just because we are friends doesn't
mean you can take advantage. I am responsible for you and I am ordering you back to
the capital before you get killed!"

"Okay, okay. I'm coming. . . ."

"How? I have no idea how to get
Durham's chopper back up to you. I don't
even know who to call."

"Don't worry, I've got a ride," said Judd.
He was standing on a small river ferry, a

331

rusty old Toyota pickup truck packed in tight by a herd of loudly bleating goats.

"You're driving back to Bamako? Are you fucking kidding me, Judd? Is this one of DoD's crazy ideas? Are you with the contractor?"

"No, Durham's guy had to leave. He didn't say why. I'm driving myself back. In the Grand Imam's pickup truck." Judd smiled to himself, knowing what was coming next.

"You are fucking kidding me!"

"The Imam lent it to me."

"For God's sake, don't tell Washington."

"A good sign. Maybe I'm a diplomat after all?"

"When will you be back here?" asked Larissa, ignoring Judd's attempt to lighten the mood.

"I need to stop in Bandiagara, but I will be back in Bamako late tomorrow afternoon."

"Bandiagara? What the hell for? You aren't making any sense. Do you have any idea what's been going on back here? Any idea at all?"

"It will all make sense soon, Larissa. You have to trust me. I'll be back tomorrow, no later than five o'clock."

"The Pentagon is having a fit that one of

their envoys got shot on an unauthorized mission in a mosque up in a restricted zone, the embassy is on lockdown because of a new security threat, the intel guys have their hair on fire, and I've got the goddamn Senate Foreign Relations Committee chairman arriving!"

"McCall? He's coming here? To Mali?"

"We've had a break in his daughter's abduction. The Malians have received proof of life from the kidnappers and they assure us they can quickly resolve the situation. McCall is coming to try to get his daughter back and make sure we don't screw it up. He lands tomorrow afternoon. See what you've been missing?"

"By the Malians, you mean Idrissa? His people are handling the hostage negotiations?"

"Right."

"I thought we don't pay ransom to terrorists."

"We don't. We also don't ask questions when one of our allies offers to safely recover a senator's daughter."

"That's bullshit, Larissa, and you know it. You served in Central America."

"What are you talking about, Judd?"

"School of the Americas, death squads, you remember all that? Not the finest moments in American foreign policy. I just want to be sure we aren't making the same mistakes all over again."

"We won the Cold War, in case you've forgotten."

"Of course we did. And the Soviet Union could have annihilated us. Just like al-Qaeda wants to do. But I also know we also got played by every tin-pot dictator who knew we would jump whenever they shouted, 'Communist.' Jump or turn a blind eye."

"Judd, you aren't making sense."

"That's why I'm up in Timbuktu. That's why I'm going to Bandiagara."

"What do you know that I don't?"

"I can't say for sure yet, but this whole thing is wrong. I think you know it, too. It's all ghosts."

"I don't know anything of the sort."

"Okay, fine. What about Maiga? Any news on him?"

"Nothing. Right now we are on heightened alert. That's all we are focused on. We are anticipating an attack on a military installation or possibly a foreign embassy. We are pulling everyone in. That includes you."

"Attack? What kind of reports?"

"I can't say anything on a goddamn unsecure cell phone."

"Is it Ansar?"

"Come on, Judd. It's credible and imminent, that's all we need to know. The fact that they tried to kill you and Durham only corroborates the seriousness of the threat. They have already targeted U.S. personnel and wounded a special Pentagon envoy. You see where this is going, don't you?"

"Actually, I don't."

"Well, you better get yourself together, Judd. A Task Force Mali meeting is scheduled for nine p.m. tonight. You are supposed to be back here to run it from the embassy videophone. I don't know what to tell them."

"Postpone it. I need more time."

"You can't do that. Rogerson is already wheels up. Everyone knows he's on his way back and they are just waiting for it. Once he lands in Washington tomorrow morning, it's his task force. You are being overthrown."

A coup d'état. How ironic.

"Judd, it's over."

"Don't give up on me now, Larissa. Patch me in at nine o'clock and I'll run it by phone."

No reply.

"I'll take that as a yes, Madam Ambassador."

"Judd, you've got another problem."

"What is it?"

"I was hoping to talk to you in person, but it obviously can't wait."

"What is it?"

"Does the name Papa Toure mean anything to you?"

"Why?"

"He's the guy in Idrissa's photographs. The courier. The one accepting the envelope of cash."

"Uh-huh."

"The Malians now say they have a thick dossier on this guy. They say they have evidence he is running money from radicals in northern Nigeria into Mali. And they believe the envelope pass they witnessed on Monday evening was part of the payoff for the current terrorist plot. Idrissa is willing to share the whole file with us, but on the condition that we help take the target down. Houston wants to unleash his guys to help the Scorpions capture or kill this Papa Toure. And his coconspirators. Before it's too late."

"But our military cooperation is suspended."

"Houston can request an exception, given the circumstances, and what do you think Washington will say? I'll be forced to agree."

"We can't let that happen."

"Why not?"

"They're wrong."

"Is that because . . . you do know him?"

"Larissa, I can't explain on the phone."

"Judd, Malian intelligence is linking Toure directly to . . . you. Is that true?"

No answer.

"And it gets worse, Judd. They also claim they have proof that you have been feeding this man information. Judd, is this true? Have you been in contact with this Papa Toure? Why would you be in touch with such a person? Fine to lie to Idrissa, but why would you be lying to me?"

Fuck.

"Judd, my neck is on the line here, too. What the hell is going on here?"

"Larissa, look." Judd took a deep breath. "Yes, I do know him. I've known him for years. But he's not what they're saying. He's no radical. He's a goddamn hydrologist. You have to trust me on this. The reports are all bullshit. Papa is straight. I'll stake my career on it."

"You already have, Judd."

"Don't worry, Larissa."

"It's too late, I'm beyond worried. Either you have gotten way out of your depth, Judd, or someone is coming after you. Someone serious. I hope you know what you are doing."

"I'll handle it."

No reply.

"Just hold off Houston as long as you can. Will you do that for me?"

No reply.

"Larissa, will you? Please?"

"Yes," she said, with a loud exhale. "I will try. But you better hurry up. Once Rogerson is back, I won't be able to protect you."

"I understand. One last question. Were any of your people from the embassy in Britain last week?"

"What? Why?"

"Please, Larissa. Were any of your people in Great Britain last week?"

"Well, yes, Colonel Houston was in Wilton Park outside London for a security conference. How is that remotely relevant?"

"It's relevant. He's the soccer fan, right?"

"Yes. He's a big soccer fan."

"I'll bet he roots for Chelsea, right?"

"Who knows? Judd, at a time like this, how can a soccer team possibly matter?"

"Thank you, Larissa. It does." Click.

46.

The ropes were so tight they had rubbed away the skin around Katie's wrists, creating bracelets of red, raw flesh. But her hands had gone numb, so it wasn't her wrists that hurt. It was her ribs. Each time the truck crested and then skidded down a dune, she slid helplessly, like a sack of yams, against the side of the open truck bay. Engine roar, slide, thud, crack.

Katie was blindfolded but could see speckles of waning daylight through the cloth wrapped around her eyes. She could feel the Saharan heat that had yet to subside. She'd lost track of time, but comforted herself with the small knowledge that it was still daytime. And she knew that she was being taken far away. It had been several hours of driving, a daylong roller coaster up and over the soft sand dunes. Painful, but probably good signs. *Progress?*

The rhythmic motion reminded her of the summer she'd spent sailing across the Atlantic on her college roommate's father's yacht. What a summer! Sailing from Boston to the French Riviera sounded so glamorous, so luxurious and carefree. The kind of thing she dreamed about. What it meant to be worldly. She hadn't bargained for the hard work, the sleepless nights, the exhaustion. The seasickness. She was especially unprepared for the endless, relentless waves of the open sea. Desert and ocean, perhaps not the opposites she once thought.

At the peak of the next sand dune, she could hear the truck's engine roar. She clenched her teeth, her stomach churned, and she tried again, fruitlessly, to brace herself. Slide, thud, crack. *Please, God, when will this end?*

No, wait, she thought. *That's not the right question. What I really need to know: Where are they taking me?*

47.

"Sorry, everybody, we had to reschedule this task force meeting so many times. I appreciate the flexibility. I'm also sorry I can't be there in person, but these are unusual circumstances. It's now four o'clock Eastern Standard Time. Let's get down to business."

"Where exactly are you, Dr. Ryker?"

Good question. "I'm sorry. I can't say." Judd rotated 360 degrees, peering out into the darkness over the vast desertscape all around him. *I'm not lying.*

Judd was alone atop a desolate sand dune. He held his cell phone to his ear, underneath a head wrap keeping the blowing sand from his face. Even though it had been several hours since sunset, his shirt was drenched with sweat.

341

"We've got Embassy Bamako on the line, right?" asked Judd. "We should be scrambled and secure. Ambassador, what are the latest conditions on the ground?"

"Thank you, Dr. Ryker. Bamako appears to be calm. We are unaware of any significant changes in the political situation." Larissa had an odd waver in her voice. "However, everyone, we have a new and serious security development, to which I'm turning the floor over to my defense attaché, Colonel Randy Houston."

Judd realized he recognized Larissa's waver. *Terror.*

"Thank you, Ambassador James," said Houston. He sounded hyped up and confident. Bordering on giddy. "A few hours ago, we received a disturbing report directly from the Malian military that early this morning a Scorpion strike team, one of the units that we trained under the regional security platform, was ambushed while on patrol north of Timbuktu. All indications are that the Scorpions were attacked by an active cell of Ansar al-Sahra, led by a notorious terrorist named Bazu Ag Ali. We are gathering additional information on this character and his whereabouts. Because of the pullback order following the coup, we did not have any Americans embedded with the strike team at that time. That means no U.S. casualties. I repeat, no American personnel were directly involved or have been harmed. But the exclusion order also means we have no U.S. eyes to corroborate the attack or any of the details. We believe the entire team is KIA. The initial report indicates that their throats were slit, the bodies dismembered and displayed in a gruesome manner that I will not describe now. The killings are similar to what we've seen terrorists do in Iraq and Afghanistan. This attack by Bazu Ag Ali's cell has all the hallmarks of al-Qaeda."

He waited a moment to let those listening use their imagination. "The bodies were discovered by a Tuareg civilian who is now in custody for his own protection. We will assess photos when they come in to verify the reporting, and we will attempt to debrief the civilian in coming days. In the absence of countervailing evidence, we are treating this incident as an indicator of the acceleration of the ambition and capacity of Ansar al-Sahra."

Houston paused and the line was dead silent. He continued, "Our initial assessment was that the attack was designed to send us a message, but we weren't sure what that message might be. Now I believe we do know. Within the past thirty minutes, we received new information that Ansar's next target may be U.S. Embassy Bamako. We have indications that Bazu Ag Ali is planning an imminent attack, possibly within the next twenty-four hours. As a precaution, we have locked down the embassy, shut down consular services until further notice, expanded the setback perimeter, and pulled in all our people. Most have now complied."

Judd shook his head. *Subtle dig.*

"We are, of course, still assessing the information and cross-checking it with SIGINT data and other intelligence. But as of now, the local authorities believe the threat is credible. Our assessment concurs. We are therefore treating the threat as credible."

We get it. You think it's credible.

"This is State counterterrorism office," interrupted a voice. "Does this new information suggest that Task Force Mali should be shifting from coup reversal to a security and counterterrorism mandate? My office would support such a change, given the circumstances, and I have it on authority that the White House and Pentagon concur. What does the seventh floor think? Has Landon Parker weighed in here?"

"No," interjected Judd. "I have no new

344

instructions directly from Mr. Parker or the Secretary. That means no new mandate. This task force is chaired by S/CRU and we are still under direction to reverse the coup. Those are our orders. Embassy Bamako, continue with lockdown protocols. I am confident that Ambassador James and her team will take all necessary measures to keep everyone safe. And please keep us apprised of any additional developments. Do we have any updates on President Maiga or his condition?"

"This is narcotics and law enforcement. We have new reporting that President Maiga may have been using his old bank, Bamako-Sun Bank, to transfer funds for a Russian mining company that we now believe is a front company for narcotics smuggling in West Africa. There are Russians running cocaine from the coast, up through the ungoverned parts of Mali, and then into Europe via Algeria and Tunisia. We have other sources indicating suspicious Russian Antonovs landing at a remote airfield in the north, coming in via Yemen with unknown cargo. The new Malian attorney general has shared with our FBI liaison that he has a growing dossier on President Maiga's business interests and plans to bring formal corruption and money-laundering charges, possibly as early as tomorrow. He shared in confidence that presidential immunity from prosecution may be on the table as part of his resignation negotiations. We understand those negotiations are already under way."

Resignation negotiations under way? A new attorney general assembled a dossier in just two days? Nothing in Africa happens this fast.

"Mali's attorney general has also requested that the U.S. Department of Justice freeze bank accounts linked to Maiga here in Washington. His daughter, Tata Maiga, is living here and has an account at the Georgetown branch of SunCity Bank. They are asking DoJ to scan for suspicious transactions and to put an FBI tail on her."

"This is S/CT again. We also have fresh reporting on Maiga. We suspected he was soft on extremists, but there may be additional evidence that he was channeling Saudi funds to disaffected Imams in the north using couriers based out of Nigeria. We will check for a SunCity Bank link, or anything connected to his daughter."

"Hold on!" interrupted Judd. "Everyone knows the situation is highly fluid and early reporting is usually wrong. All these new reports need to be assessed. As of right now, our policy and the directions of the Secretary are clear: We are to restore the democratically elected president to office. That is official policy. Our job today is to break this coup. Let's remember this is the same President Boubacar Maiga that sat next to the Secretary of State at the Jakarta Democracy Summit. He was fully vetted. So let's not get ahead of ourselves with unconfirmed raw reports. We should allow the intel confirmation process to work before we do anything rash. Let's stay on task here, everybody. Now, do we have anything further?"

Silence.

"Very well. This meeting is adjourned."

Judd pushed the button on his phone.

Christ. Deep breath. *Where is this flood of reporting coming from? It's a fucking hatchet job.* He rolled his thumb over the side of the phone, scrolling, scanning for Sunday's name.

u there?

Judd took another deep breath. A hundred yards away, across the dead sea of sand, atop another stark dune, rested the old truck. A small fire flickered next to the pickup. Above him, the stars were so plentiful they appeared like fog. It was even more beautiful than watching the sky from the mountains in Vermont. . . . A welcome bong rang out from his phone.

Sunday: Roger
Judd: New reports on BM pouring in but r they true?
Sunday: Unclear. 2 early 2 say.
Judd: Suspicious?
Sunday: Yes
Judd: Why?
Sunday: Sole source. Same source
Judd: Meaning??
Sunday: Don't know. Still working on it.
Judd: One more favor: your friends have any info on a PAPA TOURE? Very discreet please.

Judd slid his phone into his pocket and gazed into the Saharan night sky. It was clear and the stars were a milky white, a bright sliver of the moon shone down like a spotlight on Judd, standing alone on the dune. *Who is Idrissa really working for? What about Diallo? Papa? Luc? Houston? Durham?*

Come to think of it, who am I really working for?

Judd's contemplation was interrupted by his buzzing phone. It was too quick for a reply from Sunday. He drew out the phone, which was flashing "Jessica cell . . . Jessica cell . . . Jessica cell." *Shit.* Deep breath, push.

"Hey, Jess."

"I won't ask where you are, but I do want to know *how* you are. You owe me at least that."

"You're right. I'm fine. Please don't worry."

"I won't if you tell me not to. Are you sure?"

"Yes."

"There's nothing on the news about Mali. Nothing at all."

"I guess not much to report. How's the beach?"

"Toby has the flu. Been throwing up all day. You making headway with Idrissa?"

"I'm sorry to hear that. Who gets the flu at the beach?"

"Your five-year-old son, apparently."

"I'm sorry I'm not there. Give him a hug for me."

"You're not doing anything . . . *dangerous,* are you, Judd?"

"Of course not, Jess. I've hardly seen the outside of the embassy. Don't worry. Larissa and diplomatic security keep me wrapped tightly in the bubble."

"Hmmm." She doesn't sound convinced. "Did you see Papa yet?"

"No. He's upcountry. In Dogon. But I did call him. He's well. Keeping busy."

"Stay in touch with him."

"Jess, um . . ." He paused.

"Yes, Judd? Are you cutting out?"

"Jess, I'm still here. Have you ever had any reason to, um, to doubt Papa? Anything you've ever worried about?"

"Never."

"Now that I'm in government, I need to be extra careful. What do we really know about Papa? Doesn't he seem suspiciously well connected?"

"No, no, no. He's just a networker. Remember, he helped introduce us. That's what he does."

"I suppose."

"That's why he's valuable."

"If you say so, Jess."

"Why are you asking?"

"It's nothing. Never mind."

"You know, people often say terrible things about successful people. Try to cut them down just when they are getting ahead."

"Uh-huh."

"You should know that as well as anyone."

"Right."

"You can trust Papa. He is our friend."

"Okay."

"Judd, I'm telling you. You know I'm a good judge. You. Can. Trust. Papa."

"Okay. I know, I know. You're right. Jess, love to the boys."

"These things can quickly get complicated," she said, ignoring his attempt to get off the phone. "You have to stick with those you can trust. Don't go looking for new enemies. And watch your back."

"I will. I gotta go."

"How did that Colonel Durham turn out?"

"Uh, yes, great guy. You were right about that, too."

"Of course I was. Judd, the Special Ops guys can be very useful. They can do things others can't, you know."

"I'm learning that."

"You never answered how you were doing with Idrissa. Are you pushing him out?"

"I'm trying my best. I've really got to go."

"That doesn't sound very promising. Come on, Judd, let me help you. Have I been wrong yet?"

Deep breath. *She's right.*

"Jess, it's all moving too fast. I can see that something just isn't right, but I don't know what it is. What *is* crystal clear is that the tide is turning against Maiga. I feel like he's losing. Like I'm losing."

"What did I just tell you? You have to stick with those you know you can trust."

"That's part of the problem. I can't even keep Washington on board. I've been trying to play it straight, trying to make the case, but I keep hitting a wall."

"Maybe you need a different strategy? If your data is all bad and the frontal approach isn't working, maybe you need to try something else?"

"Like what?"

"You're in Africa, you're in the Sahara, Judd. How do people survive there? How have they lived through the droughts, the rise and fall of great empires, just making it through the hard life? How did Malians survive the French empire?"

"How is that helpful now? I don't understand."

"Think about it, Judd. You know about the scorpion and the snake?"

"The what?"

"Do you know what happens in the Sahara Desert when there's a fight between a scorpion and a snake?"

"I have no idea. The natural sciences were your thing."

"The snake is bigger and stronger, but the scorpion is craftier. A scorpion will play dead, it will make the snake believe that it's winning, and then, when the time is right . . . the scorpion strikes. That's how the scorpion wins."

Huh?

"Got it, Judd?"

"I think so, yes."

"I knew you would. Good luck, sweets." Click.

Judd dropped the phone back into his pocket and scanned over the desert. Despite the serenity, his mind was racing. *What's my next move? Where are all the pieces?*

Judd suddenly felt very alone and self-doubt rushed back into his head. *What did Jessica really mean? Am I supposed to play dead?*

He calmed himself and twisted his neck, cracking the vertebrae and clearing his head. He conjured up a mental list of the players and where they fit.

Maybe I am?

Judd retrieved his phone and dialed the direct line of Landon Parker, who answered on the first ring.

"Ryker, I understand you have yourself on a little adventure. I've been meaning to call you. The Secretary is concerned. She is preparing for the Euro–Near East Security Partnership summit in Istanbul next week, and the spotlight will be on counterterrorism cooperation. Mali's not looking so good. We may need to adjust our strategy, Ryker."

"Mr. Parker, things have indeed changed here. That's why I'm calling you. Now that I'm here, it's definitely not what we initially thought. I know that Washington is anxious about the security situation, and things look like they are turning against President Maiga on the ground."

"I see."

"Mr. Parker, it may be time you directed Embassy Bamako to make a deal with General Idrissa. If he can deliver the Mc-Call girl and work with the United States to prevent any new attacks, then we can live with new elections next year. Given what we now know and what's happened over the past forty-eight hours, I believe this is the right course."

"I see. I'll take that under advisement."

"And if the mandate is changing, sir, Task Force Mali should be transferred to Assistant Secretary Rogerson once he returns to Washington. He can decide how to best manage the new objective. I appreciate the Secretary's vote of confidence in S/CRU, sir, but this case has become more complicated than the Golden Hour model."

"Yes. I appreciate that, Ryker. It was a

good experiment. S/CRU was always a gamble. I think we all recognized that. Hell, maybe you'll get another shot. Maybe you'll get lucky and the Solomon Islands will blow up again."

"Yes, sir."

"The Secretary thanks you for your efforts on behalf of the country and the Department. I'll take care of it." Click.

Judd scrolled through his recent calls to Diallo's cell number, pressed select, copy, and then paste, and texted the number to Sunday.

Judd dialed another number. "Larissa, it's Judd."

"What the hell was that? The task force is steaming. I don't think we're going to be able to hold Washington after that performance."

"I know. I don't understand where all this new reporting on Maiga is coming from, but it's devastating. I don't think we have a choice. I appreciate that you've been holding the line for me, but it's time to change course. I think we have to accept Idrissa's offer to recover Katie McCall. Can you relay that?"

"Yes, I'll handle it. But I don't think that will stave them off. Houston is already assembling a Special Ops team to disrupt Ansar and the attack on the embassy. I'm not supposed to tell you this, but he's got new information that Bazu Ag Ali is with the cell at a safe house outside Bamako. Houston wants to attack and destroy the cell and grab Bazu. He's worth more alive. The wheels are in motion. Once he's ready to launch the mission, I'm going to come under intense pressure to give him clearance."

"Give him the green light, Larissa. Let Houston and his Special Ops team loose on Bazu. Do it now."

"I don't understand what you're up to, but I hope you know what you're doing. Be safe, Judd."

"I will. I've got to go. And thank you, Larissa. No matter what happens."

Click. Dial.

"Luc, it's Judd. Yes, you were right. We need Diallo's help. It's the only way to break the impasse. But things are moving fast. If we are going to pull this off, it has to be tomorrow. Relay to Diallo that the United States and France are now both on board. Tell him London, too. Better to come from you than me. But it's imperative that Diallo is in Bamako tomorrow. He has to be at the Presidential Palace at Koulouba by seventeen hundred. Can you make that happen?

356

I will be there, too . . . *bonne* . . . *bonne* . . .
au revoir."

Judd's small campfire was growing, the dancing light creating long shadows on the dunes.

Another call.

"Mariana, it's Judd. . . . Yes, thank you, I got the message from Serena. Helpful as always. I've got a message for Tata Maiga to deliver to her father. You're not going to like it, but you need to hear this. Things are moving very quickly, I can't say what exactly, but the situation in Bamako has changed dramatically. The president's life is in danger and I can't protect him. I can't say any more. He needs to agree to resign. Tomorrow. For the sake of the country . . . I know . . . I know . . . Mariana, this is me here. . . . You think I don't know that? He needs to resign, but this part is very important, please make sure Tata understands this. The president must insist that any resignation is witnessed by an international guarantor. That's the best I can do, but it's essential. He should ask for immunity from prosecution and a pension and a house and cars and all the goodies. . . . Yes, I know he doesn't care about that. . . . The only absolute redline is the witness. This is the deal breaker. For his safety, it must be a well-known international witness, preferably a high-ranking American. . . . I don't know who, but Idrissa will figure that out. . . . Yes, I agree, it's a leap of faith. . . . No, he's got no other choice. . . . I can't say why. . . . Mariana, this is the only option right now, and I know you are the only one that can make this happen. It's got to be tomorrow."

Bong from an incoming text. Judd looked down to see it was from Sunday.

"Good-bye, Mariana."

Sunday: Number traced & located. What am I looking for?
Judd: McCall connection
Sunday: Roger. Anything else?
Judd: Papa Toure?
Sunday: Nothing. Must have the wrong name. Anything else?
Judd: Check on my DoD liaison, shot in TB2 today, airlifted to unknown location, name = David Durham.
Sunday: Roger

One more call before a few hours of sleep.

"Papa, it's me. Yes, yes, I saw the Imam. . . . Yes, I think I understand. What have you found in Bandiagara? . . . I see . . . I see . . . okay. . . . Papa, I'm coming to pick you up."

■ ■ ■ ■

PART THREE:
THURSDAY

■ ■ ■ ■

48.

"Rrrrrhhhhhrrrrhhhrrrr!"

Judd was jolted awake by the hollow elongated belch of a camel. The beast's open mouth and quivering lips were just inches from his own face.

"Rrrrrhhhhhrrrrhhhrrrr!"

Judd jumped up quickly and escaped out of range of camel spittle. He had been sleeping on the roof of the truck cab, and his back was stiff and achy.

"Shoo! Go away!" he said, flicking an indigo blue Tuareg blanket that was wrapped around him. The camel, now disinterested, wandered off.

Judd slipped feetfirst from the vehicle's roof through the open window into the driver's seat. "Power nap over. Time to go," he muttered to himself as he turned over the ignition. "Yallah."

After several hours' driving, he finally passed a small piece of weather-beaten wood perched on a rock. Written on the makeshift sign: BANDIAGARA 5 KM.

"Papa, here I come!" he shouted. Then he thought, *You can't be a radical. It makes no sense. You're* Papa. *I've known you too long,* right?

A few minutes later, Judd pulled into a small courtyard, where Papa was waiting. At the sight of his friend, grinning from ear to ear and waving like an excited child, Judd's anxiety evaporated.

"Ah, Judd! *Mon grand ami!* My big friend! *Bienvenue à Pays Dogon!*"

Judd exited the truck and gave Papa a bear hug. After a brief embrace, Papa held Judd's shoulders and looked him up and down.

"You have not aged a bit, my dear Judd. You still look like a graduate student. Of course, you are now a big man, yes. But you still look so young. No gray hair."

"It's good to see you, too, Papa." Judd noticed that the same didn't apply to his old friend. Papa's beard was ashen, his hair thinning, his stomach fat. "Let's catch up in the car, Papa. We have to hurry. We have to be at the palace in less than twelve hours."

"And the Grand Imam?"

"Yes, he was helpful. Thank you. A bit cryptic, given the urgency of the situation. But I think I got the message."

"You Americans always like things upfront and straight. It doesn't work that way in the rest of the world. You know that, *mon ami*?"

"I'm still learning, Papa."

"Africa is complicated. More than you know. Sometimes we have to make difficult choices. They won't always be what they appear. It's not always black and white."

"I know, Papa."

"It's not always clear who is the angel and who is the devil."

Judd narrowed his eyes.

Papa continued, "We don't always know who is who, Judd. Sometimes we shake hands with the devil. We may know, we may not know."

"What are you saying, Papa?"

"Sometimes we don't *want* to know, Judd. That's how to get things done."

"*I* want to know. Is there something you need to tell me, Papa? Are you in trouble?"

Papa stared directly at Judd. "How long have we known each other?"

"Eleven years. Since Kidal. With BJ and Jessica."

"Correct. That is why I am helping you.

363

That's why I always help you. And one day, if I need it, I know you will be here to help me."

Judd paused for a moment. "Yes, Papa."

"Good. Then let's go to Bamako."

The two men climbed into·the truck, Judd turned the ignition, and jerked down on the transmission handle, but held his foot on the brake.

"Papa, I forgot to ask the most important question! Did you find it?"

"Yes," said Papa, holding up a small backpack. "Yallah!"

49.

The lights were off in the cube farm that was the CIA's Africa Issue office. It would have been completely dark if not for the faint glow from Sunday's computer screen.

Sunday pulled a small reporter's notebook from inside his jacket pocket and read down the list of telephone numbers that he had scrawled. Carefully, he typed the numbers into the keyboard and watched as locations on a map were highlighted by blinking red lights. When he'd finished, he studied the screen, narrowing his eyes, puzzled. He rubbed his chin. "General Diallo, you have been a busy man," he said aloud.

Sunday held up the notebook again to check the numbers against the map co-ordinates, drawing his finger along the screen to be certain he hadn't made a mistake. Confident he'd done it correctly, he raised his eyebrows, bit his top lip, and slapped the desk.

"Aaay, *Mu Je,*" Sunday whispered to himself, instinctually falling back into a Hausa phrase that he'd commonly heard around his house as a young boy. "Yeeeesss. Let's go," he said, and he hurriedly picked up the phone and dialed. After three rings, the other end answered without a word.

"Purple Cell. Code two four one zebra Charlie," said Sunday. "Sorry for calling in the middle of the night, but I think I've found something. I will send over the details via SIPRNet, but we will need an airborne Special Operations snatch-and-grab team in Mali ASAP. And I mean we need them ready to go within the next twelve hours. There are complications, so we'll need a diversion mission order, and the team leader must be someone we can absolutely trust. It's got to be all black. Repeat, all black."

No reply on the other end of the line.

"Does Purple Cell acknowledge?" he asked.

Pause . . . Pause . . . Then a woman's voice answered, simply, "Yes."

50.

Inside the brightly lit room, a dozen men
and women in suits sat in high-backed black
leather chairs around a long wooden conference table. In a concentric ring around the
room were younger suits, holding thick
notebooks and fidgeting with their Black-
Berrys. The large flat-panel monitors on the
walls were blank. At the end of the table
was a lone empty seat, its vacancy a growing but unmentioned irritation for those
present as the minutes after nine o'clock
ticked.

In strolled a tall, thin man with wavy gray
hair, his usual patrician aura undermined
by tired, sunken eyes and a face so pale it
would have been hard to believe he spent
more than half his days in tropical climes.
"Okay, people," he said as he took the head

367

seat and arched his back. "This is meeting three, or is it four, of Task Force Mali?" he asked no one in particular. Without an answer, he continued, "I've just gotten off an eighteen-hour flight from Johannesburg and come straight here from the airport. I haven't slept or fully read in yet, so I'm still catching up. I understand that the Ryker kid has been running things while I was busy fixing Congo. Where is he?"

"He's gone to Mali, sir."

"How, then, may I ask, has he been running this little State Department task force?"

"Last meeting was chaired by phone from an unknown location."

"I see. No wonder I've come back to such a mess. No one is home minding the store," said Rogerson, nodding with satisfaction.

"Sir, now that you are here, we've got an immediate decision for the task force. This is agenda item one."

"Proceed," responded Rogerson, with a royal wave of the hand.

"A Special Operations team is preparing for an urgent mission to intercept a cell of Ansar al-Sahra led by Bazu Ag Ali. Our people believe, based on new information from Malian authorities, that the terrorists are en route to attack U.S. Embassy Bamako, likely today. We have already put the embassy on heightened alert, increased the setback by another one hundred meters, and accepted an offer from the Malians for additional troops along the outer perimeter."

"Very good. But what about this Bazgali character?"

"A Special Operations team and two Black Hawks are already en route to Mali. Their plan is to rendezvous with Malian intelligence officers who have the target location, and then they will intercept the cell and capture the cell leader, Bazu Ag Ali. The mission was delayed because of a State Department freeze on military cooperation after the coup."

"Did Ryker do this?"

"The freeze, yes, sir. But Ambassador James lifted the hold late last night."

"Good girl," he said under his breath. "So what is our agenda today?"

"The original mandate of Task Force Mali was to reverse the coup against President Maiga. But given new concerns we have about Maiga's activities and this new security threat, we could back-burner that priority and focus on the security threat. That would imply State counterterrorism assuming the chair of the task force."

"Is that the view of the task force? Is that

the position of S/CT?"

"Yes, sir," said an eager voice from the chair immediately next to him. "We are in the midst of disrupting a credible and imminent terrorist threat against American interests and personnel in Mali. We had an American soldier shot by terrorists in Timbuktu yesterday and have fresh reports of a major attack last night on Malian forces by Ansar al-Sahra in the northern sector. The security posture is further heightened by the arrival of Senator McCall today and ongoing efforts to secure the release of his daughter. We are working closely with Malian security on all of these priority tasks."

"Holy Jesus," said Rogerson under his breath. "What has Ryker been doing?"

"Frankly, sir, he's been blocking us."

"Where exactly is Ryker now?"

"Dr. Ryker is somewhere in northern Mali, as far as we know. He refused to get on the extraction helicopter in Timbuktu."

"Well, then he's on his own." Rogerson tsked. "No one on this task force is to communicate with nor assist Dr. Ryker. He is shut down. Is that understood?"

Nods all around the table.

"State counterterrorism is ready to assume the chair of Task Force Mali and to direct the U.S. policy response. If you deem it appropriate, Mr. Assistant Secretary."

Bill Rogerson looked around the room, all eyes on him. He glanced down at the thick briefing book lying unopened on the table in front of him, then back to the assembled team.

"Yes. Yes, I do. S/CT, you have the chair. Now, if you all don't mind" — Rogerson stood to leave — "I'm back on a plane to Nairobi in . . ." He squinted at his watch. "In fourteen hours. So I'm going home to get some rest. And to check on my horses."

51.

Katie sat cross-legged on the dirt floor. A plate of overcooked goat meat and tomatoes rested to the side, untouched. A warm Coca-Cola was half-empty. She stared at the bottle, watching the bubbles floating to the top, trying to count them.

The walls of the small cell were all dried mud. A window the size of a mail slot allowed sun to peek through. *It's daytime,* she thought. *At least I know that.*

Katie's tears had run dry and her mind had settled into a regular routine. Fear had steadily been replaced by boredom. And anger. *If only my father knew,* she told herself.

She was suddenly jolted from her daydreaming by approaching footsteps. She scampered up and backed against the far wall. She could feel the cool mud through

372

her T-shirt. Next was the clack, clack of a lock being released, the door opened slightly, and an arm reached in and set down a bucket inside the room with a folded yellow cloth lying on top. The door quickly shut again, clack, clack.

Katie slowly approached the bucket, picked up the cloth, and shook it out. It was a dress. A traditional silk dress with embroidered stitching. And a bucket of warm water. Without thinking, she dropped the dress, crossed her arms, and yanked her filthy T-shirt over her head. With her hands she cupped the water and threw it against her body, splashing some on her face and under her arms. She dropped her skirt and slipped on the new dress. It was a little too large. She thought, *At least it's better than the sticky T-shirt I've been wearing for the past five days. Or is it six days?*

She pulled her hair back into a tight ponytail and brushed the front of the dress, taking stock of her newly refreshed look. Then it hit her, right in the throat: What's really happening? Why did they give me new clothes? For an execution? That makes no sense. *Am I being sold?*

Just then was a knock at the door. "American girl!" said a rough voice.

Katie backed again to the far wall.

373

"American girl!" shouted the voice again.

"Yes," she said meekly.

"Yallah! Let's go!" And the door opened, a man in desert fatigues, his head wrapped in a black scarf and his eyes covered by sunglasses, entered the cell. He was holding a burlap bag in his hand.

"*Pardonnez-moi,* American girl," said Bazu softly, as he slipped the sack over her head and led her out the door.

52.

Vrrrooooooomm, roared the old pickup engine as it crested over a sand dune, landing with a thud that bounced Judd and Papa inside the cab.

"All this racing will be pointless if we crash," said Papa, holding on to the handle above his head.

Both of Judd's hands were tightly squeezing the steering wheel, which he was jerking back and forth in an exaggerated motion, not unlike how a child pretends to drive a car.

"Yes, Papa. But if we arrive late, it'll be wasted, too," he replied with a smile, briefly stealing a glance at his old friend sitting next to him.

To emphasize his point, Judd pressed down hard on the accelerator, forcing the truck engine into another steep dive.

As they accelerated over the next sand dune, an unexpected sight appeared right before them: a herd of goats. Judd slammed on the brakes, skidded hard to one side, and yelled, "Yaaaaahhhh!" He spun the wheel the opposite way, pulling the truck out of the fishtail, narrowly missing a goat, and sending the rest of the herd scampering away.

"Oh, shit! That was close!" said Judd, turning back to double-check he hadn't hit anything.

"Inshallah," whispered Papa to himself, shaking his head.

53.

Ambassador Larissa James stood on the far end of the Bamako airport runway surrounded by bulky security men, a lone zebra among the wildebeests. A line of black SUVs and a single police car were humming behind them. There was no breeze today, and the tiny flags on the front of the ambassador's car rested in the heat. She fiddled with her wristwatch and checked the time.

"Is that it?" she asked one of the guards, pointing at an approaching light in the sky.

He peered through his binoculars while mumbling into his wrist.

"No, ma'am. That's a commercial flight. BA from London."

A few moments later, Larissa watched a British Airways jumbo jet land and taxi, stopping on the tarmac several hundred yards away. The airport sprang to life, busy

377

service vehicles moving into place, surrounding the huge airplane as it shut down
its engines.

After several minutes, a security guard approached Larissa. "This is ours, ma'am," he
said, pointing to a light in the sky, far off in
the distance. The target grew closer and
came into focus. A small white unmarked
plane landed in front of the ambassador's
group and then taxied back toward them.

Larissa straightened her jacket and
combed her hair with her fingers. "He's
here," she said to herself.

54.

The blades of the Black Hawk helicopter started their slow, lazy spin. The whump, whump, whump built in volume and speed. Within a few seconds, the whirl had accelerated into a violent tornado of wind and white noise.

Half a dozen Special Forces soldiers sat in the back of the helicopter. They were clad in all black, with Kevlar vests and shiny M4 assault rifles. Each man completed a last-minute weapons check and confirmed his code sign that dictated his role once they reached the target. Like the idling chopper, they were vibrating with energy, ready to launch.

The pilot, his head covered by a black helmet and sunshield, scanned the helicopter's control panel in a final systems check. Outside his window, another identical Black

Hawk was performing the same takeoff ritual.

"Sandpiper One, all clear," he said into the headset.

"Sandpiper Two, all clear," was the immediate reply.

The pilot turned to the man in the copilot seat. They were no more than four feet apart, but the noise of the engine meant they, too, had to use radios to communicate.

"Sir, Sandpiper One and Two are ready," he said into the headset, nodding to the other man. "Operation Harmattan is ready when you are. We are just waiting for your go, Colonel."

The copilot pivoted in his seat for one last look at the soldiers in the back. He received a visual thumbs-up signal and then turned back to the front, shifting more gingerly than usual as his left arm was wrapped in a heavy sling.

"Operation Harmattan is a go, Sandpiper One," said Bull Durham, flashing a thumbs-up sign to the pilot with his right hand. "Let's go!"

55.

Senator Bryce McCall deplaned ready for battle. His navy blue pin-striped suit was crisp, his silver hair perfectly parted. The senator gave no indication of the shock of emerging from an overly air-conditioned plane and hitting the wall of Sahelian heat. The sunlight seared his face, but he effortlessly slid on sunglasses and scanned the crowd waiting for him at the bottom of the stairs.

"Which one is ours?" he asked gruffly out of the side of his mouth.

"Ambassador Larissa James is at the front, in the peach pantsuit," said the escort standing just behind him. "The woman. The only white woman," she added unnecessarily.

The senator grunted, and then glided down the stairs heading right for his target. "Ambassador James, is there any news on my daughter?"

"Welcome to Mali, Mr. Chairman. I will brief you in the car."

"I don't want to waste any more time. Are we going to get her back today, like I was promised?"

"Senator, please understand. I will brief you shortly, but not here."

"Goddammit, Ambassador, just tell me if my little girl is safe and coming home."

"Yes, yes, Senator, our current information is that she is safe. There's a last-minute hitch with the deal for her release. She's been held in a very remote part of the north, so communications are difficult. General Idrissa has taken personal command of the negotiations and he assures me that he is working on it."

"Do we know who the bastards are yet?"

"No, sir. But the good news is that she's been brought down south, we believe to a safe house not far from the capital. This is a good sign that negotiations are progressing and they intend to complete the handover. But we aren't done yet. I'm hopeful we'll have a break and some more good news within the hour."

"Well, if she's close, then why the hell don't we just go get her?"

"It doesn't work that way, Mr. Chairman.

I'm sure you understand. Please be patient. Let the Malians work it out."

They were interrupted by loud shouting coming from the direction of the British Airways plane. A stream of black pickup trucks with flashing yellow lights emerged from every direction and formed a ring around the plane.

"What the hell's that?" asked McCall.

Larissa turned to one of her security men. "What is it?"

"I don't know, ma'am. I'm checking with the Gendarmerie," he said, turning away from them to whisper into his wrist.

The commotion across the tarmac grew. Scuffles broke out. Soldiers poured out of the trucks, waving batons high in the air, yelling in rough French.

"In the vehicle now!" directed one of the security men, pushing Larissa and the senator into the back of an SUV as they craned their necks to see what was happening. The entourage accelerated away.

"What on God's green earth is going on around here?"

Larissa turned to the security guard in the front seat. "Well, what was it?"

The guard, one finger in his ear, replied, "I'm still checking, ma'am. Some kind of VIP arrival, I think."

"Is that how they treat VIP guests in Mali?" asked McCall.

"The Gendarmerie are definitely arresting someone off that plane," said Larissa, ignoring the senator's question.

"Not Gendarmerie, ma'am. Those are Red Berets, General Idrissa's personal security."

"Looks like a riot to me," said the senator. "We've got no time for getting mixed up in local politics, Ambassador. What's the plan for getting my Katie back?"

"I'm afraid those two things can't be separated, Mr. Chairman," she said as the vehicle exited the airport. "The Malians are assuring us that she is safe, but there is some kind of last-minute delay. We don't yet know the problem, but we are working on finding a way to get her back in U.S. custody and then down here as soon and as safely as possible. We are heading to the Presidential Palace in about an hour. General Idrissa has a request before any handover."

"What?"

"He has invited you to witness his formal installation as president."

"Why in the name of sweet Jesus would I do that?"

"A gesture of gratitude. For their co-operation. On security matters and the safety of American citizens."

"Is that a quid pro quo? Is that a goddamn quid pro quo? Are they blackmailing a United States senator with his own daughter? I won't do it!"

"No, of course there's no quid pro quo. They don't see it that way, and neither should you."

"Ma'am," interrupted the security guard. "Our Gendarmerie liaison confirms that there was an unexpected VIP arrival on that British Airways flight, and that he's been detained on national security grounds. He said there is no longer any threat. We don't need to worry."

"VIP? Who?"

"General Oumar Diallo."

56.

"Go! Go! Go!" yelled Durham into his headset. The Special Operations soldiers threw ropes over the sides of the helicopter and rapelled to the ground.

The Black Hawk was hovering just 120 feet over a small compound, but Durham watched the action via infrared satellite on a monitor on the helicopter's dashboard. The screen showed red ghost figures in tight formation surrounding a small structure. Then, like a choreographed ballet, half the group fanned out to a perimeter and the other half, with an eerie combination of grace and extreme violence, entered the building in precise synchronization. On the screen, bright flashes showed live fire as the troops reached their target and destroyed any resistance. They grabbed a single body and exited the structure.

"Chalk One, area is secure! We have the target, Chalk Two! Moving to the extraction zone now!" were the reports coming into Durham's headset.

His Black Hawk landed just east of the compound, while the other chopper set down on the west side. The doors swung open and in poured the soldiers, carrying the captured body, wrapped tightly in a gray blanket.

Once Durham confirmed that all were on board, he gave the pilot an aggressive thumbs-up. "Go! Go! Go!"

The Black Hawk elevated slowly, the engines whined louder, and then, like a cannon shot, it vanished over the horizon with its valuable cargo.

57.

"Darling!" bellowed Mariana Leibowitz. In a tight lavender gym outfit, full makeup, and dangling gold earrings, she paced impatiently around her office as she talked into her headset.

". . . I know, Derek, I know that the *Washington Post* doesn't give two shits about a coup in West Africa. I have been reading the papers and the overthrow of President Maiga didn't get more than a two-inch summary on A22. This was a major story, and you wedged it between a bus crash in El Salvador and another flood in Bangladesh. You *missed* the story, Derek!"

Her stride accelerated. "This is me you're talking to. It's Mariana, remember? I know how your business works, but you can do better than that, Derek."

Through her floor-to-ceiling window

overlooking McPherson Square, she could see Lafayette Square and, through the trees, the gates to the White House.

"Yes, okay, well, what if the Pentagon was involved? What if there is a link to a drug kingpin? Is that sexy enough, Derek? Would that get your attention?"

On the streets below, crowds of tourists intermingled with the white-collar suits of K Street, the lawyers and lobbyists. The worker bees of the American political machine.

"No, I don't have anything on paper I can share with you. You know that already. But I am sure an experienced professional like you knows exactly whom to call for confirmation. . . . Yes, I can get you someone, but off the record, of course. Not today. Soon."

58.

"You have failed me."

"No . . ." said Oumar Diallo, spitting blood onto the dank stone floor. "It is not too late."

Mamadou Idrissa shook his head in pity. "You have failed. You were once great and powerful, but no longer."

Diallo stared up at his former protégé, in a freshly pressed navy blue banker's suit, so out of place in the filthy prison cell. "No!" he screamed.

"No one can hear you down here, Oumar."

"You were always the smart one, Mamadou," he said, twisting his wrists to strain the ropes holding him to the chair. "Who is the one who found you when you were small and insignificant? It was me. Who promoted you above all the others? It was me. Who gave you the opportunity? It was me."

Idrissa turned away and angled his head sideways, his vision following long streaks on the grimy wall. He wondered if the stains were mold or dried blood.

"Mamadou, it was me!"

"Yes," said Idrissa, turning back to his captive. "I was grateful. But that was long ago. Now you have failed. It is a shame." Idrissa gazed tenderly at his former master, Diallo's face barely recognizable with his eyes swollen nearly shut, his cheeks puffy and dark. "Now *I* am the big man."

"Yes, Mamadou."

"I am sorry. That is our fate. It cannot be avoided now."

"No . . ."

"It can be no other way. Our deal is finished. You did not fulfill your part. There is nothing more I can do."

"No. It is not over. Please, Mamadou," pleaded Diallo. "You can keep the money. The business, too. I will go back to Europe. I will be quiet. I know that my time has passed and your time has come."

"It is too late for that."

"I can fix everything."

"You promised me that you would handle the Americans."

"Yes."

"You assured me that you knew how to manage their fears."

"Yes."

"You and that Tuareg Bazu were supposed to take care of the girl."

"Yes! It is not too late, Mamadou!"

"No." General Idrissa calmly drew a pistol from inside his jacket, licked his lips, and fired a single bullet though the center of General Oumar Diallo's forehead.

"No," he repeated softly. "No."

59.

Judd rolled down the window and tried to explain in simple, impatient English.

"We are part of the American government delegation. Do you see that convoy? We are with them!" Judd pointed through the gate at the ambassador's SUV. He could see Larissa James and Senator Bryce McCall walking through a reception line of boubous and military uniforms. It looked like the whole embassy was there, too. Cyrus, Colonel Randy Houston, and a train of protocol and security officers. A field of TV cameras were set up to one side to record their arrival.

"You must let us through."

The soldier clearly didn't understand English, but he was repeating, "No." He was obviously nervous: His fingers tapped the

AK-47 strapped across the front of his chest; his yellow eyes darted from Judd to Papa and back. Soldiers in desert camouflage and Red Berets were now emerging from behind sandbag barricades to surround the vehicle. "No." He was shaking his head. "No."

Papa Toure leaned forward. "Let me try." Papa looked directly at the soldier and took off his sunglasses.

"Grand homme, mon ami . . ." and then switched to a local language Judd didn't understand.

He spoke softly and raised both hands, and then with one hand slowly opened the door. On the clack of the door, the soldier suddenly pointed the AK right at Papa. A circle of other soldiers leapt up, all guns pointing at the pickup truck. Papa continued to talk calmly, with his hands raised, and moved to the front of the vehicle to continue the conversation. The other soldiers were becoming increasingly agitated; some were shouting, one was talking nervously into a radio.

Beyond the gate, Judd could see that the ambassador's group had finished with the welcome party and was now entering the palace. "Papa, hurry. Tell him we've got to go. *Now.*"

Papa nodded, but his eyes were locked on the soldier. The last of the entourage had now disappeared, but the standoff outside the gate seemed no closer to resolution. *Hurry, Papa.*

60.

U.S. EMBASSY, BAMAKO
THURSDAY, 5:02 P.M. GMT

Guards were nestled behind a wall of sand-bags, two blocks away from the gate to the embassy of the United States of America. Their commander had positioned them to create an extra buffer zone around the embassy gate protected by U.S. Marines. They knew something was different tonight because they had been given live ammunition and were barred from sleep rotation. Their commander claimed the orders were because of a visiting American VIP.

But the men were suspicious. Why would the world's most powerful nation need them for protection? They also knew, despite the praise of their commander, that the outer security perimeter was less a first line of defense than a trip wire for an attack.

As the soldiers traded cigarettes and complained about late paychecks, one of the men shared a rumor circulating among the troops: A new terrorist group, of Libyans and Egyptians trained in Saudi Arabia, was planning to attack one of the foreign embassies. Maybe even tonight. He'd heard they are fierce, fearless, and, a fact especially unsettling to the others, that they use Egyptian magic to turn invisible.

A guard peered cautiously over the sandbag wall, aiming his .50 caliber gun across the street, sweeping his eyes and the gun back and forth for anything suspicious. So far, he saw nothing. Nothing to shoot, yet.

61.

Papa smiled and nodded. He exchanged an elaborate handshake with the soldier that ended with a snap. *Breakthrough!*

Papa climbed back into the truck. "Yallah, let's go."

"We're in? How'd you do that?"

"It's okay, let's go." The soldiers stood aside, the gate opened, and they pulled into the circular driveway of Mali's Presidential Palace at Koulouba. Judd and Papa raced from the car and headed through the elaborate front door, beelining for the salon. *I've been here twice before; I know my way.*

When they reached the main room, Judd and Papa paused and made eye contact. They exchanged quick, knowing nods. Then in unison they pushed open the large wooden double doors, straining with both hands, the two of them bursting through the doorway.

Inside, it was suddenly dead silent as all eyes turned to the intruders. General Idrissa, dressed in an immaculate blue business suit, was perched high on a throne, a faux-baroque table in front of him. Senator Bryce McCall and President Boubacar Maiga were also seated at the table, each with a pen in hand.

On either side of them stretched a long line of chairs. Sweeping to the right was Idrissa's new cabinet, with a wall of uniformed soldiers in red berets at attention behind them. To the left were the Americans: Ambassador James beside the senator; the defense attaché, Randy Houston; the CIA station chief, Cyrus; followed by half a dozen other embassy suits. Security men, all Oakleys and earpieces, stood behind them. Two perfectly symmetrical arcs of diplomacy and security. All in suspension. *All staring at me.*

"Mr. President, you don't need to resign."

"Judd, what are you doing?" Larissa was distraught.

"What is going on? Who the hell is this?" demanded McCall.

"Judd Ryker, Crisis Reaction Unit, U.S. Department of State. Do not sign anything, Senator."

General Idrissa stood up aggressively. "Security! Arrest this trespasser!" Several soldiers moved toward Judd and Papa. The ambassador jumped up and blocked their path, shielding Judd and Papa.

"No! Let him speak!" The American security team rushed to her side, forming a perimeter around the three of them. *A stand-off.*

Larissa turned around. "Judd, you better be right."

"This is an outrage!" yelled Idrissa. "You are insulting Mali. You are endangering our security! We must have security!"

"Senator," said Judd, as calmly as he could, "you are today being asked to witness President Maiga's resignation and General Idrissa's installation, but it is a vast web of lies. The charges against the president are untrue. Our partnership with General Idrissa is based on a carefully constructed fiction. Virtually everything in your briefing book, everything that General Idrissa has told you, everything that he has told us, is a fabrication."

Now the American side was looking uncomfortable, too. Cyrus and Colonel Houston shifted in their chairs.

"It's all been too easy. Only today have I finally been able to figure out why. To put all the pieces of the puzzle together. With me here is Papa Toure from the Haverford Foundation. I picked him up in Bandiagara this morning and raced here so you can hear it straight from him. You can see what he's found."

Papa stepped forward and held up a small brick, wrapped in burlap. "Heroin," said Papa nonchalantly. He tossed the package onto the table in front of Idrissa, where it landed with a heavy thud.

"And there's more. There are hundreds of these bricks in caves in Dogon Country." Papa bowed his head deferentially. "Mr. President." He passed his cell phone to President Maiga, who looked at the image, shook his head in disgust, and then handed the phone to Senator McCall. On the screen was a photo of a small cave containing hundreds of identical burlap bundles. "Taken yesterday in Yaba."

"This shipment came in by plane from Pakistan. And it was unloaded and guarded by the Scorpion strike force," said Judd.

"What are you talking about?" asked a confused Senator McCall.

"The poppies are grown in Afghanistan, collected from farmers by the Taliban, and then moved into Pakistan for processing into heroin. They then smuggle the heroin by plane, truck, and camel into weak states as a funnel into the streets of Europe and North America. Mali has become a major hub of the heroin pipeline. And the profits go directly to the Taliban. We built and trained the Scorpions to fight terrorism. But Idrissa has turned them into a private protection racket for his own drug smuggling. And it's a business that is killing American soldiers."

"Lies!" roared Idrissa.

Colonel Houston shook his head and leered at General Idrissa. "The Taliban, Mamadou?" he muttered. "How could you?"

The Red Berets stood their ground.

"Everyone in the village knows, even the children," said Judd.

"Who do you think showed me where to find the caves?" asked Papa coolly. President Maiga nodded gently.

"Who is this stooge? He has no standing here!" growled Idrissa. "This man is the terrorist. We have proof. Arrest him!"

"No," said a deadpan Cyrus. "I have known Papa Toure for twenty years and vouch for him. He is highly credible." Cyrus and Papa exchanged subtle nods of recognition.

Judd shot Papa a shocked look. Papa raised his eyebrows in acknowledgment.

"What about the terrorist attack?" asked Houston. "The Scorpions were ambushed yesterday by Ansar al-Sahra. And they are planning to attack the embassy today. That's why we dispatched a Special Operations team today, to disrupt the cell."

Judd turned back to the crowd. "How could that massacre have happened in Timbuktu when the unit was in fact in Bandiagara? Has anyone seen the bodies?"

"The Scorpions are from the same area of Dogon. I spoke with the families this morning," said Papa. "No one knows anything about an attack."

"How could that be?" asked Judd. "Perhaps the attack never happened. It's another fabrication."

"How is this possible?" demanded Senator McCall.

"I've been asking myself the same question," said Judd. "Then finally it all started to fit together. Everything, one way or another, comes from a single source. The terror attacks. The intel on Ansar al-Sahra. The corruption charges against President Maiga. The supposedly terrorist bomb that nearly killed Ambassador James and me eight months ago. The sniper who shot Colonel Durham yesterday. It all comes back to one person, and all the rest is just circular. That one source: General Mamadou Idrissa."

"I still don't understand," said McCall to no one in particular.

"Ansar al-Sahra is probably not even real," added Judd. "We've been buying everything that Idrissa has been selling us. That's likely why our own military, through General Oumar Diallo in London, gave him a green light for the coup against President Maiga."

"Randy, is this right?" Larissa whipped around toward Colonel Houston, who was looking at the floor and still shaking his head.

"Of course it's right," said Judd. "And I'm hearing from a friend back in D.C. that the *Washington Post* already has the story. They know the Defense Department was too close to the coup maker and they are ready to run the story once they get a government source off the record to confirm it."

"We can't allow that," said the Senator McCall. "We can't let one loose cannon defense attaché undermine all our counter-terrorism operations. It'll be like the Church Committee in '75 all over again. The press will have a field day. Congress will be forced to react. Probably to *over*react. If our training and equipment unwittingly went to drug traffickers, then we have to stop it, but we can't have this in the newspapers. I won't allow it."

"It gets worse, Senator." Judd held up his phone. "We've got new signals intelligence that proves your daughter's kidnappers have been in direct contact with General Diallo. We thought it was initially a negotiation contact, but now the CIA can confirm that Diallo has long been in touch with a well-known gun and cigarette runner who has been holding your daughter. His name is Bazu Ag Ali. He's a smuggler and a mercenary, not al-Qaeda. Cyrus can check with his colleagues back in Virginia if you need further confirmation. Diallo is the mastermind behind her disappearance and the ransom. Bazu is just a pawn in their game."

Judd paused to let that sink in. "And if General Idrissa is promising to recover Katie safely, then that means he's also been in direct contact with his old mentor Oumar Diallo. He is presenting himself as her savior, but he's obviously in league with the kidnappers."

"Diallo is dead," said Idrissa dismissively.

"But I saw him at the airport!" insisted Larissa James. "Barely an hour ago! We all saw your men take him into custody!"

"Yes, he arrived home today. But General Diallo died in an unfortunate accident. It

405

happens in Africa."

"What about my daughter? Where is she?" demanded the senator, turning sharply toward Idrissa.

"I don't know. Your Dr. Ryker and his wild fantasies have put her life at risk," said Idrissa, shaking his head. "She is still in the custody of the terrorists, and there may be nothing we can do to save her now."

The doors burst open. "Daddy!" Katie McCall rushed into the room and into the senator's arms. They were quickly enveloped in a bubble of security men.

Judd looked around, as surprised as the rest of the room. Trailing behind the girl was a calm Bull Durham, his arm wrapped in a sling, wearing a huge grin.

Judd gave Durham a puzzled look.

"Who else can get a Black Hawk in Mali on short notice?" He was still smiling. "Not you."

Judd nodded in agreement.

"You know, there's an old saying we use in Afghanistan about working with what you have," continued Durham. " 'Until the desert knows that water grows, his sands suffice.' "

"Jessica?" asked a wide-eyed Judd.

"It's Emily Dickinson. Who's Jessica?" asked Durham, with a shrug.

Larissa turned to Cyrus. "Did you have anything to do with this?"

"No, ma'am," he replied firmly.

Senator McCall interrupted. "I still don't know what in the name of sweet Jesus is going on here. Why on earth would they do all this to us and to my little girl?" he asked.

"The bombing, the kidnapping, the sniper attack, the terrorist warnings," said Judd, regaining his composure and stepping forward. "They were all meant to create a false sense of insecurity. To get us nervous about terrorists, more forward-leaning on equipment and cooperation. And to soften us up for his power grab. When President Maiga learned what was happening and tried to stop it, Idrissa arrested him. Then Idrissa set up Diallo and Bazu Ag Ali to take the fall. And we played right into his hands. It very nearly worked."

Larissa James then asked the question suddenly on everyone's mind: "So . . . now what . . . ?"

All eyes turned to President Boubacar Maiga.

Maiga looked around, assessing the room. He nodded in satisfaction. Maiga gracefully stood tall, puffed out his chest, and inhaled deeply.

The crowd was frozen in anticipation. The

big man had yet to speak, but he had already recaptured his audience. Idrissa sunk meekly into his chair. The Red Berets surrounding the Americans retreated, then silently stood at attention behind Maiga.

President Maiga spread his arms wide. "My brothers . . ."

62.

Senator Bryce McCall stepped up to the podium. A volley of camera flashes erupted, and the television cameramen zoomed in close to record this historic event. The podium was adorned with a bouquet of microphones on top and a seal on the front that read UNITED STATES DEPARTMENT OF STATE. Behind him were the red, white, and blue of the American flag, alongside the green, yellow, and red of Mali's flag. Ambassador Larissa James stood behind him, just within the camera shot. Next to her was Colonel Randy Houston, wearing a freshly pressed formal service uniform adorned with medals, and a dark green beret. Judd leaned against the back wall, strategically positioned near the exit.

"Thank you for coming to this press conference on such short notice. As you all

409

just heard a few minutes ago, President Boubacar Maiga addressed his nation on national television to report the successful resolution of the political crisis in Mali. President Maiga, a long and reliable friend of the United States, has fully resumed the powers and duties of head of state of the Republic of Mali. The military officers who were responsible for the temporary situation have agreed to stand down and retire to their home villages. This is a triumph for democracy in Africa and for the peaceful resolution of political differences.

"The events of today are also a victory for American diplomacy. I began my peace mission to Mali today with modest hopes for bringing together the parties and avoiding bloodshed. I am so pleased that my efforts as mediator produced this positive result. Our quick and responsive diplomacy contributed to today's outcome, and our bilateral security cooperation provided the enabling environment for the transition of power back to President Maiga this evening. Thanks to the hard work of the mediators, harmonious cooperation of the different branches of the United States government, and extensive support from the international community, we have been able to resolve this situation in a way that will strengthen

Mali's democracy and cement the resolve of Mali and her partners to fight the international scourge of terrorism.

"I want to also congratulate President Maiga for his leadership at home and his partnership in the region. I cannot confirm any details at this time, but an attack by a new and even more lethal terrorist group known as Ansar al-Sahra was successfully repelled earlier today by Malian security forces, working hand in hand with American advisors. While this new threat is disturbing, the failure of today's attack, even in the midst of our political negotiations, is a sign of Mali's growing capability to secure its own borders and its importance as a national security partner of the United States. Therefore, I am pleased today to announce that the United States will soon launch the U.S.–Mali Transnational Threat Containment Initiative. The USMTTCI is an expanded partnership that will include enhanced training, advanced high-tech equipment, joint exercises, advisors in the field, and other collaborative efforts to further strengthen our mutual commitment to fighting terrorists like Ansar al-Sahra in every corner of the earth. . . ."

Judd quietly slipped out the door before the senator finished his speech.

EPILOGUE

*KITTY HAWK, OUTER BANKS, NORTH
  CAROLINA
FRIDAY, 6:05 P.M. EST
HOURS SINCE THE COUP: ONE
  HUNDRED FOURTEEN*

Jessica reclined in a beach chair at the water's edge. The sun was just starting to touch the horizon. She watched over her two young boys playing in the sand. Building a castle with tall spires and perpendicular sticks protruding from the corners, they were just out of earshot.

Jessica wore a simple black bikini and straw cowboy hat, which mostly obscured the headset into which she was talking quietly.

"Let's make sure the whole Purple Cell team gets recognized for their work this time. I don't want it to play out like the Nairobi affair. We need to avoid that. You understand?"

"Yes, ma'am," replied Cyrus.

"And our man in Germany, too. Let's take care of him. We may need to conjure up a chopper again, and we're going to need his assets. Let's keep him sweet."

"Yes, ma'am. Anything else?"

"I'll be recommending service awards for Ezekiel and Sunday. They certainly deserve it. Papa, too."

"I agree. They performed above and beyond. I hope the senator sees to it to weigh in on their behalf as well."

"I doubt it." Jessica spied the headlights of a taxicab pulling up to the beach house. "I think we are done here. Until next time."

"Ma'am . . . I'm sorry to ask, but do we need any . . . er . . . cleanup on your end?"

"Meaning what, precisely?" Jessica watched Judd step out of the cab and pay the driver.

"Is your cover blown, ma'am?"

"No." Judd was on the pathway, walking toward the beach. "I think we are all set."

"Are you certain, ma'am? We can have a team put together a new backstory. We can have the whole Purple Cell sanitized."

"Negative. Not necessary." Jessica unclipped the headset and slid it into her beach bag. She removed her hat to let the gentle ocean breeze blow through her hair.

She turned away from Judd's approach and picked up a goblet of chilled white wine, the glass speckled with drops of condensation.

"Hi, Jess." Judd dropped his duffel bag in the sand and bent down to plant a long, soft kiss on her lips.

"Daddy, Daddy! Look at our sand castle!"

"Fantastic, boys. Looks just like the Great Mosque of Timbuktu."

"So, did you fix it?" Jessica got right to the point while handing him a glass and pulling a wine bottle out of her beach bag.

"Not really. Things are calm in Bamako. Maiga is president again."

She delicately poured wine into his glass. "Well, that sounds fixed to me. Isn't that exactly the outcome we wanted?"

"Idrissa will retire. Diallo is the scapegoat, but he's dead."

"I see. Not ideal, but still a good result."

"Yes, I suppose."

"And you did it in less than a hundred hours, right?"

"I guess so, yes. About eighty-five hours. If I were counting."

"Right. So you just proved the Golden Hour? Let's toast." She held up her glass.

"No."

"No?" She dropped her arm. "Well, then

maybe you need to go back to the drawing board."

Judd didn't answer.

"Maybe your little experiment in government is coming to an end and it's time for you to go back to your students. Maybe it's time for us to all go back home?"

"I don't think so. Not yet."

"Maybe you need to go back to your data, Judd."

"My data didn't reverse the coup in Mali. Neither did whatever you'll read tomorrow in a tiny story buried in the back pages of the *Post.*"

"I see. . . . Then, Judd, dear," Jessica asked with a suppressed smile, "how did you do it?"

Judd finally raised his glass. "Backchannel."

ACKNOWLEDGMENTS

The Golden Hour would never have been possible without the opportunity to work inside the U.S. government, an experience for which I am grateful to many people, but especially Jendayi Frazer and Bobby Pittman. I want to thank all those who read early drafts and helped to make the story both more readable and more realistic, including Bill Trombley, Bobby Pittman, Tony Fratto, Charles Kenny, Markus Goldstein, Dennis Moss, Kassy Kebede, and Liya Kebede. I am appreciative of the many supporters who helped me to navigate the new world of fiction, in particular Evan and Leslie Semegran, Charlie Spicer, Jeffrey Krilla, Stephanie Hanson, Tammy Poggo, Lynne Rienner, Dennis Wholey, Arvind Subramanian, Basia Sall, and Tammi Sharpe.

Some of the references in the story come from Eamonn Gearon's wonderful *The Sa-*

417

hara: A Cultural History.

Huge thanks go to my agent, Josh Getzler, for championing this project with such energy and support. I'm also thankful to Amanda Newman for her enthusiasm for the book and her fortuitous timing in watching BBC News. Thanks to Danielle Burby at HSG and Sara Minnich at Putnam for their patience and diligence.

I'm eternally grateful for the advice, and humbled by the trust, from my editor, Neil Nyren.

Most of all, I thank my family, Gabriel, Leo, Max, and especially Donna, without whose love, encouragement, and sensible editing this never would have been completed. Yallah!

ABOUT THE AUTHOR

Todd Moss is Chief Operating Officer and Senior Fellow at the Center for Global Development, a Washington, D.C., think tank, and an adjunct professor at Georgetown University. From 2007 to 2008, he served as Deputy Assistant Secretary of State, where he was responsible for diplomatic relations with sixteen West African countries.

Previously, Moss worked at the World Bank and the Economist Intelligence Unit and taught at the London School of Economics. The author of four nonfiction books on international economics affairs, he lives in Maryland.